Darcy
Quarry Hall, Book Four

Michelle L. Levigne

www.MtZionRidgePress.com

Mt Zion Ridge Press LLC
295 Gum Springs Rd, NW
Georgetown, TN 37366

https://www.mtzionridgepress.com

Published in the United States of America
Publication Date: November 15, 2025

Editor-In-Chief: Michelle Levigne
Executive Editor: Tamera Lynn Kraft

Welcome to Quarry Hall, where the wounded find shelter and healing, and train to share that healing and the lessons they have learned with other hurting souls.

Quarry Hall is the mansion home of the Arc Foundation, a philanthropic foundation dedicated to finding the people who have fallen through the cracks and give badly needed assistance, one person at a time. The daughters of Quarry Hall are the walking wounded, and still have some growing and healing to do as they face a wounded world. Accompanied by their guard dogs, trained in self-defense, aided by innovative technology and with intelligence and military connections, they put their lives on the line for the One who did the same for them.

Chapter One

If this were a life-and-death situation, Vincent would have died ten minutes ago.

He stumbled backward, his foot turning as his heel jammed between two workout mats. Joan acted before consciously registering her teacher's uncharacteristic clumsiness, lunging and bending low, to catch him around the knees with one arm, turning with all her body weight and yanking his legs out from underneath him. Vincent tumbled backward with a muffled shout, eyes widening in surprise.

Joan flung herself back, out of arm's reach, fully expecting him to slash upward with his legs, vault back to his feet and tackle her in a move too rapid to see. Instead, Vincent slammed into the mat with a loud smack-thud… and stayed flat, spread-eagle, staring up at the drop ceiling of the basement workout room of Quarry Hall.

"Are you sick?" she asked, when Vincent took his time sitting up and stayed sitting, his expression bemused.

No, not bemused, she decided a moment later — distracted.

"A thousand miles away," he said, and rubbed both hands over his shaved head, wiping away sweat.

"Please don't lecture me that I should have followed up on that. You're close to freaking me out. You've been distracted ever since we came down here to work out."

"You're right." He got to his knees and stood, moving slowly, but showing no signs of any damage from his rare fall. No stiffness, no limping.

He glanced over his shoulder at her once as he crossed the tile floor to the racks of equipment on the far wall — hand weights, jump ropes, bamboo poles, bokken, and various other bits of martial arts equipment. Joan didn't react, although in the year-plus since she had joined Quarry Hall, her sparring sessions and self-defense lessons had yet to include any of that equipment. She suspected sometimes Vincent hung it on the wall just to play with the minds of his students.

Her companion, Ulysses, did react when Vincent reached up and took down two of the six gently curved wooden practice swords, bokken, in dark-stained wood. The big, dark gray Akita let out a snort and put his head back down on his extended forelegs.

"Since when do *you* use any weapons?" Joan asked.

"Uh, yeah, I use weapons. Despite what the other troublemakers around here say, we wouldn't have any of this stuff here if we didn't use it at some time. I just haven't taken your training in that direction." Vincent tossed one of the swords to her, underhand.

Joan stepped forward, reaching to catch it. The smooth wood smacked into her hand with enough force to make her palm sting.

"Ready, Inigo?" He cocked one eyebrow at her and stepped up onto the practice mat again.

"Only if you're the six-fingered man." Joan resisted the temptation to make a fancy, silly bow, slashing down with her sword. After more than a year of tutelage with Vincent in self-defense, she knew better than to split her attention for even a few seconds. She grinned, as lines from *The Princess Bride* flashed through her mind. Vincent had joined her, Kathryn, Su-Ma and Jennifer in the TV room two nights ago to watch the silly movie. Having him point out all the errors in the fight scenes just added to the fun, instead of ruining the experience.

She saved the question for later, of why Vincent would be thinking now of Inigo Montoya and his quest to avenge his father's death. Somehow, it made no sense for a fantasy-adventure movie to influence his self-defense lessons.

However, influence coming from whatever had distracted him a few minutes ago did make sense.

"Are we going to Japan soon?" she asked, poised to jump out of the way when Vincent made his first move.

"Samurai, we are not," he muttered, and drew back with an elegant economy of movement that told her Vincent and the wooden sword were old friends.

"Going for sushi?"

A snort and a flicker of one corner of his mouth rewarded her effort.

"Connor MacLeod of Clan MacLeod?"

"Remind me to lecture you later about how much force would be necessary, as well as the sharpness and strength of the blade, to lop off someone's head with one swipe like they did in those totally unrealistic movies."

"Uh, excuse me, but haven't you ever heard of fantasy?" Joan stuck her tongue out at Vincent's sardonic, raised eyebrow.

She knew better than to react to his preparations, because whatever move she made, Vincent would know how to counter it. Trying to predict his attack and prepare for it was wasted effort. Better to stand where she was, both hands on the sword, holding it out in front of her at waist level, parallel with the ground. She wondered if she should even try for the clichéd smack between the legs if he came at her. Not that she would succeed, but the audacity of *trying* might distract Vincent enough to let her ward off his next blow. Sometimes it seemed four-fifths of self-defense was psychological.

Ulysses let out a grumbling sigh. Amazingly, Vincent glanced slightly at the big dog, both corners of his mouth twitching. Joan swallowed down a warrior's cry—he had pounded into her, literally, the harsh lesson of never warning her opponent that she was about to attack—and leaped.

She swung upward with her sword, aiming for his hands rather than the wooden curve of blade. Vincent hesitated. Now she knew something was definitely wrong with him. In that split second her blade hit its mark. He let out a grunt, part shock and part pain. The wooden blade went flying. Joan hit him high in the ribs with her elbow. Vincent grappled at her and they went down. She twisted, turning and drawing up her legs as they fell, raising her arms to ward off his arms sliding around her in his trademark stranglehold. Her sword went flying, tossed away to leave her hands free for defense. Her knee hit Vincent's hip and she flexed her leg, pushing away from him. She hit the practice mat on her side and slapped her hands down hard, pushing in an attempt at a somersault. The angle was wrong and something strained and tried to pop from wrist to shoulder in her left arm. Joan rolled away and braced for Vincent to pin her to the mat in a lightning-swift wrestling move.

Nothing happened. She twisted around, getting to her knees and staggering up to her feet and turned, to find Vincent lying on his side, shaking his head and grinning, just watching her. Ulysses got up and crossed to the mats and bent down to lick Vincent's head.

"Now that's adding insult to injury," Vincent said with a groan, raising his hands to ward off the big dog.

"What's wrong?" she asked. "I know there's no way I'm that good. Really, are you sick?"

"Feeling old, I guess." He stretched out on his back, gaze on the ceiling panels. Again.

"I'm calling Brooklyn." She didn't move, except to drop to one knee on the edge of the mat.

"My past is catching up with me, that's all." Vincent pressed his arms and hands flat on the mat, then inhaled sharply, flung his legs upward, twisting into a backward somersault and landing on his feet. He winked at her. "Don't worry about me."

"Easy for you to say."

"What you need to worry about is this morning's board meeting." He gestured with his chin at the clock on the far wall by the stairs. "Might want to make a good impression, starting with a shower."

Joan stuck her tongue out at him again, only slightly reassured when Vincent let out a bark of laughter. She headed for the stairs, Ulysses at her heels, while he retrieved the wooden swords. At the top of the stairs, Joan bent to look down and shivered a little at the sight of Vincent just standing there, staring at the swords resting across both hands, a distant expression on his ebony face.

"Okay, Lord, I don't know what's going on, but please... If something bothers Vincent, it has to be bad." She sighed as she hurried up through the multiple staircases of Quarry Hall to her room in the former servants' wing of the house. "If not bad, then at least weird."

Then she didn't have time or energy to think about the puzzle of what could distract Vincent. After a year of lessons, going out on the road to help with assessments, handling the records and paperwork and learning all the procedures and rules of the Arc Foundation, she was about to meet all the current members of the Advisory Board at once. More important, they were about to meet her—Harrison Carter's long-lost daughter and future leader of the foundation. True, she had met several of them over the past few months, but her father hadn't told anyone she was his daughter, the answer to their constant prayers. Today would be the official "unveiling." She knew she had the financial and intellectual skills and understanding to handle all the work that came with running the philanthropic foundation her father had started. The problem, and what made her feel uneasy, lay in the personalities who would assemble in the main library in a little less than an hour.

She expected them to be cautious, reserving judgment until they got to know her. The ones who had met her already would likely be upset that they had been deceived about her identity. Certainly they would have reacted differently to her if they knew she was the heir and future leader, rather than just the newest recruit. That was part of why she had met them as an Arc Foundation employee. People were more natural in their actions, reactions and attitudes if they thought the person working with them was an equal or an underling. Knowing she would be their superior, possibly seeing her as a threat and interloper, would change everything.

Joan hoped most of them would be happy for her father and have the common sense to trust Carter's judgment. However, Kathryn and several other Quarry Hall "daughters" had dealt with misogynistic and power-hungry members of the board in the past. Some of the troublemakers remained on the board, despite the purging that had occurred while dealing with problems they had caused. Joan expected several to be opposed to her inheriting leadership someday because she was illegitimate, and female, twisting some biblical teaching to justify their refusal to grant authority to a woman. Her father had warned her of the attitude and found some amusement in it.

"They don't seem to realize their illogic, their bigotry. We are not a church, nor associated with any specific denomination. Your authority is not dependent on having the 'right' gender. And if anyone should be censored for immoral actions, it is me," Carter had said just two weeks ago, as they started preparing for today's meeting.

"I wonder what they would say if you told them you had already handed the reins over to me, based on the fact that you are morally corrupt," Joan had said.

That had been one of her father's good days, and he had been able to laugh long and loudly without breaking down coughing.

Joan went over the biographies of the Advisory Board members in her mind as she showered and dressed and debated how much or how little makeup she needed to use. Elizabeth, her stepmother, had been a treasure trove of wisdom and insight over the last year, teaching Joan elements of dress, makeup, jewelry, and deportment, using them as weapons in the refined warfare of social interaction.

Today, she chose a long, pale gray shirt-dress with a stiff collar and three-quarter sleeves, sedate silver studs in her ears, and a thick silver ring with a diamond set in an oval of ebony, a smaller copy of the ring her father always wore. Joan smiled as she put it on, remembering that first flash of understanding and pleasure that washed through her when she opened the box at Christmas. She wondered how many members of the board would even notice the ring, much less recognize the significance.

"Please, God, guide my tongue today. Help me speak with wisdom and tact and not leap over the table to give someone a good right hook," she whispered as she studied her reflection in the dresser mirror, trying to decide on which shade of face powder to use.

Ulysses walked at her side when she left her room, rather than going ahead of her, claws silent on the thick carpet runner down the center of the hallway. The massive neo-Tudor mansion seemed to hold its breath as Joan walked from her wing, across the upper level of the house, then took the main staircase down to the ground floor. She glanced out the narrow strips of window, filled with antique, amber-tinted, wavy glass, as she descended. No signs of cars approaching the long, tree-lined driveway from the main gate. She supposed no one else was eager for this watershed meeting, either.

Stepping into the library, she found that assumption was wrong. A husky, broad-shouldered man, standing a good head taller than her, was already in the room. The cut of his tan suit, slightly pulling across the back, fit the stereotype of a Texas millionaire, five generations away from riding the range. When he turned around and she saw the insets of contrasting material on his lapels, she muffled a chuckle at this confirmation of her assessment. Where was his ten-gallon hat? Any chance his car had a wide set of horns affixed to the front grill?

The momentary startled pause, and then the head-to-toes glance the man gave her, accompanied by a slight curling of his upper lip, warned her what attitude he had brought into the room. His gaze barely flicked across Ulysses before dismissing the dog's presence. That made him one of those Advisory Board members who thought the presence of the guardian dogs was a waste of resources and caused more problems than they solved. Adding that to her assessment, Joan guessed he had come early to choose a strategic spot at the long table. Today was a day for political maneuvering. She wouldn't be surprised if he greeted everyone who walked in, taking on the position of host even though this wasn't his house or his foundation.

She mentally matched a more jovial photo with the wary, cold, assessing expression facing her now. The biography sheet that accompanied the photo flashed through her memory. Rance Pendergast, chairman of a major Protestant, interdenominational defense organization. They funded lawsuits to protect the rights of parents to home school and to keep the government from imposing humanistic curriculum on private schools and church schools, among other endeavors. Joan put him in the "women should be seen only rarely and not heard at all" category.

"Well, that didn't take long." Pendergast dropped into a chair at the end of the table closest to the door.

Joan wondered if he chose it because it let him see everyone as they came in, or because the chair at the other end of the table was her father's. Or rather, it was usually her father's. Today, Carter had awakened with an aching in his legs that usually meant a rough day, so he would spend it in his wheelchair to avoid strain. An empty place to the right of the head chair indicated where he would sit, and Joan would take his usual chair, as they had agreed.

"Make yourself useful, honey, and get me some coffee, 'kay?"

She wanted to slap that good-old-boy genial grin off his face and ask him if that molasses-and-cornpone accent was real, or part of the mask he wore to try to disarm his opponents before he got nasty. Joan kept her hands hidden in the folds of her full skirts and stepped around Pendergast to the intercom sitting two places further down on the table. There was another intercom at the other end of the table. She chose to ignore the urge to walk all the way down there, putting the length of the table between them.

"Brooklyn, is the coffee ready for the meeting?" she asked, pressing the button for the kitchen intercom.

"Now lookee here, I could have done that," he blurted, over Brooklyn's response.

"Yes, you could have. I'm sure you've been here often enough, you know how the intercom works, and that the refreshments will be delivered before anyone else arrives." Joan found it easier to hold a calm, pleasant expression on her face than she originally thought possible. Maybe that bubbly sensation in her gut was amusement when Pendergast's face took on a reddish tint. She pressed the button again. "How soon will it be here? Mr. Pendergast is thirsty. It must have been a long trip." She met his gaze and fought down a bubble of laughter when he flinched, startled that she knew his name.

People like Pendergast, she realized, didn't like being behind on knowledge. She knew just from the way he scowled at her, he didn't realize yet who she was. Joan made a mental note to ask, later, how many other daughters of Quarry Hall had attended the Advisory Board meetings and were treated like second class citizens, maybe even treated like they were invisible. Unless someone gave them orders, to fetch and serve. She knew no one would dare such tactics when Elizabeth attended the meetings. How exactly did her stepmother manage to deflate these self-important, sexist windbags, without having to say or do anything?

"Five minutes. Ten, tops," Brooklyn said, her voice rich with laughter. "Still taking the muffins out of the oven."

"Please tell me you made the cranberry orange ones?"

"Now why would I waste those goodies on a bunch of men who don't appreciate the finer things in life?" A ripple of laughter was abruptly cut off as the intercom connection closed.

Joan suspected Brooklyn had heard Pendergast's *harrumph* of wounded pride at her words.

"Run on down to the kitchen like a good little girl and get me some coffee," he said.

"By the time I get to the kitchen, the cart will be halfway here. Waste of time and energy." She gave him a smile that she hoped was a fair imitation of the gracious, cool smile Elizabeth deployed more effectively than a guided missile. She saved it for self-important politicians and various religious leaders in the surrounding counties. To a man, they thought they could declare their titles and Quarry Hall would open its doors and provide whatever they wanted, including unthinking, instantaneous support for whatever was on their various agendas.

Pendergast didn't growl, but Joan sensed it in the air as she turned her back on him and walked around the table. He *harrumph*ed again when she stopped at the tall, French Provincial secretary, pulled open the angled top, and retrieved her leatherbound folio and the stack of collated and stapled papers, containing the information the board would deal with today. Joan felt his gaze digging into her back as she continued to the other end of the table.

"That's not real hospitable of you," he finally said.

"Hospitality is a two-way street. There are codes of conduct and decorum for both the host and the guest." She put the stack of papers down to the left of her chair and made a production out of tapping them into place so they made a neat pile. "It might be interesting to find out from the rest of the board where that dividing line is, the point at which a guest goes too far and the host no longer owes him civility."

Then she tugged the chair out from the head of the table and settled into it, carefully smoothing her skirts out underneath herself.

"Now see here, girly, I don't know who you are—"

"That is very obvious," Carter said from the doorway.

"Carter, this new girl doesn't know her place." Pendergast got up from his seat, gesturing at Joan while taking a few steps toward him.

"No, actually, she knows her place quite well." He glanced over his shoulder into the hall, and in the moment of silence, Joan heard the rattle and chime of the tea cart, loaded with refreshments for the meeting. Carter pushed the toggle of his wheelchair and rolled into the room, making room for Jennifer, who had volunteered to help in the kitchen today.

Pendergast scowled, dropped into his chair again, and turned his head away from Jennifer as she approached the table, with her Dalmatian Puck close on her heels. Lidded carafes of tea and coffee filled the top level of the tea cart, while trays of cups, sugar and cream and spoons filled the shelf underneath it, and baskets of muffins and nuts sat on the bottom. She deftly slid a tray or basket from each layer of the cart and set them on the end of the table in front of Pendergast, then moved to the center of the long table, repeated the process, and put the last set of trays and baskets on the end in front of Joan. Puck sat down on the edge of the carpet, his unblinking gaze fixed on Pendergast. Jennifer wore that slightly wide-eyed expression she had perfected for giving troublemakers enough rope to hang themselves. Kathryn had labeled the expression, "I'm so cute I'm going to die of sugar overload."

Chapter Two

Joan knew Jennifer had volunteered to take care of refreshments for the meeting because Pendergast would be there. The man loathed her, yet he had no right to make any complaint about her. Joan didn't have all the details of the story, other than Pendergast had decided to take a private tour of Quarry Hall several years ago, and ignored the discrete signs indicating the private living area of the mansion. Despite the clear statement that only residents were allowed past that point, he walked through, opening doors and investigating whatever he wanted. He walked into Jennifer's bedroom while she was getting dressed. Puck had barked loud enough to break glass, according to Kathryn, and hit the man hard enough he stumbled across the hall before slamming into the wall. Pendergast hadn't seen anything he shouldn't have, but instead of apologizing and admitting he was in the wrong, he tried to twist the incident around to put the blame on Jennifer. Supposedly, she should have known there were strangers in the house and locked her door when she was "indecent."

"She hopes to provoke him into exploding and maybe even quitting," Kathryn had said, when she related the bare bones of the embarrassing, amusing incident to Joan. "While he was still stunned and on the floor, he called her the Whore of Babylon, parading around naked—she wasn't— to tempt good Christian men. Uncle Harrison decided to laugh, and the other members of the board who were here laughed at him so long, he gave up on that accusation. Honestly, why do the really hardline sexist jerks hang on and the only mildly irritating creeps go away when you want them to?"

Now Joan fought hard not to laugh, remembering Kathryn's words, but it was hard, watching Jennifer flutter her eyelashes as she went about her duties. Looking at Pendergast wasn't any better. The man sat taller and stiffer and his face got darker with red. She thought about a scene she had read in an old novel once, describing someone as being apoplectic and the heroine wondering if his head would swell up like an enormous blood blister and explode.

That didn't help her self-control either. Joan turned to her father, who had wheeled around the other side of the table and came up to the empty spot to park his wheelchair.

"Coffee or tea, Dad?" Joan carefully did not look at Pendergast as she got up to pour for her father.

His muffled gasp was loud enough to be heard at her end of the table. Was he upset that she served Carter but not him? Or had he caught the word "Dad" and realized who she was? Did he understand how badly he had started out?

"Tea, please. Brooklyn finally found that container of the holiday tea she hid so well nobody could find it."

"Oh, yum. Tea for me today, too." She picked up the carafe and poured for both of them. The rich black tea, heavy with cinnamon and nutmeg, dried apple, cherry, and orange bits had become her favorite. She hoped Brooklyn had saved the treat for their end of the table, and it wasn't being wasted on Pendergast and his ilk.

"Extras," Jennifer said, wheeling the cart around to tuck into the nook between two bookcases right behind Carter's wheelchair. "Do you need me for anything else?"

Joan glanced down to Pendergast's end of the table. He was finally pouring for himself. His hands shook so she could see the carafe going up and down.

"Try to feel sorry for him," Carter murmured. Then louder, he said, "No, that seems to be it. Run for your life."

Jennifer laughed and scurried down the length of the table to the door out of the library. She paused in the doorway, waiting for Puck to leave the room. Holding the library door open, she looked back to say, "They're hee — er," pitching her voice just slightly like the little girl from the first *Poltergeist* movie.

Pendergast didn't seem to catch the reference at all. He tore open four sugar packets and dumped them into his coffee, scattering crystals across the table. Jennifer vanished through the doorway, and a few seconds later four more members of the board walked into the library.

Joan mentally matched them with their photos and bios and classed them as allies when all four greeted her by name, welcoming her to the meeting. Pendergast grumbled and snorted when two of the four remarked they were delighted to finally meet her and said they had been praying with her father for years now, that she would be found and join the Arc Foundation.

~~~~~

"Not as bad as we feared, was it?" Carter said, six hours later. The final echo came down the hall as the massive door of Quarry Hall closed behind the board members.

"Exhausting, definitely." Joan tugged the tea cart out of its nook and started gathering up the dirty cups and spoons. "You're pleased?"

"Oh, absolutely. I wouldn't call it a moment of triumph, but definitely a high point, when Wallace and Hanes spoke up at almost the same time,
~~~~~

telling Pendergast if he didn't want to play nice, he should take his ball and go home."

"Meaning resign from the board, I hope."

"Believe it or not, he really is a good man. A reliable ally. He just has some old-fashioned ideas, and an inability to admit when he's wrong or apologize when he's wronged someone. Some misguided belief that it's weakness to acknowledge his flaws. God is slowly tearing down some of his long-held beliefs, though. I hope by the time I have to turn everything over to you, he'll be your friend."

"We should both live so—" Joan fumbled a stack of cups. "Sorry, Dad. I didn't—I'm tired. My head hurts."

"We should both live so long?" Carter shook his head, his smile wry. "Most of the dead wood, the poisonous element on the board, has been driven away. Believe it or not. Looking back, I can see how the Lord was protecting us, using small, embarrassing, uncomfortable problems to drive away some people before they became loud, visible problems that would destroy our effectiveness." His gaze went distant and he nodded slowly. "A severe mercy."

"C.S. Lewis, in his letters to Vanauken," she offered.

"Hah. We're starting to think too much alike."

His eyes sparkled, and Joan felt that momentary heavy, sharp, dropping sensation that hit her at the oddest times. These glimpses of the sharp-witted, energetic man her father had been just emphasized how little time she had left to get to know him, to learn to carry on the legacy he had built specifically to put into her hands.

"It's a good thing I'm sending you out on the road. You need some fresh air, test your wings, and a couple more metaphors I'm too tired to think of right now."

"Dad—"

"There's a file in the top drawer of my desk. Get it for me?"

Joan hesitated a moment, then nodded, put her load of dirty cups and empty baskets on the tea cart, and stepped over to the massive desk sitting in the nook at that end of the library. At that time of the day, it was awash in splotches of color from sunset spilling through the floor-to-ceiling stained glass window. The desk was old-fashioned, the drawers deep and made to hold hanging files. The front file was blue, indicating it was an organization or ministry needing funding or support of some kind. The Arc Foundation had to thoroughly investigate it before becoming involved.

"The Spike Center?" she asked, reading the tab, to make sure. When her father nodded, she pulled it out of the drawer and brought it back to the table.

"Vincent is especially interested in this one." Carter didn't open the file but rested his clasped hands on it.

"He isn't saying why, is he?" She thought about how distracted he had been during their workout that morning.

"Not yet, but I'm not letting him go out on the initial assessment visit until he does."

"And you're sending me out with him." Joan weighed all the things she could say in response to this unusual development. Usually, Vincent only got involved at the later stages of investigating an organization or worthy cause, such as when the companion dogs reacted to the presence of danger or duplicity. If Vincent knew the situation with this Spike Center was rotten from the start, he wouldn't let anyone investigate, and he would say so. Why the delay in revelation? She decided not to voice any of her theories, simply because Vincent was silent at this point. "Is he babysitting me, or am I babysitting him?"

That earned a snort from her father. He sat back in his chair and tipped his head to one side, studying her. His smile softened before he nodded and flipped the file open. Several photos filled the top sheet of paper. Two featured a massive, old-fashioned building that had probably started out as a warehouse or factory more than a century ago. A cluster of men in jeans and blood-red t-shirts filled the third. The fourth photo was of a family: bearded, stocky, graying man, white-blonde wife, in their late forties or early fifties, and a dark-haired young woman who had her mother's angular, elegant features.

Once Joan had a chance to look at all the pictures, her father turned the paper over, revealing an emblem that she realized was a close-up of the logo on the t-shirts. A white circle with a black spike slashing across it, and a single drop of blood hanging from the tip.

"Okay, I get the symbolism. I get the feeling it was chosen to catch the attention of some pretty rough elements. Judging by the building, a decaying part of town, big city?"

"The entire southern portion of the city is referred to as the Zone. Battle zone, most likely." Carter closed the file and sat back, clasping his hands in his lap. "The Spike Center started out as a rescue mission in a storefront, mostly offering hot food in the winter, a place to get out of the heat and have something cold to drink in the summer. Everyone who worked there was a volunteer, risking their own safety, investing their own funds in the work. When they started to make a difference, funds started trickling in and they got noticed. Bigger names decided they weren't a fly-by-night operation and gave their approval and support. They made more of a difference in the neighborhood, moved to bigger quarters, and started doing more for people. Beds, showers, daycare, job leads, basic medical help, counseling. Two years ago, the men in the picture put everything on the line and bought the warehouse, intending to turn it into a community outreach center. Adult education, clothes closet, free clinic, food pantry, women's shelter. You can do an awful lot with all that space."

"But?" Joan asked after he fell silent and rested his gaze on the closed folder.

"A month ago, the fall from grace began. Rumors only. Exploiting the girls who came to them for help. Misappropriation of funds. The usual accusations that are so much worse when aimed at people who are trying to do good."

"Anything that will make Christians look like hypocrites, you mean." She reached back to the cart and brought the half-empty carafe of tea to the table. When she gestured, Carter nodded and she filled the two remaining clean cups for them.

"Everything is still rumors, but the longer they circulate unchecked, the more people want to believe them. Funding has been withdrawn. Demands have been made that the leadership step down. The Clay family joined maybe two months ago and are considered uninvolved with the alleged problems. They are in essence holding everything together, keeping the renovations going, continuing the outreach efforts, until the scandals and rumors have been dealt with."

"So are we investigating the rumors?"

"We are, but you aren't." A smile crooked one side of his mouth when Joan didn't react. "One of the accused is cousin to a friend of Elizabeth's. You've met her, Saundra Ashmore. She asked if Arc would consider stepping in and helping. On the surface, we're only filling in the gap in funding. I've already contacted Xander and asked Sophie to start working her magic, investigating the accusations, digging into the histories and activities of everyone in leadership. However... Vincent has admitted he knows Rev. Clay, but nothing more. So far. I'm going to hazard that he knows him from the 'bad old days,' as he calls them."

"Uh huh. I'm guessing Vincent was in the office when Elizabeth got the first bundle of information. He took one look at the picture and went so quiet he seemed to be invisible. She noticed when nobody else would, and when she asked what was wrong, he wouldn't answer one way or another."

"If it were anyone else, I would accuse you of having a hidden camera in my office to spy on me." Carter picked up the cup of tea and swirled it around in his cup for a moment before taking a long drink.

"Maybe..." She bit her lip and slouched down a little in the chair, her thoughts swirling through one theory after another.

"What are you thinking?" he asked, his voice soft.

"How soon after the Clays joined the Spike Center did the rumors start up?"

"You're thinking Vincent's old friend is the source of the trouble. A power play, out with the old administration, in with the new. That was my first theory." He exhaled loudly, emptied his cup, and put it down on the table. "I'm afraid that is Vincent's first thought, too, and he's second-guessing himself."

"So I *am* babysitting Vincent, in essence." Joan fought a shiver that tried to work its way out of the core of her. The mere thought of Vincent being uncertain of his own judgment threatened the stability of the new life she had found at Quarry Hall. Vincent was as much a pillar of the household as her father, stepmother, and Brooklyn.

"Support. A sounding board. If you speak his doubts, you enable him to face the questions and examine the situation from all sides."

~~~~~

"They referred to us as the Three Horsemen," Vincent said, coming out of the evening shadows around the lagoons in the lower level gardens of Quarry Hall.

Joan smiled, mostly because she had actually sensed him coming up behind her and hadn't been startled when he spoke. She had come out here to enjoy the twilight cool and let Ulysses run for a while after dinner. She had helped make dinner tonight, so someone else had clean-up duties. At Quarry Hall, everyone pitched in, sharing all the chores, avoiding the necessity of strangers coming within the walls. The old mansion was a sanctuary, shutting out the outside world as much as possible.

That was about to change. The outside world — specifically Vincent's dark, unspoken past — was coming in to fetch them.

"You ate the fourth Horseman?"

"Keep it up." He sauntered over to the bench sitting next to the little bridge that arched up over the channel leading from one lagoon to the next.

"So Rev. Joshua Clay was one of the Horsemen." Joan settled on the edge of the bridge. Ulysses trotted out of the underbrush on the far side of the lagoon and came over to settle next to her.

"He was... support staff. The three of us were Snow, Javelin," he tapped his chest, "and Shadow. The ones who recruited us tried to make us forget who we were, take away all our identities except our functions, our code names. Who Joshua Clay was before he became Daedelus... who knows? He was a loose cannon in a lot of ways, but I seriously doubt he's so reckless he would take back his original name."

"Daedelus? As in the Minotaur's labyrinth?"

"A genius engineer. You need to know how things are made, what makes them strong, before you can destroy them. That was his job, his talent. Midas was the fifth member of the team, and his job was to find money, conjure it up out of nothing, siphon funds away from the target to
~~~~~

cripple them and finance our missions."

"Do you think Clay is behind the problems with the Spike Center?"

"It's possible. But Geneva… I can't see her either helping him do it or being so fooled by him she wouldn't notice."

"Geneva?" Joan thought back to the pictures in the folder. "His wife?"

"The woman I met in Afghanistan wouldn't be blind to this kind of long-term plan, if Daedelus is holding true to form. If he's still Daedelus. Her first husband died, Daedelus stepped in…"

"So the girl isn't his?"

"He's her father now." Vincent leaned back, staring up through the canopy of leaves. "Shows just how much I've changed, that I'm letting this bother me at all."

"You're trying to figure out if he's changed that much, too?"

"We're all hypocrites about something." He scrubbed his face with his palms, then met her gaze. "It's a shock when your hypocrisy smacks you in the face. If I can change, if the Lord can salvage the scraps of a soul remaining to me, why can't I accept that Daedelus is reborn, too?"

"Maybe you should stop thinking of him as Daedelus. I mean, you don't think of yourself as Javelin anymore, do you?"

Vincent's eyes narrowed and he tipped his head slightly to the side, an oddly birdlike mannerism that made Joan think of one of the little sparrows that congregated on the lower roofs of Quarry Hall in search of the birdseed and crumbs regularly strewn there. She had to fight not to laugh at that imagery. Something big and predatory, like a condor or even a pterodactyl would be more appropriate.

Then Vincent laughed. He sagged slightly on the bench, shoulders shaking, the sound soft, rippling through the gathering darkness.

"Okay, Joshua it is."

"When was the last time you saw him?"

"Afghanistan." He let out a long, deep sigh. "Funny… I was trying to earn my way into Heaven in those days. Risking my life to make up for all the truly evil things I did. Dae— Joshua came after me. At least, he started out coming after me. No one was supposed to leave our… our organization… alive. Somewhere along the way, hunting me, his soul started to come back to life, and he wanted out, too. Or so he claimed. I wasn't ready to believe him, and Geneva was part of the mix. He always had a weak spot for the ladies. I could believe he'd reform, or at least try to reform, to win her."

The mountains of Afghanistan, twenty-three years ago

Vincent smiled and nodded and stumbled through a mixture of sign language and bits of the local dialect, bargaining with the farmer's wife.

After three days of eating dried food and stale bread, the refugees in his care needed some fresh food. Ordinarily, he could always scavenge up something from the surroundings, living off the land. It might not be easy to swallow, but it would provide energy. However, the weather had been cold and dry so long, there was nothing to find. This was supposed to be spring in Afghanistan? Weighing the need for food against the need for shelter, he had been grateful for the weather. Until now.

This little village and the outlying farms were far from anything even remotely resembling a city, the rise and fall of political factions, the Taliban and all the other currents of unrest in the country. Far enough the people weren't afraid to help strangers. Vincent knew just a smattering of the several different tongues the tribes hereabout used. Between that and sign language, he could get by. All he had to do was get this group of elderly missionaries and their child charges to the safe house and his contacts on the other side of the border in China.

They would spend the day resting and hiding in this tiny, nameless farming village just a few miles west of the pass that was the next goal in their journey. Vincent had just bargained for a resting place in a barn, soup, tea, and bread. He bowed and thanked the farmer's plump, graying wife with gestures, then hurried back to the stone fence where the refugees huddled against the biting spring wind.

"We can stay here," he announced, and handed out the warm, flat rounds of bread she had given him as soon as he admitted there were children in his care.

The adults thanked him and handed out the food to the children, urging them along with clipped, sing-song words softly breathed. There was barely anything for the adults to eat by the time they were satisfied the children had enough. Vincent admired them for that.

Three men, two women, all wrinkled and worn out from hiding from the current regime while they preached and worked as doctors. None of them had been heard from for more than ten years. Their mission boards had given them up for lost, thanks to blocked communications over the border and the crack-down against all foreigners, especially followers of any religion other than Islam. When the team had managed to smuggle word out to their superiors that they were alive, they had asked for help in crossing the border. They also said they were bringing children with them, some entrusted into their care by their parents, the others orphans.

Chapter Three

At this point in his life, Vincent had reached the end of his reserves. Every favor had been used up, and the few people he had thought he could trust had either turned him in or refused to help, in terror for their lives. He had grown desperate enough to try to pray, remembering a few blissful years with his paternal grandmother, who took him to Sunday school. In answer to that stumbling prayer, help had appeared in the form of missionaries living on the fringes. They found him exhausted, hiding in their barn in northern Spain, fighting a raging infection from a bullet he hadn't been able to dodge. In return for shelter and healing, Vincent gave them his experience and skills. He had to argue his new friends into accepting his help — they didn't want him to risk his life until his soul was ensured entrance into Heaven.

Now, Vincent led his little group into the barn, a cave enlarged with sod bricks and ragged boards, and closed the door. The farmer and his sons and their oxen had already gone out for the day, plowing the chilly spring fields. He gestured for the children to sit down while he rearranged the piles of hay into beds. Eight, ranging in age from four years to eleven. They were good, obedient children, terrified into silence and compliance. After so many days walking, they were identical in their weary looks, dark smears under their enormous eyes, hair lank and dirty, clothes clotted with dust. Vincent felt more tired just looking at them and hoped that he too would be able to curl up in the hay and steal a few hours of rest. Sleep would have to wait until they were over the border, at the safe house, and he could trust someone else to help with the guarding.

He dished up the soup and passed it around to the little group after everyone was settled into their scratchy nests in the hay. Vincent made sure the adults got as much as the children. Then, when they had scraped their bowls clean, he filled them with the cooling tea. There were only so many bowls to go around. He settled down in his own sparse nest by the door, breathing in the scents of cattle and chickens, moldering hay and dirt, and listened as the adults led the children in prayers before they went to sleep. It had been years since he had last been in Afghanistan, nowhere near this province, and the language was just different enough he had to concentrate to understand what they were saying. Something about the children's sweet innocence and trust in their guardians, despite their fear, made him smile as he listened.

Such simple faith the children had, despite the harshness of their lives. He remembered back to his own boyhood, when he had believed and trusted so easily. Memories turned into misty fragments of dreams.

Vincent sat up and reached for his gun with one hand, reaching for the long knife strapped to his waist, before he came fully awake. Long, bitter experience had taught him that when he started to relax, that was when danger and disaster were most likely to strike.

He glanced around the barn. Everyone was asleep, though Rev. Morris tried valiantly to stay awake, his head bobbing and his deep blue eyes flickering. The man sat up and ran his fingers through his thinning, snow-white hair.

"Trouble?" he whispered, meeting Vincent's eyes.

"I don't think so. I'm going to take a look outside, just to be careful." Vincent nodded to the man and slowly got to his feet. The hay rustled around him, but none of the sleepers were disturbed.

The yard around the cave-barn echoed in the silence. Even the softly moaning wind seemed far away from the rocky, weed-strewn oval.

There. He caught movement, a flicker of rare sunlight on something metal. Someone peered around the side of the stone farmhouse.

"We're just tired travelers. Old people and children," he announced, stumbling through what he knew of the local dialect. "Show yourself."

"Doesn't anybody around here know decent English?" a man drawled and stepped out from behind the farmhouse. The sun glinted off the curved, heavy blade of his knife. The fact that he seemed to be only armed with a blade made Vincent wonder what kind of trouble he had faced recently.

A man with his back against the wall was doubly dangerous. Add to that the long gap of time since Vincent had seen his former teammate, that made the situation even more dicey than he cared to handle. The need for stealth and to attract as little attention as possible kept him from listening to gut instinct and pulling out his gun as soon as he recognized Josh. His aching hunger to reform and make up for the sins of his past had nothing to do with his hesitation.

"Daedelus?"

"It's Josh Clay now." He grinned and scrubbed at his beard, just as black and just as dusty as always, and considerably longer. He tugged his wool-lined cap off his head and batted it against his thigh, raising more dust. "How you doing, Javelin?"

"Vincent, now. A little busy. And you?"

"Lost."

"Another treasure hunt gone wrong?" Vincent smiled, despite the odds that the blade pointing in his direction would be flying toward his throat at any moment. What were the odds of Josh *not* being here on the bidding of their former superiors, to kill him if he couldn't haul him all the way to headquarters?

"Trying to get some friends out of trouble, actually. We got separated and..." Josh finally seemed to see the blade he clutched in his hand. He sheathed it and pulled his long, stained, dirt-colored coat over it. He nodded toward the barn. "You staying there?"

"Until night."

"Nobody comes to this part of the world for the fun of it. Knowing you—"

"That's the problem, isn't it? I've been trying to become invisible." He stepped sideways a few inches, to keep Josh from seeing if anyone stepped out of the barn, looking for him. The fewer people involved in the inevitable confrontation, the safer they would be.

"I hear you've taken up playing knight in shining armor." He nodded toward the barn. "From the tracks, you've got a gaggle of little ones under your care. Big change from the old days."

"At least we never hurt or killed children. Coming down in the world, Daedelus?"

"I'm not Daedelus anymore," he snapped, managing to keep his voice down.

"As of when?" Vincent concentrated on keeping himself relaxed, as if he expected nothing.

"About three borders ago. Amazing how much easier it is to breathe, the more hostile territory I put between the powers-that-be and me." He shrugged, and a moment later his weary attempt at a smile cracked and crumbled off his face. "Yes, they want you skinned alive and roasted over hot coals. And yes, they sent me after you. As far as I know, they lost track of me about..." Another shrug. "Who knows?"

"That kind of attitude doesn't keep your head on your shoulders."

"What's the use of living if you don't enjoy it?" Josh gestured over Vincent's shoulder. "Could you use a hand? For old time's sake?"

"I could use an extra set of eyes and ears," he admitted after considering. Better to keep the man close, where he could keep an eye on him and ward off any trouble he might try to cause. If any xenophobic extremists learned about the existence and movements of the missionaries, this exhausting trip could turn dangerously exciting. Josh would keep them safe just to guard his own neck.

"Great." Josh followed him back into the barn. "You don't happen to have anything to eat, do you?"

Vincent stifled a sound that was half-laughter, half-groan. Josh certainly hadn't changed, even if his name had.

Josh joined their company and pitched in as if he had been a volunteer from the beginning. Vincent waited for him to complain about the lack of food, the lack of alcohol, and walking by night and sleeping by day. Josh said nothing about it. He carried the children on his back with a smile and carved tiny animals and people for them out of roots and twigs when they stopped to rest. He spent hours in murmured conversation with Rev. Morris. Vincent wondered if that was part of Josh's restraint, some sort of ancient memories of a religious upbringing. Then again, what did he know of Josh's past?

A day from the safe house, the spring flood coming down from the mountains intervened. It was dawn and they still hadn't found a place to hide for the day.

"Hear something?" Josh asked, lifting a hand to signal for quiet. Immediately, the children dropped to their knees and pressed their hands over their mouths.

It sounded like a truck engine, coming from near the river. According to Vincent's map, they had one more rocky hill to cross, then the road dipped down into a steep river valley.

He and Josh went ahead, following their ears. They had barely crested the last hill when they saw the source of the noise. A tarp-enclosed truck sat in the middle of the river, facing them. From the regular pulse of the engine, rising and falling and the slight jerks forward and backward, the truck was stuck and the driver tried to rock it free.

"Think if we help him out, we can hitch a ride?" Josh murmured. He started down the incline before Vincent could consider the question.

Halfway down, Vincent glanced upriver and frowned. The rushing water of spring thaw looked… wrong. Josh had reached the water's edge.

"Josh," he shouted, "it's flooding!" Vincent gestured at the wall of mud and stones and snow-melt rolling down the river, pushing the water over the banks, heading straight for the trapped truck. He ran.

The other man jumped into the water and splashed through it, thigh-deep, yelling and gesturing at the driver of the truck. The driver looked out the window and waved at Josh, then opened the door and stood on the running board of the ancient, army-surplus-style truck to look upriver. He slid back into the driver's seat quickly.

Josh reached the back of the truck and shouted, then threw himself against the tailgate. The truck engine roared. The wheels spun, splashing muddy water up in a long, creamy brown wave. Josh closed his eyes and gritted his teeth and pushed. Vincent reached the edge of the river and flung himself across the intervening yards. The icy water bit at his weary muscles and sucked the feeling out of them. He threw himself against the tail of the truck and pushed. A twin wave of muddy water doused him.

"It's moving!" Josh bellowed in triumph—and nearly hit his knees, coughing out a mouthful of gritty, icy water. Vincent caught him. They held onto the tail of the truck, still pushing as it ground its way up the incline of the road they had just come down.

The driver slammed on the brakes as soon as the truck cleared the bank of the river. Moments later, the leading edge of the flood reached them. Vincent and Josh jumped back several feet as the river widened instantly and watched in awe as the seemingly solid wall of debris rushed by them.

A stream of words preceded the driver opening the door. By the voice, it was a woman, hidden inside a bulky coat and head wrappings and thick gloves. She stepped out, jumped down to the ground and walked over to them on trembling legs, still spilling her words.

"Sorry, Ma'am," Josh said with a grin. "I don't understand a word you're saying."

"You're Americans?" the woman blurted. She tore off her head wrappings, revealing bright blue eyes, a tiny uptilted nose, heart-shaped face, and an amazing cascade of platinum blond curls all the way down her back.

"The last time I looked I was." Josh's face softened into a smile and his eyes brightened.

"You wouldn't happen to be Vincent, would you?"

"That's me," Vincent said, taking a step closer. Josh scowled at him, which brought an answering grin to his face.

"Thank God. Father Darius said you'd be coming through here."

"You're my — you're not my contact." Vincent wondered what Darius was thinking, to let this woman come out here by herself. "We're supposed to be meeting a team."

"There were five of us, but we got separated. I did a lot of praying and decided to come this way to try to meet you. I'm Geneva Morris, by the way. Is my grandfather with you?"

"Little Geneva?" Josh stepped back and looked her over. "He talks about you like you're a toddler."

"Last time Grandpa saw me, I was." Geneva wiped a sudden tear from her eye. "Where is he?"

They rode in the truck. Vincent drove, with Geneva between him and Josh. Vincent couldn't get a word in during the climb to the top of the hill. Josh reported to Geneva how well her grandfather and his co-workers had done on the trip. It sounded like he had been the leader from the beginning, to Vincent's ears.

The reunion between Geneva and her grandfather brought tears to almost every eye in the group. The old man knew his granddaughter before she even called his name. As Rev. Morris explained later, Geneva was the image of her grandmother. They ran to each other and hugged, crying and laughing. Josh wiped a tear from his eye, which amused and surprised Vincent. When had he grown a tender heart?

They loaded the children into the truck, wrapped them in the blankets Geneva had brought, and drove away as quickly as possible. Then, Vincent heard her story.

Geneva was part of a group that smuggled Bibles into Muslim-controlled countries and helped abused women and new converts escape when their lives were endangered. When she heard that her grandfather's team had made contact, she insisted on being part of the rescue group. Because of her experience in tight situations, Father Darius had urged the other organizers to let her join.

Their group reached the safe house at dawn of the next day. They waited three days before the other members of Geneva's team arrived, somewhat shame-faced and bedraggled. In those three days, Vincent watched Josh begin his campaign for Geneva's attention. He tried to interfere, mostly because Josh would soon have a price on his head. Geneva didn't deserve that kind of trouble. Besides, Josh had never truly been serious about any woman. He seemed to enjoy the chase more than the prize. He was like a sport fisherman. As soon as he caught one, he threw it back. It wasn't like the relationship would last once they got on the plane and flew to England.

So Vincent focused on looking outside the safe house for trouble. Despite the certainty that disaster would swoop down on them from out of nowhere, he felt oddly at peace in the cramped little house. He enjoyed inventing quiet games for the children, to keep them amused and settled in one room.

Josh, however, destroyed his hard-won peace every time he turned around. Every chore Geneva asked him to do, whether gathering fuel or bringing more water from the cistern out in the yard or even scrubbing pots, Josh did it eagerly. He seemed to spend every waking moment following her around the tiny house, listening to her speak, hunting for opportunities to do her bidding.

"He's a love-struck puppy," Vincent growled, watching Josh hurry back into the house from the cistern, with two slopping buckets of water. Then the idiocy of the situation struck him. Maybe Josh was following the same tactic he had been following — trying to earn his way to Heaven. Or in Josh's case, get into Heaven on a generous woman's coattails.

Geneva was an intelligent, discerning woman who risked herself for others, yet Josh's servile actions worked. Her eyes sparkled whenever he spoke to her. Jokes that fell flat from Josh's lips and earned groans from the others made her laugh.

The more Vincent told himself to write her off as another intelligent woman who let herself be blinded by charm, the more the growing relationship between her and Josh bothered him. He knew Josh and Geneva didn't belong together. Yet what could he do to help her?

He grew desperate enough to pray, and that meant getting somewhere by himself where he could hash things out with God, out loud. He wasn't quite ready to accept that God could hear his thoughts.

The problem resolved itself as he stumbled through his first prayer. Josh came to find him. Vincent heard his approaching footsteps, sliding down the gravel path into the narrow ravine below the house. Vincent settled on a boulder with his back to the trickle of a stream, facing the bend in the path where Josh would emerge, and waited.

"Man, I am in the lowest level of Hell," Josh muttered. He stumbled around the last turn and skidded down the steepest part of the slope to the edge of the water. "She's engaged," he blurted, before Vincent could ask.

"Geneva?"

"Their contact arranging the flight just got here and gave her a letter thick enough to choke a mule—or maybe jackass, meaning me." Josh dropped down on the boulder facing Vincent. "You know that David she's been talking about all the time? 'Oh, I can't wait for you to meet David. You two have so much in common,'" he said, his voice slipping into falsetto, as he tucked his clasped hands under his chin.

Vincent couldn't help it. He had to laugh.

"Yeah, make fun of the guy who just got his heart ripped out. It's my own fault. Should have figured she was in love and not a groupie for Super-Missionary Man."

"Sorry. You should have known a woman like her wouldn't get this far without someone putting a claim on her."

"Yeah... man, if this is what it's like to have a broken heart, I'm swearing off love for the rest of my life."

Vincent never finished that prayer, but he was impressed with the timing. After all the things he had seen, the near-misses and providential arrival of supplies and guides and transportation, he knew better than to write anything off as coincidence.

By the time they made their connections and boarded the cargo plane bound for England, Josh seemed to be recovering. Enough that he didn't wince every time Geneva talked about her fiancé—who was meeting them at the airfield in England.

"Ironic." Rev. Morris sighed as Vincent finished checking on the children and settled down next to him in the cramped confines of the cargo plane's hold.

"What is?" Vincent glanced over his shoulder. Josh had managed to sit next to Geneva. He wasn't sure if he should pity him or write him off as a hopeless idiot. They sat close together, talking earnestly, their voices muted by the rumble of the engines readying to taxi down the runway.

"It took a broken heart for young Joshua to turn his mind to spiritual matters."

"Oh, is that what he's doing?"

Vincent didn't believe it for a moment. Josh and Midas had infiltrated a cult maybe six years ago, pretending to be searchers. He had the role of soul-weary, spiritually starving, confused young man down pat. While he earned the trust of the leaders of the cult, he also romanced the daughter of the leader, to gain access to off-limits buildings in the compound where valuable items and computer software were stored.

~~~~~

"So you're thinking he's been playing a role all these years, just to win Geneva?" Joan asked.

"I should have stayed in contact, kept tabs on him. I figured Daedelus—Josh would have reached his limit of spirituality, of God talk, and decided even a woman as incredible as Geneva wasn't worth cramping his style, wearing a mask for years."

"Maybe he gave up and gave in."

"Either that, or he's still playing a role, infiltrating Christian organizations, using Geneva as a front, causing destruction wherever he can, then moving on."

"How'd he win her away from Super-Missionary Man David?"

"Didn't." Vincent heaved himself off the bench and gestured with a jerk of his head for her to follow, heading back up to the house.

"What do—"

"David and Geneva were married, and he died, killed in the crossfire of a gang war he was trying to stop, when their daughter, Darcy, was about a year old. Josh made himself their defender, got involved with the inner-city outreach, and two years later married Geneva. He even adopted Darcy."

"You think maybe he orchestrated David's death?" A heavy chill ran down her back and wrapped around her gut, in harsh contrast to the humidity that remained after the long June day.

"It's what I would have done, back in the day."

"Unless Josh's conversion was for real."

"That's what I need to determine. Have you read through the whole file?"

"Dad just gave me the overview. He's more worried about you. Especially since you didn't tell him or Elizabeth much of anything."

"Yeah, he's not easy to fool." A rueful smile softened Vincent's features. They completed the walk back to the house in silence as the evening closed in, warm and gentle and comforting around them.
~~~~~

Chapter Four

"Darcy?" Roger Lancaster picked his way across the crumbling parking lot of the abandoned Allied Glass Works. Twenty yards away, the river sent wreaths of mist through the night, obscuring what little he could see under the crescent moon. "Honey, are you here?"

Footsteps whispered through the darkness, somewhere in the black, blocky building ahead. He caught a glimmer of movement as he drew closer and saw moonlight filtering down through gaps in the roof. She waited for him inside, just like her note had promised.

Roger clenched his fist in his pocket, wishing he had a weapon, just for a moment. His steps slowed as he approached the gaping maw of the building, where the overhead door had been shattered, allowing access for anything and anyone who wanted to take shelter there.

Such as Darcy.

Prickles of uneasiness crept up and down his spine, from the sense of self-preservation he had learned in a life he gave up years ago. If this was twenty years ago, he would listen and walk away and not go into that building for the meeting.

If this was twenty years ago, he wouldn't care about the accusations, and he wouldn't be so grateful, desperate, for the help Darcy promised him. Not just him, but six other men whose reputations hung in the balance. She sent him a note, saying she had found evidence that the accusations were false, and she knew who was behind the whole scheme, trying to destroy the ministry that was the focus of their lives.

"And a little child will lead them," Roger murmured as he glanced over his shoulder at the parking lot.

That wasn't quite accurate. Darcy was nearly twenty, but she had an innocence and purity that made her seem much younger. She made him feel old and soiled and weary and yet gave him hope for the future at the same time. The first time he saw her, he had come back to the Spike Center after a four-month fundraising tour. The rumors and accusations were just starting. Darcy was bussing tables, pausing to talk to the filthy, reeking, sodden derelicts and red-eyed drug addicts who came in for a free meal. She cared, and those broken-down wrecks of humanity knew it. They kept their hands off her, and they controlled their tongues in her presence.

"Darcy?"

Roger shivered and glanced back over his shoulder. Nothing moved in this section of town except the mist. Black on black shadows. Silence. Not even the wind to talk to him. Jeans and sweatshirt weren't enough in the chill that seemed to flow out of the black mouth of the abandoned factory.

Like a monster, waiting to devour him.

When he had been a boy, he had played in the caves along the coast of Cornwall and pretended to be a knight, rescuing maidens from dragons and ogres. His parents had split when he was eleven, destroying his childhood and shredding his dreams of adventure and daring. Moving from Cornwall to Detroit had been the first step in a long, downward plunge, nearly wiping those dreams out of his soul. Darcy made him remember those days. For her, and her belief in him, he wanted to stay and fight for his reputation and the rescue mission.

Roger shook his head and ran his long fingers through his thinning, graying red curls. When had those memories decided to surface? Since he found the note from Darcy tucked under his apartment door? He wished he had returned soon enough to actually talk to her, but maybe it was better that way. With all the lies being circulated about those heading the ministry, it might be better if no one saw them talking in daylight.

He just wished Darcy hadn't chosen a place like this. It was one thing for her parents to choose to make their home in the Zone, but another thing for a girl like her to wander around so late at night, alone. True, Darcy was the most talented and natural student of swordplay he had taken on in years, but a white girl riding her motorcycle alone in the Zone after midnight—that attracted the kind of attention a sword couldn't defend against.

Darcy was too good-hearted. She needed to be defended from herself, almost as much as she needed defending from the scandal trying to tear the Spike Center down to its foundations.

"You're not a knight in shining armor and she's not a damsel in distress," Roger muttered, and stepped through the gaping mouth of the broken doorway.

Darcy as he had last seen her filled his mind. Her long, dark hair was held back in two ponytails. She wore her favorite green sweatshirt with the roaring lion on it, and scurried through the swinging door into the kitchen, carrying a tub of dirty bowls and spoons almost too heavy for her. Roger had hurried forward to help, and they laughed as they stumbled over to the huge sink to put the tub down.

"Thanks. Rescued me again," Darcy had said with a breathless laugh. Then her smile had faded. "I wish you and the rest would stay. You built this place. We're the newcomers."

"That's why you and your folks are considered innocent. We need all of you to stay and carry on the work until we can clear our names. Be a good little girl and keep safe, okay?"

"I'm not a little girl," she had said with a sigh and a flicker of humor in her eyes. "I'm nearly twenty. I can vote. I can drive. And I can go three rounds with you before losing my sword."

"I'm the best swordsman in England," he had interrupted, deliberately thickening the Cornwall accent he had worked hard to lose, so the bullies in his Detroit neighborhood wouldn't bloody him every time he opened his mouth.

He had followed his favorite childhood tales and took up fencing and then mastery with other swords to ward off many different kinds of bullies. He had held onto the swords, only selling them when the Center needed a boost of financing. Three of his precious swords had provided the funding he needed to start his dojo. If he didn't have his dojo and his students, he didn't know how he would hold onto his peace of mind while he waited for the scandal to be unraveled and the accusations proven false.

"I am not a little girl."

"Sweetheart, compared to me, you're still in diapers." He had brushed a loose strand of hair back behind her ear. "When this mess is all cleared up, when we're all back to work, all this will make sense. It's best that we step aside so our work won't be damaged by the lies of our enemies."

"You'll come back?"

"I promise."

"I wish we could find whoever is telling all those lies about you and Sam and Tyler and the others," she had said with a sniff, her pretty mouth flattening in hurt and anger. "I'd just like to take them and —" The anger that flared in her eyes, on his behalf, warmed him.

"None of that. Leave it to God to handle this mess."

"I'd rather pray for a big, mean, avenging angel to come down and start banging heads together."

"All have sinned, remember that. If you let them take your peace, then they've already won."

Roger tried to hold onto those words, that wisdom and comfort he tried to give Darcy, but it was hard. Someone with powerful connections was destroying the work of decades with vicious lies, backed up with fabricated evidence. By painting him and the other founders of the Spike Center as hypocrites, drug dealers and pimps, they were hurting more people than just the ones whose reputations had been torn to shreds. If the Spike Center folded, where would all the people turn for help, who came to them every day for food, clothes, basic medical care, a place to take a shower and feel the love of God through His servants?

When he had returned to his apartment that evening, after another fruitless meeting with the other targets of the slander, Roger had been surprised to find the note from Darcy. His heart had skipped a few beats when he read that she knew someone who might be able to help with the problem. Now, he was only a few moments away from the answer to weeks of increasingly desperate prayers.

"Darcy?" Roger stepped into a room where a thin trickle of moonlight came in through a gap in a grimy skylight. He wondered why she was hiding. "Where are you?"

"Darcy couldn't make it," a man whispered. "So sorry."

Roger turned, catching a flicker of movement from the corner of his eye. He raised his hands in reflex as the long, gleaming blade whistled out of the darkness. Fire slashed across his neck. He stumbled backward, clutching at the hot, liquid gushing. His attacker's face appeared in the moonlight, changed into something demonic with the fury that twisted it. Roger gasped, stunned, momentarily distracted by the effort to understand. A baseball bat in the man's other hand swung upward, smashing into his head. He staggered backward, stunned, unable to cry out, and tripped over a pile of rubble. Falling, he tried to roll out of the way as the long blade swung down again, finding the other side of his neck with fatal precision.

<center>~~~~~</center>

T-minus fifty-eight minutes and counting. Darcy thought she could feel the second hand speeding around the clock hanging over the sink in the Spike Center's massive stainless steel kitchen. Fifty-eight minutes until she needed to leave for her morning lesson with Roger. She yanked open the door of the walk-in cooler and slid a bus pan full of oranges off the wire shelving. She snagged six cartons of eggs off another shelf, put them in the bus pan, and backed out of the cooler, nudging the latch with her hip.

T-minus fifty-seven minutes. A harder shove with her hip slammed the door open, just short of banging against the wall. A sense of movement alerted her as she turned, narrowly avoiding slamming the bus pan into the gangly, red-haired young man standing close enough behind her she felt his breath on her shoulder.

"Doug!" She would have punched him, but her hands were full.

"Sorry." He grinned and stepped back, reaching to take the pan. "Got time for breakfast before I go to work with your dad?"

"Can't. Sparring today with Roger." She slid past him and hefted the pan onto the long worktable running down the middle of the kitchen. "Eva—*huevos*." She reached to the rack hanging from the side of the table and selected a long knife.

"Is that smart?" Doug raised his hands when she pointed the blade in his direction.

"Is what smart?" Darcy grabbed three oranges out of the pan and quartered them with rapid strokes.

28

"Spending time with Roger." He looked around the kitchen and stepped closer to her. "You know, after all the things people are saying about him."

"And you're adding to them." She took three more oranges and quartered them with more force than necessary.

"What if — I know you like Roger and you trust him, and so do your folks — but what if the rumors are true?"

"How can you think that?" Darcy turned to him, raising the knife, then catching herself. She turned back to finishing the oranges.

T-minus fifty-five minutes.

"Well, you have to figure with all the things people are saying, some of it has to be true — the odds — "

"Odds are that a lot of troublemakers are jumping on the bandwagon and trying to cash in on whatever blackmail they think will be paid." An especially vigorous slash of the knife squealed on the stainless steel surface. "Isn't the timing odd? Don't you think it's a little suspicious that *all* the members of the board have been accused of the exact same things?" She finished the last orange and reached for the pan. Four steps took her to the deep sink. She rinsed the pan and came back to the table, held it under the lip of the table and swiped all the orange sections into it.

"Perfect timing," Belinda said, reaching over the table to take the pan from her. "Dougie-boy, you're not part of the kitchen crew and I'll just bet you haven't washed your hands since yesterday. Out of the kitchen or the health inspector will be riding our backs for a week." She snatched the damp towel from her belt and waved it at him. "Shoo."

"Yes, ma'am." He hunched his shoulders and watched Belinda take the pan to the long pass-through window where other pans of prepared food were lined up, ready for the hungry breakfast crowd of homeless due to descend on the Spike Center in fifty-two minutes. He didn't leave.

"Their enemies don't have any imaginations," Darcy continued, lowering her voice. "It's all lies, and you can't convince me to think anything else." She reached for the tall stacks of paper plates, then turned back to him. "How can you think that of them?"

"I'm not — I don't want to believe it. I'm just worried about you getting hurt."

"Roger would never hurt me." She dodged three women with slopping buckets of juice, heading for the dispensers out in the dining room. "Either help or get out of the way."

T-minus fifty minutes.

Doug didn't say anything, which suited her just fine. She filled his arms with disposable plates and cups and he followed her wherever she directed so she could set up the serving line. Next, the plastic utensils. Then wheeling the carts full of plastic trays into place at the head of the line. At precisely T-minus fifteen minutes, she was done with set-up. Doug still didn't speak, but she felt his mournful gaze on her as she slapped together a peanut butter, bacon and banana sandwich on toast, wrapped it in a napkin, and snagged a plastic pint jug of chocolate milk on her way out of the kitchen through the back door.

He didn't follow her, and Darcy stumbled when a hand seemed to squeeze around her heart. There went her closest chance at a boyfriend yet, and over what? She knew with every fiber of her being that Roger and Cyrus and Hooper and all the other members of the board, all the original directors of the Spike Center, were innocent of every salacious accusation and rumor. Why couldn't Doug trust them like she did? Couldn't he see that if the volunteers and staff of the Center didn't stand together, everything would collapse? Martha staunchly believed they were innocent—why couldn't Doug trust his grandmother, if nobody and nothing else?

"Darcy? Sweetheart, what's wrong? You have an enormous black cloud hanging over your head, and on such a glorious morning, too." Karl Van Mournen's rich, British-accented voice rolled down the shadowy hallway, stopping her on her way to the loading dock.

The clock inside her head kept ticking.

He was just a silhouette at the far end of the hall. Darcy paused to slide her sandwich into the pocket of her sweatshirt jacket, hanging on a peg on the wall, and snagged it off the peg.

"I saw you and young Douglas in the kitchen. What did that young rapscallion say to upset you?"

"He thinks I should stay away from Roger, not go for my lessons at the dojo, just because of all those lying jerks trying to hurt him." Darcy cringed, hating the whiny sound of her voice. If she looked in the mirror would her lower lip be sticking out like a pouty brat one-third her age?

"You don't really care what that silly boy thinks, do you?" Karl said, his voice rich with repressed laughter.

Something bristled deep inside and itched down her back.

"I adore Martha," he continued. "She's like a grandmother to you. A wonderful woman. But no matter how much she loves her grandson, that boy isn't good enough for you."

"Good enough for me?" She tried to laugh. "Doug is a friend." She swallowed hard, fighting that aching, sinking sensation. She really had hoped Doug would be the boyfriend she had been waiting for, praying for. Her father liked him. Van Mournen liked him. Their opinions mattered more than anyone else's in the world. "Just a friend."

"And as a friend, he is worried for you."

"Are you worried for me? Worried that I'll get into trouble, going to Roger for lessons?"

"My dear, I am no longer able to wield a sword." He raised his cane, then bent to slap his bad leg. "I can teach you theory, but Roger is the best man available to spar with you. We both know how vital it is for you to learn swordsmanship." A low, rich chuckle rippled down the hall, loosening several knots of tension in her back and gut. "I hope to add another... treasure... to our private collection when I come back from my next trip. Your future guardianship demands that you know personally how to handle what will come into your care someday."

"But do you believe what they're saying about Roger and the others?" she demanded.

"Roger Lancaster is a good man. An honorable man. I know for a certainty that not one word spoken against him is true."

"Then how do we prove he's innocent, and all the others?"

"Well... I think that is more your father's province than mine, dearheart. Trust me—you do trust me?"

"Always." Darcy swung her sweatshirt jacket around her shoulders and slid her arms into place. T-minus eight minutes. Fortunately, the dojo was just a few blocks straight down the street from the Center, a matter of moments on her motorcycle.

"Go to your lessons and let older and wiser hearts and minds deal with the nefarious plans of slanderers and scoundrels."

~~~~~

Ten minutes after her lessons were supposed to start, Darcy sat on the worn cement steps of the grimy, red brick, three-story building that housed the dojo. The entire first floor was open, all the interior walls removed, surrounded by amber-tinted windows behind metal grillwork, so she could see across from one side to another. She saw the exercise mats, the punching bags, free weights, barbells, racks of equipment, and Roger's office tucked into one corner. However, no sign of Roger. No sign of movement on the second floor, where a dance teacher, yoga instructor, and massage therapists rented rooms. No lights on in the windows of the third story, where Roger had his apartment. She was ready to go behind the building, in the narrow alley between it and the building in back, to climb the fire escape and tap on Roger's window. What if something was wrong with Roger? What if he was sick, still in bed, unaware of how late in the morning it was? She couldn't imagine Roger not calling if he needed to cancel.

Ten more minutes and Darcy pushed her motorcycle around the back of the building and stood on the seat to reach the bottom rung of the fire escape ladder and climb up. The shades were rolled up over the window at the third-floor landing, and the security bar across the window was firmly locked into place. There was enough sunlight splashing across the sparsely furnished apartment to see Roger wasn't there. No signs of
~~~~~

breakfast dishes. The bathroom door was open. No movement, no signs of life.

Darcy considered climbing up to the roof and trying to force her way in through that door, but it was too close to the edge of the roof. The only way she could think of to get that door open was a running start and throwing all her weight against it. She didn't have much faith in her ability to kick hard and break the lock. She needed something hard—maybe something sharp—to break a lock on either the roof door or the window. A shudder worked through her at the momentary thought of using the katana Roger let her use for their workouts. While the blade could do the job, she didn't want to risk it.

"Moot point," she muttered, as she started down the fire escape again. The sword was inside, and she was outside, and if she could get to the sword then she wouldn't be in the predicament where she needed it, would she?

On the way back to the front steps, she made a complete circuit of the building and found Roger's car parked in the gravel drive on the far side, between it and the building next door. Darcy shuddered, looking up at the multiple gaping windows with shards of glass hanging in the frames. Odd, how the abandoned, slightly dangerous feeling emanating from that building seemed to make the shadow it cast feel thick and cold.

Where was Roger, if his car was here?

Half an hour later, Darcy was still sitting on the front steps as Mercedes, the yoga instructor, came to prepare for her first class of the day.

~~~~~

Joan expected to head out the next morning to drive to the Spike Center and was surprised to see Vincent heading for the carriage house without any luggage. When she ran to catch up with him, he wore the same distracted look from yesterday, and for a moment he didn't seem to see her. A few lines formed around his mouth, and she thought he would tell her to stay behind, that whatever he was going to do had nothing to do with her.

Instead, he just nodded as the lines smoothed away, and hooked his thumb over his shoulder at the black vintage Corvette she had seen him restoring in the carriage house workshop over the winter.
~~~~~

Chapter Five

"Taking it for a test run before we take our trip?" Joan muffled a chuckle as Ulysses left her side, trotted over to the grassy apron in front of the carriage house, and settled down. Some of the Quarry Hall dogs loved to go for rides. Ulysses preferred sleeping in the sun when he wasn't needed as her guardian.

"I need to talk to George," Vincent said. "Giving him a new toy to play with should prime the pump."

"Uh huh." She wasn't sure if she should tease him about being cryptic.

George, the foundation's mechanical genius, could be OCD and refuse to communicate, but an old car to play with always made him happy. What did Vincent need from the physically and mentally damaged man in charge of the car pool?

"Shouldn't take long. If you want to come with me..." His smile faded, and for a moment he looked so tired, Joan wondered if he had slept at all the night before.

She knew Vincent was secretive about his deep, dark, painful past, and she was normally willing to let him hold those secrets. She understood exactly why keeping ugly, painful, shameful things buried was sometimes far more comfortable than bringing them out into the light of day to be dealt with. Last night's revelations had been surprising, and humbling. Who was she that he trusted her with that much detail?

"Well," he said as he snagged the keys off their hook on the pegboard, "might save some explaining along the way if you hear whatever he has to say. For our assignment."

"If George has anything to say at all." Joan waited until they were both settled in the butter-soft leather seats before speaking again. "What does he have to do with Joshua Clay?"

"Back when he was Snow—as little as possible. Daedelus felt the same way. There was a time when the rest of us spent a lot of time and energy keeping them from killing each other."

"George was Snow." Joan kept her gaze focused straight ahead as the Corvette rolled, purring, down the long asphalt driveway to the main gate. "From some things you said... well, you didn't exactly say—"

"We hated each other. We were all we had, the Three Horsemen, so we stuck together and kept each other alive, all the time knowing we'd gladly take the assignment to wipe each other out the minute someone stepped out of line. Or like me, tried to break free. Actually, Shadow escaped first..." Vincent tapped the miniature tablet sitting on the Corvette's console and the gate swung open before they reached it.

"Did you do... all that... to George?" she asked, when they were out in traffic and gliding down Portage Trail.

"Nine years ago or so, while we were still getting things set up to take over the Hall, some of your dad's shady connections told us about him. He went over the side of a high bridge into the Ohio River in the middle of a snowstorm. He was shot up, his car exploded, he was burned and cut up and frostbitten and drowned..." His voice cracked with something, torn between weariness, confusion, anger and laughter. "My guess is, someone with a deep-seated need to make sure Snow never came after him for paybacks. The stubborn old cuss refused to die. In his pocket, they found my picture and a dozen addresses to look for me. Or at least pick up my trail."

"He was coming to kill you."

"He sure wasn't coming to relive the good old days."

"When did you ask Elizabeth to take him in? Before or after you found out he was brain damaged and crippled?"

"Does it matter?"

"Duh," she said softly.

Vincent chuckled just as softly. They were silent for the next few miles, as they headed down Market Street to get on I-77.

"She's one sneaky lady," he said, once they were on the highway and heading south. "I was away on business when the original contact was made. Elizabeth understood what that little piece of paper and my picture meant. She could have told those shady friends to forget what they found, let Snow get lost in the system. Put a 'do not resuscitate' order in his medical file. She chose to take him in and make me face my past. If I didn't love that woman more than my own life..." Vincent stayed focused on the road ahead of them. "It's healing, being responsible for the well-being of someone who would want you dead if he ever remembered who you were."

"Healing can be danged uncomfortable."

"Got that right." He glanced away from the road and met her gaze long enough to wink. "In a lot of ways, I kind of envy George. He doesn't remember who he is, what he used to do. Completely clean slate, clean conscience. He's got that child-like faith Christ tells us to want more than anything."

"I used to wish I could forget a lot of things I had to do to survive," she offered. "Forgetting can be dangerous. If you don't know who wants you dead, how can you be alert for them coming after you?"

"Alert for years, or a short time feeling no fear at all? No more nightmares. No more wondering when someone will pick up that trail you thought you erased. No more being afraid to love someone because your enemies will hurt them to hurt you."

"In Snow's—George's case—keep your enemies close, in case he remembers and finishes his job?" Joan said, when he didn't speak for several minutes.

"It's not like they show on TV, where someone recovers from amnesia and gets his life back. Not when portions of your brain are reduced to scar tissue. The man George is now, that's the man he's going to be until he dies. He's totally sold out to Christ. He'll stay sold out."

"What if he doesn't remember that he's sold out?" she asked after a moment of thought.

"You're definitely in a glass half-empty mood today."

"That's an improvement."

"Yeah?"

"Up until I met my dad… I didn't even have a glass."

Vincent sighed, the sound ending in a rough chuckle. "I'm only telling you all this because you're going into this situation with me. You might be the only one to have my back. When it came to anyone on our team, the only thing you could count on was self-preservation. They'd have your back as long as they needed you to have their backs. Nobody more reliable in a crisis, but when you got into safe territory… If something seems too good to be true, it is. Faerie tales are just nightmares, sugar-coated and painted with rainbows."

"You think Josh's conversion and his ministry are just a faerie tale."

"I need to see him, spend time with him, see him in action, before I'll know the man."

"By their fruit you shall know them," she murmured.

"Amen."

They got off at the next exit and headed for the industrial parkway visible from the highway. Twenty minutes later an overhead door rolled up to let them drive into the long cinderblock building smelling of oil and exhaust, chrome polish and leather. George scurried up from the pit where he had been working under a Jeep. His movements reminded Joan of the flying monkeys who worked for the Wicked Witch of the West. One leg was visibly shorter than the other, and the opposite shoulder constantly stayed ahead of him, his body twisted at the hips. Long, straggly hair, somewhere between white and colorless, couldn't obscure the knots of scar tissue down one side of his face, wreathing his forehead, knotting along his jaw line. His eyes were wide like a child spying a table loaded with cake and candy.

"Pretty baby," he crooned, and bent low to reverently stroke up the side of the Corvette. "What's wrong with her? What do you want me to fix? What did you do to hurt her?"

"I didn't do anything, George." Vincent gestured for him to stand back so he wouldn't be hit by the door as he got out of the car. "I thought you'd want to see her, that's all. Maybe you've got some recommendations for what I still need to do to make her like new."

"An ounce of prevention," he murmured, nodding eagerly.

Vincent popped the hood and George chuckled as he scampered around to the front and heaved up the hood. Joan stayed in the car, watching as the two men talked, Vincent in low tones and George commenting on seemingly every piece of the engine. She doubted Vincent was talking about the car, and George was too excited about his new toy to really listen.

Joan thought about Vincent's remark about faerie tales. She wondered if he was thinking about Anne, and her tendency to deal with painful subjects by dressing them in faerie tale language. Maybe he was thinking more of George, how childlike he had become. When he wasn't speaking the language of cars or making intricate origami figures, he wavered between a passion for faerie tales and in-depth Bible studies that would leave a seminary professor breathless. Knowing a little more of George's past, Joan could understand a little bit the wide disparity in how the damaged, childlike man's mind and soul worked.

"Did you ever think," George said, suddenly appearing at Joan's open door, "that King Midas destroyed everything with his golden touch?"

"Uh—in the fable, he nearly starved to death because all his food turned to gold," she said, thinking quickly.

"He had to be baptized, and he nearly drowned, to wash away the curse of the golden touch." He nodded solemnly, and something flickered in his eyes, old pain and terror and what Joan feared was rage. It died before she could be sure. "I don't really think it happened yet, do you?"

"Didn't happen?"

"I think Midas still needs to have it all washed away. Make sure you don't get turned to gold when you hold him down in the water, okay?" He grasped her shoulder, squeezing hard enough to make her hiss.

Joan thought of the killer he had once been, code name Snow, a man who had been coming to kill Vincent before someone nearly killed him.

"Okay." She met his eyes and hated the momentary fear she felt for the old man she had always considered pitiable. Somewhere between an adorable, clumsy puppy and a slightly crazy old uncle.

"Make Vincent be good," he whispered, bending down to hug her hard and fast, before scampering away, back to the service pit he had emerged from nearly an hour before.

Joan waited until they had driven out of the building, the overhead door closing behind them, before speaking.

"I assume you asked him what he thought about Daedelus and Midas. Why did you ask about Midas?"

"I didn't, but somewhere behind the scars in his brain, George remembers those two were a matched pair. Almost Siamese twins. He reminded me that Midas was obsessed with pure gold." Vincent frowned as he paused at the entrance of the industrial park, waiting to pull out into traffic.

"Actual gold? He was a thief?"

"More the purity aspect."

"Meaning?"

"Midas had a taste for very young, innocent girls."

"As in..." Joan flinched as her thoughts turned to her half-sister, Nikki. She thought about Brock Pierson, romancing a girl eight years younger than him, seducing her into running away from home with him.

"Not a pedophile. Not like that. There was something very old-fashioned, almost chivalrous about Midas. High ideals. Ready to kill for his ideas of purity. He was interested in this opera singer, when we were undercover in France. Within five days, he gave her a ring, put his claim on her. She looked and acted pure as driven snow, until she got away from her chaperones, and then she was a dog in heat." He glanced sideways at her and nodded sharply when Joan flinched. "Exactly. Midas found out. The next day, the girl and the man she was with were both dead." He frowned at the stoplight as it turned red twenty feet ahead of them. "Midas made a big deal out of the ring being missing."

"The gold meant more to him than the girl."

"The gold was pure, but she definitely wasn't."

"What does this have to do with Joshua Clay, allegedly reformed and running a rescue mission?"

"Daedelus—" He shook his head. "I have to remember to call him Joshua. Or Josh—that's what all the testimonials and character references call him. What Elizabeth's friend, Saundra, calls him."

"Josh stole Midas's girl?"

"In a nutshell."

"But Midas didn't kill him right away."

"He tried. Josh told me how they were partnered for a little while after things imploded, when Shadow got away and I managed to hide for a while. Faked my own death for the first time. He didn't even know Midas was after the girl until he saw her wearing the opera singer's ring."

"So Midas got the ring back from her. He lied about it being missing."

"No surprise there. The man's native tongue, after pretending to be a British sophisticate, was lies."

"Then a few days later, the girl was dead, the ring was gone, and Midas came after Josh," Joan guessed. Vincent nodded, the lines bracketing his mouth deepening. "But Midas still hasn't killed him?"

"He told me about it in Afghanistan, trying to convince me he had reformed, and really did want out of the Game. I even brought it up to convince him to walk away from Geneva. If he really cared about her, he would walk away to save her life. If Midas ever caught up with him, he would kill Geneva just because Josh loved her."

"Okay..." Joan relaxed a little in the seat as she caught a glimpse of the tangled pathways of George's thinking, the messages he tried to get across from memories he couldn't access. She had suspected for some time now that some ancient cultures were right when they claimed that the gods spoke through the mentally damaged — or in this case, God and the angels spoke through people like George. "Somewhere deep inside, George was warning you that if Midas hasn't punished Josh yet, he might just be waiting, looking for the best way. You could be walking into his gun sights by getting near Josh again."

"You could be walking into his gun sights, coming with me. Think about that."

"Well, between you and Ulysses..." She shrugged and wished her furry guardian had come on the short trip with them. Joan was grateful he would be with her on the trip to the Zone and the Spike Center.

~~~~~

Darcy rode her motorcycle up the loading dock ramp behind the former factory/warehouse. From far away in the building, the sounds of hammering and drilling reached her on echoes. The clean, June morning breeze brought her the odors of freshly cut wood, paint and plaster. She inhaled deeply, then turned to padlock her motorcycle to a foot-wide water pipe running down the inside of the dark, crate-filled loading dock.

"There's my darling girl!" Van Mournen's deep voice greeted her from the shadows of the doorway inside the building.

"How did your meeting go?" Darcy slung her helmet over the handlebar of her motorcycle and turned to the door.

"Swimmingly, as always. How was your lesson?" He stepped out into the light of the loading dock, revealed as a tall, lean, sharp-faced man all in gray — hair, eyes, neat beard bordering his square jaw, and gray-on-gray pinstripe Italian-cut suit.

"No lesson." She stepped around him and headed down the dark hallway. It echoed and smelled faintly of new paint and sawn wood and fresh plaster. She walked through the shadows without tripping or looking where she was going. He followed her.

"Why? What happened?"

"Roger wasn't there."

"Well, he's been rather busy of late, dealing with all the troubles, keeping them from harming the Center." He gestured upward, taking in
~~~~~

the old building.

"I waited the whole time. Even until other people showed up for their lessons. Mercedes came to teach yoga. Roger never contacted any of them, never made arrangements for anyone to come in and open the building for him, lead any of the exercise groups."

"Hmm, that is odd. He's usually so reliable, so punctual." He made a sound, half-grunt and half-chuckle. "So energetic. If I had half his energy, I'd be ten times as successful as I am."

"Then you'd own the whole world."

"And I'd give it to you on a silver platter." He hurried a few steps to catch up with her, resting a hand on her shoulder and stopping her just short of the lighted hallway ahead of them. "Don't let it bother you, sweetheart. Roger is a good man going through a rough patch."

"Not a rough patch—somebody is telling lies and lies and more lies, trying to take down the whole Center. Uncle Karl... what if it gets so bad that Mom and Dad are pulled into it?"

"I would never let that happen. You just say the word. I'll have an entire stable of lawyers hard at work, throwing up such a wall of paperwork and injunctions and writs and actions, we'll all be dead and gone before anybody can work through it all. I'm here to protect your family, dearheart. Trust me." When she didn't lift her bowed head, he shook her slightly. "Trust me? You do, don't you?"

"Sure."

"Hmm, you don't look like you trust me."

"Uncle Karl—"

"You need something to put a smile back on your face. Not that I approve of how your father spoils you rotten."

Darcy snorted, her mouth trembling upward.

"But just to show you how much your happiness means to me, what say I find you a new master of swordplay to continue your lessons—just until Roger clears away his troubles? Eh? How does that sound?"

"Well, it sounds like a waste of time, because I know everything will be back to normal tomorrow."

"Indulge a silly old man."

"You're not silly and you're not old."

"Ah, me, such flattery. You do have a way with words, my dear." He slid his arm around her shoulders, and they walked around the corner in perfect step. "If I were a younger man, I'd lay my heart at your feet."

"Sounds kind of messy, to me."

He let out a bark of laughter and hugged her closer. "Promise me something while I'm out of town?"

When Darcy was a child, she would have instantly said, "Anything!" After all, he was her Uncle Karl, who gave her treats and made it possible to have adventures her parents couldn't afford. Now he paid for her sword and self-defense lessons, and filled her head with stories about all the foreign countries and cities he had visited. Now, however, after the danger and heartache she had seen in the cities she had lived in with her parents, and the rescue missions they had renovated together, Darcy had learned caution. Even with her beloved adopted uncle, who had been the first to caution her never to make open-ended promises.

"If it doesn't get in the way of my classes and my work here."

"That's my darling girl. Always provide yourself a back door to escape through." Van Mournen stopped them, released her, and turned her to face him. "Check on the treasure room for me?"

"Like you have to ask?"

"Never assume anything, darling." He winked and patted her cheek. "Swords, even the most elegant and ancient, need regular handling. Until Roger comes back and your lessons resume, take out one each day and do some shadow-fighting, will you? Keep your hand in, learn balance, and let the swords know they're still loved, eh?"

Darcy nodded, choosing the wisdom of silence rather than letting out an exultant shout and babbling her delight. Van Mournen chuckled, leaned forward to brush a kiss across her forehead, and turned down the next hallway. She fought temptation for several agonizing moments as she threaded her way through the former factory and warehouse, down hallways that had been created in the weeks since her family joined the Center, some that were nothing more than metal framing, waiting for circuitry and drywall. At this time of the morning, the staff would be finishing up the morning assessment meeting, tallying how many had come for breakfast, how many had asked for medical help, how many had asked for clothes or took the portable hygiene packages, if there were any new faces, and if any souls had taken a step closer to Heaven. By her internal clock, she was fairly sure they would be finishing the closing prayer by the time she reached the meeting room in the unfinished suite that would eventually be divided into administrative offices. Someday. If the Spike Center didn't get shut down by scandal and rumor and the continuing loss of long-time supporters.

Chapter Six

She paused long enough outside the closed door to hear one voice murmuring. "Uncle Bob" Dempsey had served as chaplain for their core group of missionary renovators for the last twelve years, and he always said the closing prayer for the meeting. Smiling in satisfaction that everything was as it should be, Darcy slowly turned the doorknob and pushed it open. The eight workers gathered at one end of the long table that usually held twenty were just raising their heads as she stepped into the room.

"Hey, sweetheart. Back from your lesson?" Josh called. "How's Roger doing today?"

"He's missing." Darcy hated the instant concern that swept over all the faces. She gave the few details, including climbing the fire escape to look for him, as she crossed to the table and stood at the end between her parents' seats.

"The police can't do anything for more than a day," Martha said. "Does he have a cell phone? If we can rule out a trip that he told no one about, that will speed up the process." She slid her Bible into the canvas craft bag that carried her necessary equipment for the day—including a handgun, a digital camera and her newest needlework project. "We can get a lot of things done while we're waiting for the police to get involved." A grim smile touched her face and she nodded for punctuation. Darcy felt a little better. After all, Martha was a retired police detective.

It took less than ten minutes for members of the team to take tasks and start the effort to find Roger, or at least track down someone who knew where he had gone. Darcy stayed in the meeting room after everyone had left. She knew she should pray, but her head was filling with ugly scenarios of the things that could have happened to Roger to make him miss their morning lessons. The Zone was an unforgiving place. Roger and the others in the original team that had started the Spike Center had enjoyed protected status in the Zone, because everyone knew they were there to help the innocents, the downtrodden, the hopeless and those who suffered from broken hearts and minds. Even the worst of the gang leaders respected them and had told their followers that the workers at the Spike Center were hands off.

Unfortunately, when the rumors started whispering through the Zone and turned poisonous, that protection had faded. Roger and the others had fallen out of favor. Numbers dropped in important areas like GED classes, daycare, sewing and cooking and health workshops, and worship services on Sundays and Wednesdays. It was only a matter of time until someone decided to turn protection into punishment.

"Please, God, don't..." She sighed and headed for the door. "Just don't let it get any worse? Send us someone to help us? Mom and Dad always talk about the angels unawares, sent in secret to help us. We could really use some big, visible angels standing all around this place, beating up on Satan and making things right again." She swallowed hard and reached for the doorknob. "Please?"

She pulled the door open and let out a squeak of surprise when she came face-to-face with Doug, who was pushing the door open. For three seconds they stared at each other, wide-eyed.

"Uh—sorry." Doug raked the fingers of one hand through his hair. "Grandma got on me about—about before."

"Doug—"

"I was wrong. Grandma says everybody is a victim of some scheme to make this place fold." Two spots of red lit his cheeks and he couldn't look her in the eyes anymore. "She said I'm being hard on Roger because maybe I'm jealous."

"Jealous of what?" Her voice cracked. She grabbed his hand, dragged him into the office, and closed the door. The last thing she wanted or needed was someone to overhear this conversation if it was going where she thought it was going.

"You know." He stole a glance at her and looked away, pretending great interest in the tack board on the far wall.

Darcy almost said, "Uh, no, tell me," but her throat closed up and her face felt hot.

Thanks, God! Maybe Doug really is interested. Enough to be stupid. Please, don't let him be that stupid, though, okay?

"I guess Martha overheard us fighting," she said instead.

"Didn't hear, but she saw enough, and then she put me through the third degree." He let out a shaking breath and met her eyes again for a moment. "She said we just have to trust God to bring justice and trip up the enemy with his own plans, and if I was going to twist things around and see Roger as a rival, then I was insulting you and I was—" He choked.

"What?"

"You know how Grandma is. Testosterone poisoning causing brain damage. Along with a lot of hormones." He shrugged, but even though the red flush in his cheeks spread out, he grinned and met her eyes now and didn't look away.

"Aren't you a little old for hormones getting in the way?"

Darcy knew how old Doug was. Exactly five weeks after she turned twenty, he would be twenty-three.

"Grandma says when the right girl is involved, guys can get knocked off balance real, real easy."

"The right girl?" Her face definitely felt ten degrees hotter.

Was Doug going to try to kiss her? Here, in the office? At least the door was closed, so nobody would see them. Weren't couples supposed to kiss when they made up after a stupid argument?

"I sure hope so," he said, his voice so soft she almost didn't hear him.

The door banged open.

"Doug, there you are," Josh said, grabbing onto the doorframe and turning as if he was about to launch himself back down the hall. "Ready to get to work? Hey, hon, shouldn't you be hitting the books?"

"Yes, Dad." Darcy muffled the groan, but she rolled her eyes. That earned a chuckle from Doug. He nodded to her and hurried to follow Josh down the hall.

Well, maybe next time.

Darcy had a hard time toning down her grin as she made her way through half-finished hallways and rooms, up the open staircase that seemed to hang in mid-air with no visible means of support, to her family's quarters on the top floor. She had three days to take the first test of the summer term, but it was smart to get it out of the way and keep forging through her required classes. Someday, when she figured out what she wanted to major in, she was going to switch from taking college classes by computer to attending a university. Even with most of her requirements out of the way, that still seemed a long way off in the future.

Van Mournen promised her he would pay her tuition to the finest schools in Europe, if that was what she wanted. While she tried to calculate what classes would make her most useful as support for her parents' missions work, he encouraged her to dream big, to study art and literature, music and dance, gourmet cooking and fashion. He wanted her to learn all the major languages, and promised to take her on year-long tours of any country she wanted, to learn the dialects in person. The world was open to her, and he promised to give it to her.

How was she going to tell him that the only world she really wanted was the one she had right here, working hard with her hands and heart? Taking care of babies, handing out food to the hungry and clothes to the threadbare. Even swinging a hammer sometimes, and trying to hear God's voice through all the busyness of serving Him. Van Mournen wouldn't understand. Even though he had dedicated his considerable experience and skills to helping provide funds for whatever mission work Josh and Geneva Clay pursued, his soul didn't belong to their God.

"That's what I want more than anything," Darcy whispered as she settled on her bed in her closet-sized room and reached for the overloaded bookshelf to pull out her textbooks. "Please, Lord, use these problems to make Uncle Karl see that You're real? Maybe beat him up a little, so he finally gives in?"

Sighing, she flipped open the first textbook and settled down to read.

~~~~~

Elizabeth met Vincent and Joan when they returned to Quarry Hall, coming down the front staircase to the main corridor faster than her normal relaxed stride. Joan noticed the flat line of her stepmother's mouth and the sheet of paper she clutched in her hand, wrinkling with the pressure of her grip.

"Roger Lancaster is missing," she announced, and held out the paper to Vincent.

"That's one of the accused men?" Joan asked.

"Saundra just called. I've asked Sophie to start searching, track credit card activity. His car is still parked next to his business. His phone doesn't have a GPS. Saundra is positive he hasn't fled. No matter how desperate the situation, he would have contacted her before he left the city." Elizabeth watched Vincent as he read through the information printed on the paper. "We came up with an idea that requires your talents, specifically."

Joan was surprised to see a crooked smile grow across Vincent's face. She waited until he nodded, folded the paper, then crossed his arms over his chest and leaned back against the wall.

"We're not using our usual investigation mode," he said, glancing at Joan, then turning back to meet Elizabeth's gaze.

"Roger runs a dojo—all sorts of martial arts, exercise classes, self-defense, rape prevention. Saundra is a partner, so she has the authority and the responsibility to bring in someone to run things while he's gone."

"We'll go in and take over, and use that to get close to the people at the Spike Center," he said, nodding. "Solid plan."

"How?" Joan asked.

"We take over the classes Roger taught at the Center. People are a lot more willing to talk if they think you're working for them, helping them when they're in trouble."

~~~~~

Vincent went up that afternoon, to meet with Saundra and move into Roger's apartment in the top floor of the dojo. Joan drove up separately that evening, to take an efficiency apartment three blocks away from the dojo. She would get to know the neighborhood, become a known face and figure in the rough neighborhood, always accompanied by Ulysses. At the end of the week, she would go to the dojo, make contact with Vincent, pretend to apply for a job as his assistant, and use that as an introduction to the Spike Center.

She parked her car in a secure lot and hiked six blocks to the rundown apartment building where a friend of Saundra's had promised to have a spot waiting for her. Joan carried very little with her and left her computer and cell phone behind to present the appearance of someone very much down on her luck, reduced to only what she could carry on her back. She was amused to realize just how naked she felt without her technology and instant communication with Quarry Hall. It was necessary, in case the people they infiltrated decided to investigate her, including searching her belongings.

Ulysses provided a passport to the trust and interest of the children who played in the streets she walked through every day in the pretend quest for employment. He kept the dangerous elements at bay. The only problems Joan had to deal with were the loudmouths and braggarts who swaggered and talked big and spewed filth, but still kept their distance. She listened and watched the currents and byplays and interactions of the people around her and entertained herself with scenarios of how people's treatment of her would change once she applied for the job as self-defense instructor at the dojo.

In between getting to know Roger's students and settling into the neighborhood, Vincent found an office to rent in the supposedly safer part of the city. Sophie shipped him equipment from Quarry Hall, to set up their communications center. If he and Joan needed to do any computer work, and especially if they felt they couldn't confer without being spied on, they would go to the office. In a worst case scenario, it would be their safe house, where they would take anyone who needed rescue.

~~~~~

"Oh, great." Keiko stepped into the room temporarily holding the Center's daycare program. "Here comes the Shoe. I was really hoping she had caught on and was gone for good."

"The Shoe?" Darcy leaned out into the hallway. For several seconds, she had no idea what Keiko was talking about. Then she understood.

She didn't know what the woman's name was, but she was easily recognizable. Who else showed up at the Center to use the daycare, claiming she needed to go job hunting, and dropped off at least a half dozen children who definitely weren't her own? She used the Center's daycare twice a week. The children changed in numbers and details every time she came in. They were always grimy, so sometimes it was hard to tell details such as ethnicity. Once she claimed an Asian child was her grandchild, when she was dark-skinned Hispanic. Then another day she had a redhead with blue eyes and freckles — definitely not a blood relative. Workers kept a tally and took pictures of the children. Over six weeks, she had brought eighteen different children to the daycare. Last week, she was the next to last one to come retrieve "her" children and nearly left without
~~~~~

one little boy who had fallen asleep in the bin of plush toys.

Munson was the last to come pick up his children, and he came in as the woman was leaving with her children. The woman, now labeled as the Woman Who Lived in a Shoe, after the Mother Goose rhyme, stared at him, then hissed something that sounded poisonous, in a dialect of Spanish Darcy couldn't translate. Munson glared back, and whatever he said, too quiet to overhear, made her go white. She had gathered up her children and fled.

"She's no grandma," he said, after he apologized for cursing. "She runs a daycare of her own. Somebody in the 'hood was saying she must have got busted for abuse, because they see her a couple days a week checking out the smoke shops, no kids with her. Now I can see why." He looked around the daycare. "I stopped taking my kids to her more 'n a year ago. Locked my girls in the closet 'cause her grandson wanted Trini's new shoes and she wouldn't give 'em to him. She gets paid to look out for those kids she dumps on you."

Darcy hadn't been part of the investigation, but after enough questions, Munson's words were proven true. Friends of the Center searched out the identities of the children, to let their parents know they weren't getting what they paid for. For the safety of the children, a caretaker who lied for the sake of profit could not be trusted. The decision was made not to let the Shoe woman leave the children at the Center if she continued to claim she was their mother and aunt and grandmother.

"I am not dealing with her," Keiko said. "She spits in my face every time I ask if the kids have allergies we should know about."

"Go get Martha or my mom," Darcy said.

She didn't want to have to deal with the Shoe woman, either, but today was her day to help in the daycare. Standards had to be kept. They weren't obligated to help someone else make money off them. Especially a woman who smelled as bad as the Shoe and who, it was rumored, drank and slept all day, whether the children were with her or not.

Keiko stepped into the next room, the daycare office, and pulled out the file that had been assembled on the many alleged grandchildren, nieces and nephews. Darcy said a quick prayer for courage and the right words. She took the file, and her friend raced down the hallway in the other direction.

Then she closed the bottom half of the door. It served as a gate for the daycare room. Anyone who entered had to be registered, contact information provided, and nametags put on each child before they entered the daycare. Those were the regulations, the standard procedure. The Shoe woman reached over the door to pull up on the latch. Darcy had seen her do it before, so she leaned against the latch. The woman glared at her and shoved her hand into Darcy's stomach.

Darcy was pretty sure the words the woman muttered in her warped Spanish were filthy enough she didn't want to know what they meant.

"You know what the procedures are," she said, grabbing hold of the woman's hand and shoving it back to her side of the door.

"Who you think you are, telling me — "

"You know what the rules are, because every time you bring children here, we have to tell you and you yell. Every time." Darcy leaned on the bottom half of the door, resting her crossed arms on it to provide an extra barrier.

"You just a stupid — " More filth followed, some of it in English this time. "You get boss. I tell her you sass me, you get fired. If you my kid, I beat you, make you mind!" she snarled, gusting breath that smelled of rotten teeth, rotten meat, and bad alcohol.

The three children with her stood against the opposite wall, looking up at Darcy with big eyes, so somber and calm, she wondered if this filthy woman drugged them to make them obedient. No, drugging them would cut into her profits.

"I'm not your child," Darcy said. She wanted so much to say that her parents were the bosses, but she knew better. Throwing her weight around was never approved behavior. "You will abide by the rules, or you can take these children home right now."

"You can't tell me take kids home — I got rights! I pay taxes! I can leave 'em here if I want to!"

"We are not run by the government, and I seriously doubt you have paid taxes in years, if ever." Darcy smiled and stood up straight. "How about we call the IRS right now, and find out how long it's been since you paid taxes?"

That floored the woman. She probably wasn't used to someone turning one of her tried-and-true weapons against her. Darcy wondered how many times she had bellowed about her rights and paying taxes, causing enough ruckus that other people either got tired of standing against her, or were honestly afraid she could deprive them of their jobs. That wasn't going to happen here.

"What you go, makin' trouble for? I din't do nothin' wrong."

"Really?" Darcy reached for the folder she had put on the shelf next to the door and opened it. "Are you ready to register the children so I can let them into the room?" She shuffled through the stack of photos, trying to roughly match up the three children with the photos. All of them had a name written on the photo. The smallest girl, whose face was half-hidden by her grimy, half-deflated rag doll and the filthy thumb in her mouth, had two names written on her photo. "What's her name?" Darcy said, pointing at the girl.

"M'tilda," the woman spat after a long enough pause to make Darcy wonder if she didn't know the child's name.

"You're sure? And is she your daughter or granddaughter?" She tipped the folder to make sure the woman couldn't see over it. She didn't want her to see that the last daycare worker who registered the children wrote that Solly or Ginny was supposed to be the Shoe's niece.

"Daughter."

"And you're sure her name is Matilda?"

A stream of curses spilled out.

"That is enough!" Martha snapped, somewhat breathless from her race down the hall. She inserted her hand between the woman and the door. Somehow, without any visible effort, she pried the nasty woman away far enough that she could step up to the door. "Thank you, dear," she said, bestowing a sunny smile in direct contrast to the ice in her voice a moment before, as Darcy opened the door for her. Martha slid through the opening and slammed the door before the Shoe could try to shove a child through the opening. "Consuela Ramirez, you have dug a hole too deep to get out of without help."

"Don't know what you talkin' 'bout," the Shoe muttered, and astonished Darcy by backing away from the door.

What was it about Martha that her mere presence could calm the foul-mouthed temper tantrum waiting to explode?

"None of the children you have brought here for daycare are yours. The fact of the matter," Martha continued, holding up one hand that effectively stopped the woman's words, "is that you have lied to us, and to the parents of the children who trust you to watch out for them. You lied when you claimed the children were yours, and you lied when you took money for work that you passed on to someone else."

"I got a right t' make a livin'," she muttered, her voice even softer.

"By lying? By stealing?"

"Ain't nobody bringin' me their kids now, anyways."

Darcy knew at least six of the children who had previously come in with the Shoe were now dropped off at the Center by their own parents or older brothers and sisters. Would the nasty old woman's temper flare again if any of those former customers of hers showed up with their children before she left?

Chapter Seven

Martha opened the half-door and beckoned for the children to come inside. Then she took the Shoe—Consuela—by the arm and led her down the hallway, talking softly to her and leaving Darcy to get the children registered. All three were siblings: Tyrone, Tabitha and Toni. Consuela was their grandmother's next-door neighbor. She took them to her apartment when their grandmother was hung over, almost every day.

Keiko returned as soon as Martha and Consuela vanished around the corner, along with three kitchen women who always showed up to help with the daycare when the breakfast cleanup was done. Darcy handed the children over to Keiko to find out if they had eaten this morning and if they knew if they were allergic to anything and had any cuts or bruises or worse injuries. This month, they had uncovered several green stick fractures and knife cuts that needed stitches. Darcy was glad to turn such questions and tending over to Keiko, who had a gift for children. She could get children to talk to her when all other adults frightened them into silence. Usually when there was major damage to deal with, such as reporting rapes and broken bones, Martha was their go-between with the authorities. Darcy hoped Keiko found nothing wrong with these children, and that Martha would return soon.

"Oh—forgot," Keiko said, more than half an hour later, after nearly two dozen more children had arrived for the daycare. "Saundra called. Since you've worked with Roger—"

"They found him?"

"Nope. Saundra found someone to take over for him. Sorry. She wants you to call her or just go over to the dojo when you get a chance, to help him get settled."

Darcy grumbled silently about the lack of faith, that Saundra would replace Roger even before they knew for sure what had happened to him. Unless she had heard from him? Maybe he had been injured and the replacement was only temporary? That possibility lifted her mood and she was able to smile as she climbed on her motorcycle during the short lull before the lunch hour, to drive to the dojo.

Saundra's black Volkswagon beetle was still parked in front of the dojo when she arrived, and Darcy let out a sigh of relief. It would be easier to get to know this replacement with someone to make the introductions. She caught movement through the tinted windows and smiled, glad to see life in the building. It had bothered her more than she liked to admit, to have the doors locked and no movements, no sounds inside. As if Roger had died.

Two men were sparring in the corner, familiar faces even though Darcy didn't know their names. They didn't notice her, intent on circling each other, their boxing gloves raised, waiting for an opening. She looked past them and saw the blinds raised in Roger's corner office, but no one there. Creaks and footsteps told her someone was upstairs. She climbed to the second floor and saw the door was closed on the massage therapy room. Pausing, she caught a whiff of the sandalwood oil and flute music that were Selena's trademarks.

Logic said the movement was coming from the third floor. Darcy pushed down the surge of resentment. After all, where else would the temporary replacement stay, other than in Roger's apartment? She caught herself holding her breath as she climbed the open staircase from second to third floor. There was no stairwell, no doorway — the landings on each floor just opened up onto the floor. She remembered how proud Roger had been when he showed off the stairway he had refinished, the renovations he had done, with the help of young men in the community he had helped renovate their own lives. The dojo was a showplace, something to be proud of, and would continue to serve the community for years to come.

"Please, Lord," she whispered as her head came above the floor level and she got her first look at Roger's replacement.

Darcy had a tendency to compare people to characters in movies when she met them for the first time. The man standing in the kitchen, talking with Saundra, arms crossed over his chest and leaning back against the counter, looked like Samuel Jackson as Nick Fury. That was ridiculous, she knew, because he wore a sleeveless gray sweatshirt with the University of Akron splashed across it in darker gray, and faded red sweatpants, not the long leather duster and eyepatch of the leader of SHIELD. He even had the neat, pencil-thin goatee and moustache.

As she reached the top step, the man turned and looked over Saundra's shoulder at her. For a moment their eyes locked and though his expression didn't change, she felt as if she had been analyzed, x-rayed, turned inside out and assessed, and then gently put back down on her feet. She stumbled on the top step, not quite sure if she should feel insulted, afraid, or comforted. Then he smiled and nodded to her, and she felt oddly warmed.

Weird.

"Darcy!" Saundra hurried toward her, holding out her hands.

The moment they first met, Saundra had struck Darcy as one of Santa's elves, crossed with Galadriel from the *Lord of the Rings* — thin, pixie-cut red curls, elegantly long features, and a stately yet floating way of movement, even when she ran. Usually, Darcy had to check to make sure Saundra's feet actually touched the floor.

"I'm so glad you could spare time to come out. Roger swore he was going to make you his right-hand girl, so I know you'll be able to help Vincent with all the fiddly little details of keeping this place going." Saundra looped her arm through Darcy's and guided her back over to the kitchen.

"Tea? I'm going to take a leap of faith this one is yours." Vincent held up the glass jar full of tea leaves with a D in blue sequins on the side.

"Yep, mine." She was pleased when he handed her the equipment and let her measure out her preferred amount of tea mixture and pour the boiling water into the chamber for steeping. She felt Vincent watching her as she made her preparations, but oddly didn't feel nervous. Shouldn't she feel at least threatened?

They settled on the couches in the living room, which took up a third of the top floor. Roger loved books and had cases jammed between every window and short cases set up back-to-back, creating support for the long table that was always covered with paperwork for the Spike Center. He had six long, low couches, always covered with a mismatched assortment of throws to hide their battered condition, twice as many faded throw rugs on the floor, and four times as many enormous pillows made to be sat on. This was a room for relaxing and quiet contemplation and friends to sit up all night, talking and laughing and playing board games.

She was pleased when Vincent asked what she understood of Roger's schedule, the people who rented space, and the flexible schedule of exercise classes. Usually people came in for private workouts or appointments during the day, and classes met early in the morning before work, at the lunch hour, and during the rush hour right after work. Traffic trickled down as the evening progressed, and usually only a few die-hards preparing for a bodybuilding competition or boxing match were at the dojo after dark. When Roger didn't have classes, the doors were locked, and anyone who wanted to get in had to make arrangements ahead of time. Darcy sometimes came over to monitor the building and let people in for workouts or massage appointments when Roger was busy with meetings for the Center.

"That's something we're going to have to ease into," Vincent said, glancing at Saundra. "I understand Roger has a couple of classes at the Center, basic stuff, calisthenics, stretching. Until I get settled here, really sure of people, make sure I don't mess up what he's established — a week, minimum — do you think you could handle those classes?"

"Uh — yeah. Sure." Darcy blinked, hoping her grin wasn't as wide and sheepish as it felt.

"Saundra speaks highly of you, and Roger told her what a big help you are here. Besides..." Vincent shrugged. "I don't want to go stepping on any toes. Less disruption with someone everybody knows filling in for him. This is a great place, but this isn't where the Lord has planted me. I'm only helping out, and I promise, I'm praying just as hard as the rest of you that Roger gets in contact soon."

"Thanks," she murmured, and covered up her sudden certainty she might cry by taking a sip of her tea.

~~~~~

The days slid by faster than she thought possible, when she was so worried about Roger. Darcy had hesitated resuming her lessons with Vincent. He didn't know how she worked, what Roger had told her about swordplay and self-defense, and she knew she would be constantly comparing him to Roger. It was easier going to the dojo than she anticipated. Part of it was because Vincent made sure to update her on what he knew of the search for Roger. Anything Saundra told him, he passed on to her.

She liked Vincent. He presented an appearance of being big and dangerous and lethal, but she saw him with some of the children who came with their mothers for exercise classes. He would do simple magic tricks for them, or walk them through seemingly complicated martial arts maneuvers, sometimes flipping them up in the air so for a few seconds it seemed as if they flew. By the end of the first week at the dojo, some of the bolder children would sneak up on him with squirt guns or to shout "boo!' and run away, squealing with delight when he chased after them. When he caught them, the chase turned into a wrestling match, but the children always ended up on top, bouncing on his chest or his back. The mothers loved him. Darcy sometimes thought several of them would quite gladly fall in love with him if he ever showed any interest.

Twice when she arrived a little early for lessons, she found him sitting on the steps out front, reading his Bible. Once Saundra asked her to come to the dojo to fill in for Vincent. When Darcy got there, the other women in the class told her that an ex-boyfriend who refused to be ex had followed one of the women to the dojo. He had a gun. Vincent disarmed him, tied him up, called the police, and then took the woman and her children to a women's shelter where they could go to vanish.

It was the most natural thing in the world to vent to Vincent when she showed up for a lesson, still fuming about a problem that had struck the Center the evening before. Darcy hadn't meant to tell him about it. Discretion was necessary in the kind of work her parents did. Vincent noticed right away that her thoughts were elsewhere and asked her what was wrong. Before she knew it, she was sitting on a stack of mats with her borrowed katana resting on her knees, spilling the details of yet more
~~~~~

fallout from the slander hitting the Spike Center.

A missions support group Darcy refused to name, even in her fury, had donated ten sets of cots and two-drawer chests to outfit the temporary women's shelter the Spike Center planned to open by the end of the summer. Women would stay there, behind locked doors where no one who threatened them could get to them, until space was found for them at shelters far from the city. Yesterday afternoon, the head of the group called to inform them that he was sending a truck in two days to take back the equipment. In light of the accusations and negative reports surrounding the Spike Center and the board running it, his missions support group was withdrawing their support and their approval.

"They even admitted they hadn't done any investigation, to find out if the stories were true or not," Darcy said, trying not to snarl. "The truth doesn't matter — all they care about is how things look. Appearances. Jesus didn't care what people thought about Him."

"Yeah, well, Jesus is God. He kind of has the inside scoop on how things are going to turn out," Vincent offered. He sat opposite her, leaning back against another stack of mats that had started sliding sideways.

"Wimps like that make me so mad. They're so worried about not offending anybody, about being politically correct. There was this church in San Antonio when we worked there. They took all the crosses off their building because they didn't want to offend anybody. They said they would get more people to come inside if they didn't see crosses and other signs that would warn them — warn them! — there were Christians inside."

"Were there any Christians left inside?"

"Who knows? How come it's okay for everybody else to shout about what they believe in, get in your face about it, but the minute a Christian talks about what he believes in, suddenly he's offensive and violating someone else's rights?"

"From where I'm sitting, seems to me that's a good sign you're doing something right. Satan doesn't waste his time and energy attacking people who already belong to him. He loves it when people fool themselves into thinking they're doing God's work by focusing on a social gospel and forgetting to invite others into the Kingdom. It's kind of hard to tell people how to find forgiveness and salvation without telling them they're messed up and wrong and need to be forgiven."

"Exactly!" Darcy gasped for breath, feeling as if she had just stopped racing to evade something trying to crush her.

"So what'd your folks do about this guy trying to take back the equipment?"

"Dad talked him into waiting for a while. He really got him, when he pointed out that this group didn't give the equipment to us, but to God." She grinned, pleased when Vincent grinned back. "My dad is so cool.

When you think that he used to be the kind of guy who would laugh at this Pharisee jerk and maybe shoot—" She stopped, feeling as if a glacier had hit her in the chest, even as her face flamed with embarrassment.

"Hey, I know a lot of great preachers who used to solve all their problems with their fists before Jesus got hold of them." Vincent sat up and leaned forward, elbows on his knees now.

"My dad is a great guy," she insisted, and clenched her fists to keep her hands from shaking.

"I hear you." He tipped his head to one side and studied her. "Are you worried maybe things will get so bad, all the pressure, holding things together until the board can clear their names, it'll hurt your dad?"

"I heard him and Mom talking the other night. Sometimes he has nightmares, when things remind him of how it used to be. He was like all those really dark, bloody, violent destruction movies, you know? Super-evil agent, the kind of guy who doesn't have a soul anymore, because he's been doing the most horrible things to defend his country." Darcy shuddered, appalled and curiously relieved to say what she had been thinking, what had worried her. She wasn't sure why she knew Vincent wouldn't use that information to hurt her family.

"I don't know," Vincent said. "I've heard about your dad, what a great guy he is. Kind of hard to believe he was that bad."

"Just shows what Jesus can do. He can fix anything." She slid the katana off her knees and gently laid it on the mat next to her, so she could stretch and try to ease away the tension tying her into knots inside. "I heard them talking. Dad is scared... he's scared maybe the trouble is someone getting revenge for the things he did a long time ago, before he met Mom, before my birth-dad got killed, even." She closed her eyes and grabbed her feet and pressed hard, welcoming the ache in her tendons.

"That's pretty sophisticated, and cruel, destroying a lot of innocent people to get at your dad. Wouldn't it be easier to just go after him?"

"That's what Mom thought. She told Dad he was just feeling the pressure of responsibility, and then she teased him that he wasn't going to go all soft on her now and bail." Darcy sighed. "Dad hasn't talked about the past like that in a long, long time. It scares me."

"Yeah, well, you know what I learned when the ugly things in my past try to sneak up on me?" Vincent waited until she raised her head and met his gaze again. "Praying should be the first thing we do, not the last."

Her face warmed and she met his smile with a sheepish look of her own.

"Something good will come out of this. You can't burn away the dross without some fire and some melting."

"That's what—well, that's not exactly what Uncle Karl said, but it's close."

"Is this your mom's brother?" Vincent stood and held out a hand to help her back to her feet.

"Oh, he's not really my uncle." Darcy sighed. Time to get back to her lesson before the hour was completely gone. "He's kind of an honorary uncle. He e-mailed me last night. He said I should relax and not worry, that something good would come out of all this. All the weaklings will get driven away by their fears, and I'll end up where I'm meant to be." She gave her right hand to him and reached with her left for her sword and let him pull her to her feet.

"Don't relax too much." He winked at her as he stepped away. "But yeah, that's the way to handle all this. Relax and let God do what He's going to do. He'll send help in His good time."

~~~~~

"Darcy?" Vincent spied the pen that had rolled under his desk, grabbed it and started to stand up — banging his head on the bottom of the drawer in the process. "Be out in a minute," he called, wincing. One week of running the dojo had taught him great respect for the missing Roger Lancaster as an instructor, and frustration at the total lack of organization and discipline in almost every other aspect of the man's life.

"No hurry." Joan sauntered across the dusty wooden floor of the dojo and through the door of the office before she let her backpack slide to the floor. Ulysses scurried around her and slid to a stop against Vincent, thrusting his muzzle into his chest, begging to be petted.

"Joan?" He rubbed the back of his head.

"That's right. Remember me? We have an appointment." She looked around the office, her gaze lingering on the steaming jumbo mug of coffee, Vincent still kneeling on the floor with his shirt hanging unbuttoned, and one bare foot sticking out from behind the desk, giving Ulysses a vigorous rubbing with one hand. "Not a person here. Why are the doors open an hour before the posted hours of operation? That can't be safe — not even for you. Especially not with all those weapons on the racks."

She hooked a thumb over her shoulder, indicating the empty dojo behind her; practice mats spread across the floor, weight machines empty and silent, punching bag hanging perfectly still, and four neat racks full of all sorts of martial arts weapons just begging someone to take them and start wreaking havoc. Weak, 6a.m. light spilled through the tall, narrow windows.

"Private lesson." He scooted up into his desk chair, put down the pen and reached for his coffee. The other hand kept working on Ulysses, who adjusted his position accordingly.

"This early?"

"She has to go to work."

"Must be someone special."
~~~~~

"Darcy Clay." He sat back, cradling his mug of coffee, and grinned at the spark of interest and comprehension in Joan's dark eyes as well as Ulysses' whine of disappointment now that the rubdown had stopped. "You're welcome to stay as long as you want, by the way."

"Should we pretend to go through the whole conversation about you hiring me, or are you close enough to her to toss out the cover story?" Joan slowly crossed the floor to his desk, still looking around and taking in the surroundings. With her baggy, faded jeans and sweatshirt with the sleeves torn off, revealing the muscle definition in her arms, she looked the part she was ready to play, self-defense instructor down on her luck.

"Stick with the cover. I want to go to the Center, step in and see how things stand with Daedelus — "

"Joshua." She stuck her tongue out at him.

Vincent laughed. He had purposely slipped up just to test her.

"I want to test the waters there, now that I'm a known name in the community. Enough people who volunteer at the Center come here for exercise or lessons, they've paved my way. Next week, we'll know how much of the truth we can tell them."

"Fair enough. Is the coffee fresh?"

"Help yourself." He hooked his thumb over his shoulder at the corner of the office where a folding table held a hot plate, old-fashioned percolator, boxes of coffee supplies and mugs, and a cube refrigerator tucked underneath. "I filled out your paperwork, by the way. Just need you to sign it."

"If you forged my handwriting on the paperwork, why do you need my signature?"

"Smart-alec." He sat up as the door opened and a slim form in jeans and white t-shirt entered the dojo.

"As a comedian friend in Tabor constantly asks, what's an alec?" She grinned and nodded compliance when Vincent gestured for her to be quiet and crossed the floor.

"Good morning!" the young woman sang out. Her wide-boned face glowed from scrubbing and no make-up. Her long hair was pulled back in a single braid, hanging over her shoulder almost to her waist. She slung a blue motorcycle helmet into the corner by the stairs and tossed a heavy key ring into it.

Chapter Eight

"How's it going, sunshine?" Vincent said, crossing the room to the wall rack where three katanas hung on display.

"Morning comes earlier every day. How come the earlier the sun comes up, the longer I want to sleep?" She grinned at him, nearly upside down as she bent over to unlace her boots.

"Lazy." His single word, heavy with scorn, earned a giggle.

In the doorway, Joan cocked an eyebrow at him and turned to take a closer look at Darcy. Vincent noted her reaction, pleased that she was immediately intrigued by this girl. He hoped they became friends quickly.

Darcy might need Joan's friendship and support in the days to come.

"Say that when I have a sword in my hand." Darcy stood and levered her boot off her left foot with the toe of her right boot.

"Big words for a little girl." Vincent tossed a katana across the intervening space.

Darcy swooped up underneath it and caught it with a resounding smack against her palm. Grinning, she toed off her socks and advanced onto the practice mats. She shifted her grip to two-handed and held the sword parallel with the floor, chest-level, waiting.

"That's Joan, by the way," Vincent said, gesturing toward the office door with his chin. "And her fuzzy shadow, Ulysses."

"Hi," Darcy said, never taking her eyes off her teacher.

"Hi yourself," Joan murmured.

"I just hired her to help out here when I move over to the Center. Maybe later we'll see just how good you are compared to her. She might just wipe the floor with your sorry little butt," he continued, grinning.

"Don't try to distract me, Vincent," Darcy said with a chuckle. "It worked last time, but it won't work again."

"She's such a good student. Check out her technique, Joan, and see what she's doing wrong."

Joan murmured agreement as she slid down to the floor and settled down cross-legged to watch. Vincent swung, twisting his body sideways to alter the angle of descent. Darcy met the blow with an upward swing and danced out of the way. Ulysses lay down next to Joan, his head on her thigh, and she absently rubbed his back as she watched the sparring.

~~~~~

Half an hour later, Vincent abruptly stopped an attacking swing and
~~~~~

stepped back. He lowered his blade and watched Darcy's reaction. She caught herself halfway through a lunge that could have taken advantage of his sudden retreat. Both glistened with sweat. Darcy breathed heavily as she stepped back. She watched him, flexing her grip on her sword.

"Better," Vincent said, nodding.

"How much better?" Darcy countered.

"This is only our third lesson! Give it time." He chuckled and nodded toward the rack on the wall.

Darcy executed a little bow and trotted across the floor to put her sword away. Vincent walked over to Joan, wiping his face on his sleeve. He held out his hand and she handed up the half-empty mug of coffee. It was cold, but he finished it off in a few quick swallows.

"How old is she again?" Joan murmured.

"Almost twenty." Vincent chuckled. "She's very insistent on that."

"What is she doing, playing with swords at her age? Shouldn't she be in college, worrying about boys, that kind of stuff?"

"Your first assignment is to find out who's been filling her head with tales of daring-do and adventure. Not your typical preacher's kid."

"Since when do we deal with the typical?"

"Touché. You need to work on your follow-through," he continued, raising his voice as he turned. Darcy crossed the floor to join them by the office. "When you block a thrust or swing, you can't just stop and look for the next blow. Keep it moving. It's easier to change direction if you're moving than if you're standing still."

"Where have I heard that before?" Darcy grinned at him and wiped a few last beads of sweat off her flushed face.

"Then listen, okay? Hey, where are you going?" he asked, when she bent to pick up a sock and raised a foot to slide it on.

"Tests."

"I thought you were going to take those tests yesterday."

"I have three, and I took two yesterday. Today is the third. My brain was too fried after two to take the third, and today is the deadline."

"A likely excuse."

"Online college is tougher than real college!"

"Wimp." He barked laughter when she stuck her tongue out at him. "Any word on that equipment you're about to lose?"

He knew the answer, but it was better to head off any suspicions before they started. Vincent had done some investigating, getting the name of the mission group from Saundra, then passing the word on to Sophie to investigate, and then to Elizabeth, who made phone calls. The mission support group was duly chastened and repentant for their lack of faith and reassured that all the accusations and ugly rumors swirling around the administration of the Spike Center were on the verge of being proven false. Everyone involved would have to practice patience, because nothing would be revealed for public knowledge until the enemies of the Center had been identified and stopped, possibly punished.

"We're still in a holding pattern."

"What?" he said, when she frowned more intently than her boot laces deserved.

"Nothing."

"Oh. Right." He nodded to Joan.

"What is that supposed to mean?" Darcy stumbled, putting her foot down only halfway into the boot.

"Nothing. You just look that way from indigestion or something."

"Vincent!" She groaned, grinning. "Is he always like this?"

"Unfortunately, yes," Joan said. "You have my permission to thump him whenever you get the chance."

"Yeah, you and whose army?" Vincent put a growl in his voice. He was delighted to see the instant link between them, even if it was to team up against him. "What was bothering you a minute ago?"

"Nothing — nothing important," she hurried to amend, when he took a step toward her, scowling. "Uncle Karl just seemed... I don't know... disappointed? Maybe I just misread his email, but I could have sworn he wanted them to pull out, to take back their equipment." Darcy shrugged, which interfered with finishing tying her boot laces. "He just likes being our miracle worker all the time, I think. That's what he does, finds money for us, finds equipment, gets things approved by governments and officials and such when nobody else will help us."

"Sounds like someone has a Prince Valiant complex."

"Sounds familiar," Joan muttered. She wrinkled up her nose at him when he glanced at her, unsure if she was teasing or not.

"Okay. Do good on your test." He nodded toward the door. "See you tomorrow."

"Definitely." Darcy nodded to Joan. "Nice meeting you."

"Same here," Joan murmured. She watched Darcy snatch up her helmet and scurry across the room to the door. "I think I need a refill." Ulysses, half-asleep, didn't move when Joan got up.

Vincent just nodded and stayed where he was, leaning against the side of the office door, and watched Darcy jump down the front steps and get on her motorcycle. When she was gone, he stepped back into the office.

"Something tells me you're her first crush," Joan said, raising her fresh mug to drink.

"What are you talking about?" He peeled off his sweaty shirt and tossed it into the hamper for dirty towels, then walked over to the basket where a supply of clean ones waited.

"You didn't see the way she watched you?"

"I was a little busy fighting off her attacks."

"She is good, isn't she?" Joan mused. She watched him over the rim of the mug. "How good with the sword is her father?"

"Stepfather."

"Maybe she got the fascination for swords from him."

"Midas was the weapons man. Blades and gold. Josh was the builder and destroyer, but was good with blades of all kinds, too. Not as good as Midas. According to Darcy, who is very proud of him, he's renovating most of the Spike Center almost single-handedly."

"Doesn't sound like someone who's out to destroy the place."

"What better way to hide his true intentions?" He shook his head and made a brushing gesture with one hand, pushing aside her retort. "I know, I'm depressing myself. Low blood sugar."

"You just don't want to be disappointed. Build up your hopes for total reformation and have them crash down on you."

"True."

"If the situation was reversed —"

"I'd be lecturing you about praying. I know." He picked up his mug and studied the thin layer remaining in the bottom. "Funny how all the years of growing and learning just fall away when the past comes back to haunt you."

~~~~~

Darcy gave herself the evening off, to celebrate finishing her online test in record time and getting a 95 percent score. That meant she curled up in her bedroom with a bowl of ice cream and a book she actually wanted to read, rather than one she needed to study, and read until her eyes were fuzzy. She heard her parents' voices out in the living room as she rolled out of bed to replenish her ice cream. She couldn't hear the words, but the tone of their voices made her pause and move slowly when she did leave her room.

"You great big worry-wart idiot," Geneva said, as Darcy stuck her head around the corner.

Her parents sat on the sofa in the far corner, with a single torch lamp throwing light up against the wall and ceiling and falling down on them. Photo file boxes and her father's battered old trunk sat open on the carpet in front of them. Geneva thumped Josh's arm with both fists half a dozen times.

"When are you going to learn?" She caught hold of his beard between two fingers and tugged until he looked at her. "Stop gnawing on the past."

"It's gnawing on me, hon," he said, his voice thick with exhaustion and worry.

Darcy pressed a hand against her mouth to muffle any sound that might escape. It felt like a giant fist squeezed at her heart.
~~~~~

"Since when do you have to carry the burden by yourself?" her mother demanded.

"I just can't help thinking—what if they've caught up with me?"

"Since when were any of that crew this subtle? You've told me enough stories about that part of your life, I'm pretty sure of their mode of attack. If any of those others found you by now, they'd have struck already. The Center would be a pile of smoldering rubble around us." Geneva got up and stood in front of him, bending down until their foreheads touched. "Are you listening to me, Joshua Clay?"

"Would it do any good if I said no?"

She sputtered, fighting not to laugh. Darcy relaxed, sagging against the wall, and felt as if her heart had started beating again. She watched as her mother tugged her father to his feet. Arms around each other, they walked over to the room full of her father's books and his computer and the speakerphone. Darcy guessed they were going to call one of her father's mentors, as they had done three times already since this crisis hit the Spike Center.

When the door of the office clicked shut, Darcy stepped out into the living room. Curiosity pushed her for another glimpse of these mementos of her father's painful, ugly past. Josh had been open with her while only giving her the bare bones of the heartless, violent things he had done, and enjoyed doing, back when he was a highly skilled, destructive mercenary.

Most of the contents of the box and trunk were documents, maps, sketches, diagrams of what looked like electrical circuits, and building plans. Among the papers, Darcy saw something glossy and colored— maybe a photo? She stepped carefully through the papers, trying not to disturb anything, and bent to catch it between index finger and thumb. Yes, it was a photo.

Five men. Filthy, running with sweat, smeared with grime, laughing, holding up slopping glasses of something amber. Probably beer or something stronger. She searched for Josh's features and found him.

Darcy stared and time seemed to stand still. How long she stood, not even breathing, she wasn't sure, but her chest ached and her pulse thundered in her ears. She stepped back blindly, not bothering to watch where she put her feet.

Vincent was right next to her father—and Karl Van Mournen was next to him.

Was Vincent his real name? Josh had told her very little about that part of his life, just enough to impress on her that the more she knew, the more danger she might face someday. He never even told her what his real name was, before he was trained and programmed, his soul replaced with ice and his name changed to Daedelus. He didn't know what anyone's name was before they were formed into a team, and didn't want to know. He had no idea what they had done with their lives when the team fragmented, if any of them other than he and Van Mournen had escaped to freedom and a new life.

"Well, now we know," Darcy whispered. She settled on the couch and drew her legs up to her chest, still holding the photo out and staring at Vincent's filthy, sweaty, smiling face.

That was not a nice smile. Not the kind of smile he gave her now, when they laughed together and worked together and he taught her how to defend herself and use her sword.

"Darcy?" Josh and Geneva paused, clearly on the way to their bedroom. As the seconds ticked by, both sides looking at the other, Darcy saw the warmth and relaxation seeping out of her father's face. She glanced at the clock on the DVD player and realized she had been sitting there for nearly half an hour, looking at the photo, her mind spinning and going nowhere.

"I know," she finally said, and unbent her legs to put her feet on the floor again. "I shouldn't have looked in the first place, but... well, I know all this has been bothering you lately and..." She gestured at the papers scattered across the rug. "Your old team, Dad. What were they like?"

"I told you."

"Tell me again. I need to understand how you're scared of them, but you hold onto things like this picture."

"You see? She agrees with me," Geneva said. She stepped through the papers and settled on the sofa next to Darcy, sliding an arm around her shoulders and drawing her back to lean against her.

"What can I say? When you've got nobody else in the world, even your worst enemies become your family. All those dysfunctional idiots they show on those reality shows on TV, they've got nothing on the mess we were in." Josh scrubbed at his face with both hands and dropped into the battered old easy chair facing the couch. "We were best enemies, worst friends, family, and we hated each other because we couldn't live without each other. That doesn't make any sense—"

"Kind of does. That's why you didn't kill each other, at least," Darcy offered.

"Got that in one." He sank into the flattened old cushions and put his head back with a sighing groan. "I still pray for them. Sometimes I pray they're dead, out of their misery. A lot of the time, I just pray they're dead so they don't come after you and your mom to hurt me. I've got a lot of unpaid debt, baby. Men like that, it doesn't matter what Christ did, what price He paid, they're going to take their justice in my flesh and blood, and the ones who mean the most to me."

"But you still pray to find them someday, and hope to get them to listen to the truth?" she whispered. It was hard to speak when her throat and mouth felt full of dust and pressed flat.

"Absolutely."

"What would you do if one of them walked into the Center tomorrow, Daddy? Would you be scared or mad or glad?"

"Depends on what they carried with them, I guess. In their hearts and in their hands. If they walked in empty-handed, then I can hope God sent them back into my life for a purpose."

"What if they came for revenge?" She swallowed hard, and it hurt. "Would you fight them?" Darcy thought of the treasure room and the weapons Van Mournen hid there, secrets he let her help him guard. Yet what good would swords do against men who knew how to kill with their bare hands, who spilled blood like farmers spilled water in their fields?

"That kind of fighting isn't part of my life anymore, baby. When I put my weapons down and left that way of life, I had to trust God would be my defender." Josh shook his head. "I'm sorry, honey."

"For what?"

"Putting my worries on you. This isn't any of your concern."

"But—" She stopped, wanting to tell him about Vincent, the man who laughed with her and gave her advice and talked about God as if he knew Him very well.

"I just had to have it pounded through my thick skull that I haven't been praying enough. Don't make me have to pound it into you now, okay?" Josh pushed himself out of his chair and reached for the photo. Darcy reluctantly gave it to him. "I'm going to pray myself to sleep, and you need to do the same, okay? This is in God's hands. My past is not coming back to haunt me. Nobody is out for revenge. Saundra assured us she has friends with a lot of influence and power in the right areas, and they're investigating. Any day now, they're going to find the source of all our problems and get everything straightened out. It's just a matter of time. Any day now, Roger is going to come back and we're going to find out it's all a big misunderstanding, a big mix-up in communication, and we'll laugh about it. Okay, baby?"

"Okay, Dad." Darcy got up when her mother did, kissed her parents goodnight and went back to her room. She waited, lying still and listening, as Josh put away his trunk. She stayed still, listening to the night until she knew her parents slept.

Then she got up and found the trunk, took out the photo box and found the photo of her father and Van Mournen and Vincent. She put it on the shelf next to her bed and stared at it, even through the darkness after she turned off her tiny lamp. She tried to pray, until the words grew fuzzy in her brain and she slept.

When she woke, she couldn't remember her dreams, except that she felt strangely at peace. The only clear image in her head was of Vincent and her father, standing back-to-back. Vincent held a sword while her father's hands were empty, but both of them defended the other. Darcy knew then what she needed to do.

~~~~~

Vincent had Joan work out with Darcy on the mats the next morning. He watched the girl's self-defense technique, trying to decipher if Josh had tutored her in the same methods their trainers had pounded into them. He was pleased when the girl proved almost awkward when it came to barehanded self-defense. She hadn't learned the dirty, street fighting techniques, where awareness of her surroundings dropped to the subconscious, instinctive, almost precognitive level, and everything turned into a possible weapon. Darcy was too self-conscious. Where swordplay bordered on becoming a dance for her, hand-to-hand was an uncomfortable exercise she got over with as soon as possible.

As he and Joan agreed when planning their strategy yesterday, she engaged the younger girl in conversation about the Spike Center as they worked out. Darcy lit up despite her breathlessness and constant falls, revealing her passion for the mission and the work her family was doing. Vincent listened to them and prayed with half his attention, begging God that everything about the Clay family was just as it seemed. In a week's time, he had come to care for Darcy, just like all his other students.

"Tomorrow's Sunday," Darcy said, when Joan signaled the bruising session of tumbling and lunge-counter-parry had ended.

"Usually comes after Saturday." She wiped her face with her palms, then raked the sweat through her hair.

"Come for breakfast and the service?" The girl turned to include Vincent, who sat on a stack of mats against the wall. "I mean, some of the things we've talked about, the way you talk about praying and... I mean, Saundra found you to fill in for Roger, so I figured you... well, it'd be stupid to assume you're Christians. I should have asked sooner."

Joan glanced at Vincent, one eyebrow raised. He had sowed enough seeds in previous conversations to get a clearer picture of her family's true spiritual status. They had planned several lines of approach to get the girl to invite them to the Spike Center. They just hadn't planned on it being so soon, or so easy. Vincent had hoped that several lines of questioning he had put out in the neighborhood would yield news about Roger before he had to face Josh. He nodded — let Joan interpret that any way she wanted. She was good at improv.
~~~~~

Chapter Nine

"Yeah, you should have," Joan said, before Darcy could turn to face him again, her face flushed with more than exertion, her eyes widening into that pleading, little girl expression he was afraid he wouldn't be able to resist. "In fact, I was asking about the Center because I'm looking for a church to join in the area. They let monsters in, don't they?"

Ulysses let out a deep *whuff-snort*, his ears perking up but his eyes never opening. Vincent had considered checking over the big dog, slightly concerned about how he seemed to do nothing but sit and sleep whenever he wasn't following Joan around. Ulysses had nuzzled Darcy when Joan introduced him to the girl at the start of the lesson, then settled down and seemed to go to sleep right away, no interest whatsoever in his surroundings.

"He'll be mobbed by all the little kids," Darcy said, nodding. "Once you convince them he isn't going to bite them. There are a lot of dogs in our neighborhood, but most of them seem to be strays. You'll want to keep a close eye on him, in case the animal control people come by on one of their sweeps." She hunched her shoulders. "Rumors are they don't even wait the minimum forty-eight hours they're supposed to before they put dogs to sleep."

"Thanks for the warning," Joan said.

"Are you coming, Vincent?"

"Thinking about it. Who's preaching?" He got up to bring over hand towels for them to wipe their sweaty faces and arms.

"Dad, of course." Her gaze wouldn't meet his for more than a few seconds at a time. That was drastically unlike the Darcy he had come to know.

"What's bothering you, kid?" he asked, pitching his voice low. Joan paused, the towel balled up in her hands.

Darcy held out her left hand. She was right-handed. Vincent held out his left hand and had to consciously keep his arm extended when the girl grasped his wrist and turned his arm to reveal the underside, and the tattoo in red and black ink on his bicep, just above the cup of his elbow.

Vincent had thought about removing the tattoo for years. The insignia—a stylized Omega wreathed in flames—had been designed by someone among the powers-that-be who had tried to program him to be a heartless, cold-blooded killing machine. He had considered it like a brand, proclaiming the ownership someone had tried to take on him, body, mind and soul. The tattoo was marred by a thin line of scar tissue right down the middle, from where he had dug out the subcutaneous transponder that let his trainers track him down no matter where he went in the world.

"Dad has the same tattoo, the same scar," Darcy said. Her hand grasping his wrist started to tremble. Vincent snatched at it when she let go and tried to pull away.

"What'd he tell you?" he asked, keeping his voice soft.

Behind Darcy, Joan waited, watching him, arms spread slightly, as if she thought the girl would try to run and she had to stop her.

"He doesn't know you're here. What do you know about him?" She licked her lips and had to visibly fight to meet his gaze. "Were you telling the truth, that you're a Christian?"

"Only thing keeping me sane, sometimes. What has your dad told you about me—about us?"

"Not much." She reached into her sweatpants pocket, pulled out a square envelope, and handed it to him.

Vincent watched her as he opened the envelope by feel. Inside was a photo—an old-style Polaroid, by the thick, square stiffness. He wasn't sure what he waited for as he watched her, trying to anticipate her purpose. Then he looked at the photo and felt just like he did when he saw Josh and Geneva smiling in the photo on top of the stack of data in the Spike Center folder. Like the floor had dissolved underneath him and the lights had gone out for a moment. Like he fell downward and backward through time, and the sands of memory that engulfed him threatened to suffocate him.

All five of them, twenty-five years younger, filthy from a successful mission, gathered around a table in some backwater dive. Snow, Javelin, Shadow, Daedelus, and Midas. Vincent marveled at the callous hardness in their faces, could hear the boisterous voices as they raised their glasses in a toast, splashing bad beer over each other and the cluster of glasses that filled the table from three previous rounds of drinks. All of them young, strong, full of life and fury, and for a brief moment united in celebrating their success. Handsome in a glaring, dangerous way. So young, unscarred.

He remembered the thin, hungry girl who took their picture with an old Polaroid before they knew she was there. He remembered how Snow had cursed her and Shadow laughed, using charm to try to get her to hand the picture over without having to pay for it. That was how the poor child earned a living—selling people photos of themselves having a drunken good time. Despite her terror, the girl had understood that they wouldn't pay for the photo and they wouldn't let her leave with it, and she had run.

Daedelus went after her, chasing her out of the bar, and came back with the photo less than ten minutes later.

Vincent's hand shook, remembering how Snow had vanished from the table a short time later. When they left the bar maybe an hour later, he stepped out of the shadows with the camera in his hands and a cold smile on his face. Vincent hadn't thought until just that moment what Snow had probably done to the girl to get the camera. He liked torturing children. When the powers-that-be sent him on solo jobs, they knew he would get the job done if the targets had children he could torment after he had murdered the parents.

Funny, how Darcy had been able to match him up with the man in the photo, despite the years, the bad lighting, the filth, and the fact that his lack of soul showed so clearly. Vincent slid the old photo back in the envelope and handed it back to her.

"What did your dad tell you about us, about the men in that picture?" He found some amusement in the realization that he didn't want Joan to see the photo.

"It was a bad time in his life, when he did bad things, but he prays for all of the men who used to be his friends. One found us, and God made everything right. Dad hopes someday he'll find the others and make things right. He says if God could fix all the things that were wrong with him, He could fix anybody." She slid the photo back into her pocket. "I sure hope that's true."

"Uh huh." He felt the cold, tight muscles in his face relax, enough to offer a soft smile. "You think I'll go into ninja mode and come after your dad with some of these swords in the middle of the night?"

"I hope not, because I really like you, Vincent."

"Yeah, well, got news for you, kid. I really like you, too." He glanced over her shoulder at Joan. She widened her eyes slightly and shrugged. Whatever he decided to do, she was with him, but she had nothing to offer. "Okay." He sighed loudly. "Guess I'd better get over there and find out what your dad is up to, get things out in the open."

"When? I hate keeping secrets from my folks."

"Well, I have some classes… around lunchtime, okay?" He held out his right hand, and Darcy's face regained some color as she nodded and shook his hand, sealing the promise.

In between those classes, Vincent fully intended to do some heavy-duty praying. He would leave it to Joan to call Quarry Hall and update everybody back home on what had just happened, and get them praying, too.

~~~~~

The sign, painted on three sheets of plywood, proclaimed in foot-high red letters that the old factory building was the new home of the
~~~~~

Spike Center. Smaller letters announced the soup kitchen, clothes closet, free clinic, and neighborhood food cupboard were open during renovations.

The former factory and warehouse stretched the length of the block, grimy red brick with a door every thirty yards. A few touches of Neo-Classical architecture showed through the years of filth, in the arches over the doors and plywood-covered windows. All the weeds had been pulled from between the cracks in the sidewalk. The broken glass and beer cans and crumbled pavement visible in the surrounding streets had been removed from the street in front of the Center. The doors were heavy, new and made of metal, with reinforced glass windows in each panel. Someone had sandblasted the brick up to ten feet from street level, removing years of grime and neglect. A section of wall between two doors had a mural of children playing underneath spreading green trees.

Studying it as he approached that morning, Vincent wondered how long the mural had been there, and how long it would be until one of the local gangs defaced it with graffiti. If they held back, that would show how much influence the rescue mission and its workers had on the neighborhood.

Halfway down the length of the building was an opening twenty feet wide, with a driveway leading up from the street. Vincent assumed that was the loading dock of the old factory. As he approached, a flatbed truck pulled out of the gap, with Stimson's Hardware and Lumber painted across its sides. Vincent grinned — this was a side of Daedelus/Josh Clay he remembered with fondness. When he had a hammer or a saw and a piece of wood in his hands, Josh was at peace with the world. Then again, nothing made him happier than watching something crumple to the ground, entirely destroyed. He was an artist, in that regard.

Pausing for two seconds, Vincent continued the prayer that had been whispering through his heart and soul since seeing that photo in the file folder: that Josh was as dedicated to his new life and his regained soul as he had been to destroying things.

Vincent tried three doors before he found one that was open. The sign above it advertised the soup kitchen and the food cupboard. He walked down a short hallway smelling of fresh paint and sawdust, which opened out into a long room filled with tables and folding chairs. The far wall had a four-foot high pass-through, starting at waist height, running the entire length of the wall opening into a kitchen full of stainless steel tables and cabinets, stove and walk-in cooler and freezer. It was also full of people, moving back and forth between the worktables and the stove. Vincent checked his watch. It was closer to eleven than noon. He smelled the mixed aromas of chicken broth and tomatoes, baking bread and cinnamon. How soon would the first hungry customers come trickling through the door behind him for their lunch?

"Can I help you?" a woman said, pausing in the doorway, a few feet down from the serving window. "We're not quite ready to serve lunch yet, but there's plenty of food left over from breakfast." She was little more than a woman shape, lost in the shadows, but as she started across the long room to meet him, details became clear.

Blue jeans, washed until they were faded almost white; a long, golden, tunic-style shirt with the sleeves rolled up and water spots down the front. She had a red-and-white checkered dishtowel caught through the belt of her shirt, and she wore sandals that clicked softly across the gleaming tile floor. Her eyes were bright blue, her face heart-shaped, with only a few wrinkles around eyes and mouth to mar her ivory and gold-toned skin. Vincent knew those lines came from laughter, not anger or fear or pain. The years vanished. She had changed, aged, but not in ways worth mentioning.

Those bright blue eyes widened. She reached up to tuck a few platinum blonde curls behind her ears as she stared at him.

"I know… Afghanistan… Vincent?" Geneva whispered. A nervous laugh broke out of her. "Vincent, is that really you? Talk about an answer to prayers!" Laughing, she spread her arms wide and hurried the last few yards to meet him.

A not-unpleasant shock went through his body as she hugged him. Her head barely reached above his shoulder. How had he forgotten how small she was?

"What are you doing here? You look wonderful."

"So do you."

"You always were the charmer. Even in the middle of that horrible time in Afghanistan, I could tell you were a gentleman." She stepped back and looked him up and down. "How strange. Darcy has been asking about Josh finding his old team. With all the problems we've been having, Josh has been half-afraid that one of you — well, one of them. He was sure you wouldn't be out for revenge."

Vincent felt a dropping sensation in the pit of his stomach, but oddly, it was as much relief as shock. Geneva did know about their team. Josh had actually told her about his old life, told her enough about the horrible things they had done in the name of so-called national security that she could calmly admit the past might endanger her family, and yet she didn't flinch. Josh had warned his family about the threats that lingered from his former life.

Even more important, Josh believed that the reformation had been real in Vincent's life, so he didn't expect danger or threat from him. What did that kind of faith say about the change in Josh?

Maybe, just maybe, the reformation, the regained soul, the spiritual life, were all real? *Please, Lord…*

"How is Josh?" He muffled a grin when he felt a flicker of shock at how easily he said the name now, instead of Daedelus. Supporting this new identity and life was as vital for Josh as being simply Vincent, head of security for the Arc Foundation, was for him.

"Busy. Never happier than when he has a hammer in his hand, or he's doing some of his fancy woodwork. Come on, let's go surprise him." Geneva slid her arm through his and led him across the room and through the kitchen.

"How surprised?" he had to ask.

"Well, when he confessed to me that you thought he had been sent to kill you, in Afghanistan, I was shocked. You were more likely to be the hunter, taking retribution on the rebel. You didn't turn your life over to the Lord at that time, but we all felt sure you were close. As long as you didn't rely on earning your forgiveness through good works and putting your life on the line."

"Yeah, I did learn that lesson."

"And?" She paused, turning to look up at him, her eyes searching and somber, almost pleading.

That funny hitch that twisted his insides, that he only felt when Elizabeth pressed him about spiritual matters or when one of his students came to him with their fears and sorrows, filled him now. Vincent knew it wasn't just an automatic, almost unthinking spiritual platitude that fell out of Geneva's mouth. She and Josh had indeed been praying for him.

"Washed in the blood and trying to get others on the straight and narrow."

Geneva hugged him briefly, blinking momentary happy tears away. Then she caught his arm with hers and led him away at double-speed.

The workers barely paused to notice Vincent and Geneva's passage through the bustling, white-tiled room. She led him down a long hall, past three rooms stacked floor-to-ceiling with cans and jars and bags of foodstuffs, and four that seemed to be crammed with all kinds of clothing.

"We're hoping to open a clothes closet four times the previous size in another week," Geneva said, noticing his glance as they passed the room. "Feed them and clothe them, and when they're able to pay attention, teach them to take care of themselves. That's what Grandpa always said."

"How is Rev. Morris?" Vincent asked automatically.

"He's been home with the Lord eight years now. He died in his sleep. Watch your step," she added, as they left the remodeled section of the building.

It was an abrupt change from tiled floor and painted walls to empty wall studs and joists, new cement, wiring hanging everywhere, and the pervading aroma of newly sawn wood.

Vincent had a good idea where Josh was hard at work, the moment they reached an intersection in the gutted building. The right-hand hallway showed signs of restoration, while the left-hand hallway was dark, showing nothing but thorough gutting. The thuds of three different hammers echoed down the partially restored hall, bouncing off drywall. Sawdust filled the air, golden motes dancing in the lights.

When they reached the end of the hall, Geneva let go of Vincent's arm and gave him a little shove so he would go through the open doorway first. She winked and smiled at him and made an exaggerated shushing gesture. He smiled back, shook his head, and stepped through the door. Funny, but he actually felt nervous. It wasn't like Josh was going to drop his charade of decades and shoot him with a nail gun.

If Geneva was so happy to see him, so positive that Josh would be happy to see him, what did he really have to be afraid of?

"What's up?" Josh said without raising his head from the framework he was assembling on the floor.

Some things hadn't changed, obviously, including that almost preternatural sensitivity that let Josh sense when someone stepped into a pitch black room, in the middle of a rainstorm pounding on a corrugated metal roof. The fact that he didn't turn immediately to assess the newcomer told Vincent his former teammate was at peace with the world.

Josh Clay had gained some weight. Vincent admitted it looked good on him, gave him a sense of dignity and maturity he didn't have when he was a ragged, straggly bearded mercenary. He wore his ebony hair just past his collar in the back, short around his face. His beloved beard was a thin, neat, dignified line around his jaw. Silver streaks at his temples and a faint silver-gray sheen to his beard surprised Vincent for a moment. He felt as if he hadn't aged, so he didn't expect Josh to have aged.

"Didn't expect you back to help so fast. Or didn't the Plinkney sisters have to go to the bank after all?" Josh continued. He paused and glanced to his right. "Hey, Doug—this section is ready to go up." Then he wiped his hands on his red flannel shirt and began to get up from his knees. "Want to help us—" He stopped short, his mouth hanging open, as he lifted his head and looked directly at Vincent.

"I don't know if you look more like a carpenter or a school teacher," Vincent said, offering the first gesture of peace. "What's with the gray hair?"

"Vanity," Josh said with a weak grin.

"Excuse me? Vanity is using something to hide that gray. It's a sign of weakness."

"Gray hair is supposed to earn respect." He wiped his hands on his jeans and shrugged. "So—vanity."

"Not my vanity, that's for certain," Geneva said from the doorway.

"This was your idea, wasn't it?" He waved his hammer at his wife. "When I get hold of you..." Josh burst out laughing. He dropped his hammer and stepped across the piles of two-by-fours and boxes of nails between him and Vincent. "I can't believe it's really you!"

"It's really me." Vincent winced as Josh grabbed his hand with both of his and shook it hard. The grin, the delight sparkling in the other man's eyes could not be denied. It was exuberance, not an attempt at one-upmanship that made his grip so tight.

"What brings you here? What are you doing with yourself? How long are you in town? Wait a minute. Doug," Josh called to the red-haired young man who approached them now. "Break time. Go see if you can steal some of Martha's peanut butter cake before everybody else gets to it, okay?"

"You got it, Josh," Doug said with a grin. His grin faded for a moment, as his gaze raked over Vincent's face. He hurried out of the room through a gap in the wall joists, avoiding the door.

Josh thumped Vincent on the back and led him out through the door.

"We can sit and talk here," Josh said, leading him into another room where the drywall had been hung, though not painted yet.

A few wobbly, paint-spattered carpenter stools furnished the room. Geneva sat. Josh stood next to her, his hand resting on her shoulder. Vincent stayed standing.

"So, tell me—how long are you going to be in town? How did you find us?"

"I'm on temporary assignment for a foundation that I work for." Vincent grinned, deciding to relax and enjoy their surprise. Their welcoming delight was almost intoxicating. "How long have you been here?" he added, though he knew. He had read and re-read the file on the Spike Center and all its workers until the data was imprinted on the underside of his eyelids.

Chapter Ten

"Going on three months. Renovations are my specialty, neighborhoods and buildings." Josh shook his head as he looked Vincent up and down, taking in his chinos, tan sport shirt and dark green blazer. "You look great. Life been good to you?"

"It has its ups and downs. God sank His hooks into me about three years after we met up and hasn't let go."

"Uh huh. I know the feeling." He tipped his head to one side, giving Vincent another, deeper assessing look, like he used to employ on a building or other structure that stood in the team's way, or they had to infiltrate to reach their objective. "Do you ever envy the people who don't have a gory, filthy testimony? The ones who can say they've known Christ all their lives, never had anything to cleanse or heal or repair?"

"Sometimes."

"What are you doing in town?" Geneva asked. She gestured around. "I don't suppose we can put you to work, make sure you stay for a while?"

"I haven't done carpentry work in years," Vincent said, raising his hands in mocking protest. "A few rooms, maybe, but nothing on this scale. My forte is defense."

"Uh huh," Josh said again, a grim smile putting punctuation on that assessing look. "I wonder, if we ever catch up with the others, if they'll be doing the exact opposite of what they were doing before God smacked them between the eyes and saved their souls the hard way."

"Hmm, not exactly."

"You know where they are?" His hand on Geneva's shoulder tightened visibly for a moment. She raised one hand to rest on his, not in protest but in a comforting gesture.

"Just Snow." Vincent took a deep breath, listening to the quiet voice of guidance inside, and just a little stunned and shamed to realize he didn't want to listen. For only a few seconds. "He was after me, but someone got to him first."

"I'm sorry. I was hoping all of us could be redeemed," Josh murmured.

"He is. The damage he survived… in a lot of ways, he's a child. No memory of the man he was. Children love him. I think he'd throw himself on a bomb for a child."

"You're looking after him, aren't you?" Geneva asked, her voice soft, while Josh visibly digested that ironic last detail.

"Three down, two to go."

"Four." Josh shook his head when Vincent opened his mouth to ask who he had found. "So, before Doug shows up with that cake, what brings you here? Something tells me it's no coincidence."

"No such thing as coincidence, for those of us who've been saved the hard way, as you put it." He settled on the unsteady carpenter's stool. "My… employer is a friend of Saundra Ashmore. When Roger Lancaster vanished, she asked me to come fill in."

"You're that Vincent?" Geneva said. "Darcy has been telling us…"

Vincent knew the moment she put together the pieces.

"Your daughter is a very good student. Very observant. She recognized me from that photo in that bar, after we got back from…" He shrugged. No need to speak the details of that bloody, destructive mission. "She confronted me this morning—after inviting me and my assistant to church tomorrow."

"That's our little girl," Josh muttered, only managing a flicker of a smile.

"I didn't come here to cause trouble," Vincent hurried to say. Then he wondered if that was strictly true.

"You didn't. I'm sure Darcy knew exactly what she was doing when she confronted you," Geneva said, and stood. "If I know her, she's gearing up for World War III to start, imagining the two of you setting off a nuclear explosion in the middle of the gym or some such thing, and putting herself in the middle as the mediator and hero of the hour. We need to talk, as soon as possible. Do you know where she is?"

"Walking the Plinkney sisters to the bank to cash their checks," Josh said. A lopsided grin brightened his face. "Let's you and I go meet her, while Geneva cools down."

"I'm not the one with a temper, Rev. Dr. Clay," Geneva said. She rolled her eyes and sighed, but she was grinning.

"Reverend? Doctor?" Vincent teased. After all, he couldn't let on that he knew everything that was available to know about Joshua Clay and his family and what he had been doing for the past twenty-plus years.

At least, not yet. A quiet voice whispered that secrets had to end quickly, to avoid disaster. Vincent knew better than to ignore that guidance, or to delay obedience.

"What can I say?" Josh said, shrugging. "Marriage and a family make a man settle down and grow up. Bet you never thought I'd be a good student."

"No. Not in a thousand years."

Josh led him down another length of dismantled hallway, cutting through partially divided rooms, stepping around piles of lumber and drywall sheeting, cans of paint, crates of nails. He proudly told Vincent they were already ahead of schedule for the renovations and coming in under budget. That meant more money could be saved for the really important things, like medicine for the expanded clinic, which would open in another three weeks, or more food for the soup kitchen.

"We'd have more money, and be able to get more done, but we're running into some difficulties... Granddad Morris warned me, when you're busy working for the Lord, one good sign that you're on the right path is when the devil steps in and uses you for target practice. We've got prayer warriors on alert all over the city, and spreading across the country. We'll get through this."

"Anything I can do to help?" Vincent smiled faintly at a sharp twinge over the lies he told by pretending not to know what was going on.

"Not like in the old days." He grinned and shook his head. "How are you at praying until the walls come down?"

"Lots of practice, believe me."

"You'll tell me about it some time?"

"Soon," he promised.

Once they stepped outside, Josh's smile faded. They walked in silence down the block, and he said nothing until they had crossed the street.

"So... " Josh said. "Is she any good?"

"I assumed you've been teaching her, along with Lancaster. Can't you tell?" Vincent said with a smile.

"I'm her father. I'll always think she's the greatest thing God ever made. And, I'll always be worried she isn't quite fast enough or tricky enough. Half the time, I'm worried that letting her learn self-defense, letting her have fun with it, is only setting her up for trouble. I mean, who is the most obvious target for terrorists and organized crime? The ones who are able to defend themselves. They have to be taken down before the little people can be beaten into submission."

Vincent grunted agreement. He had seen that happen often enough on assignments for the Arc Foundation. Bullies were content to limit themselves to threats and petty violence, until someone showed up who wasn't afraid to defy them. Then they got nasty and blood was spilled. Too many times, the blood had come from the daughters of Quarry Hall.

"There she is," Josh murmured as they turned a corner. He pointed down the block. "My little girl, probably doing her twentieth good deed for the day."

Darcy walked down the sidewalk through the canyon of grimy, five and six-story buildings. She was little more than a recognizable figure in blue jeans and green sweatshirt, tall between two little old ladies who barely reached her shoulders and who dressed exactly alike. The same silver-blue hair; same little blue straw hats with shocking-pink cherries;

the same prim navy-blue dresses and white cardigans. They hung on her arms. From so far away, Vincent couldn't hear their voices, but both women smiled, doubling the wrinkles on their pointed little faces, and chattered away nonstop. Darcy wore a pleasant smile. Vincent couldn't tell if she was in a daze or actually enjoyed the women's chatter.

A figure six feet tall, topped with a shaved head, dressed in torn camouflage pants and jacket, leaped out of an alley, three feet in front of Darcy and the ladies. Two more hulking figures dressed exactly alike stepped out and flanked him.

"Coals," Josh murmured. "A new gang," he flung over his shoulder as he broke into a run. Vincent followed. They were only half a block away from Darcy, but right that moment it seemed like miles.

Knives flashed. The three Coals blocked Vincent's view of Darcy. The sidewalk cleared and the traffic on the cluttered street seemed to come to a standstill. A little old lady shrieked. It sounded more like injured pride than pain to Vincent's ears. Then he heard dull thuds and sharp smacking sounds; flesh against flesh.

"Darcy!" Josh shouted as he flung himself onto the back of the nearest Coal. The two went down in a heap.

A second gang member turned, swinging his knife at Vincent. From this close, it looked more like a short sword than a knife. Vincent ducked and turned, kicking high. His foot hit the target, bones snapped, and the Coal went down, shouting in pain, holding his hand. The knife went flying. Vincent turned, looking for the third. Josh had his opponent well in hand, kneeling on his back and twisting an arm behind him.

The leader of the trio faced Darcy. He had her backed into a doorway, surrounded by barrels and crates of trash, with the Plinkney sisters cowering behind her. Darcy held a four-foot length of rusty, one-inch pipe in a two-handed grip, crouching low, eyes narrowed as she studied her opponent. Her sweatshirt sleeve gaped where it had been sliced and blood soaked into the material, radiating out in a spreading stain, turning the green cloth purple. Darcy seemed not to notice the wound.

Vincent paused. He had taught Darcy that stance two days ago. She had caught on in only three repetitions. Her gaze flickered away from the Coal towering over her, rested on Vincent a moment. He nodded and gestured for her to continue. The corner of her mouth quirked up.

"Why don't you go pick on somebody your own size?" she said, her voice cracking. It sounded suspiciously like a giggle.

"Like you, sweet thing?" The Coal leader shifted his knife to his other hand and took another step closer.

Darcy struck, swinging out with the pipe, changing direction at the last moment, ducking under the reflexive swing of the knife, twisting down and then up again with the pipe. Vincent winced, foreseeing the target. He hadn't taught her *that* particular blow, but all was fair when fighting for her life.

The Coal went down with a choked shriek, dropped his knife and curled up in a fetal ball. Darcy took a step out of the doorway and dropped the pipe when she saw Vincent helping Josh subdue the last of the trio.

"You were told the Spike Center was off-limits to gang fighting and gang planning and gang colors," Josh said, yanking the Coal he had been fighting to his feet.

The gang member stood four inches taller than him, but Josh appeared to tower over him. He spoke quietly, almost calmly, but the sparks in his eyes and the intensity of his voice made Vincent stand still and listen.

"You were also told that the people belonging to the Center were off-limits. Remember?" Josh continued. He shook his prisoner until the youth nodded, tears threatening in his eyes. "That's my little girl. I don't like it when people even think bad thoughts about my daughter. I don't like it when people try to hurt her friends." He twisted the Coal around until he faced the Plinkney sisters. "Take a good look and remember what they look like. Don't ever go near them again, and you make sure nobody ever threatens them again, hear me?" He waited, squeezing tighter on the youth's twisted arm until his prisoner responded.

"I hear you," he choked.

"Get out of here." Josh released him with a shove. He looked around himself, at Darcy and the Plinkney sisters and Vincent watching him. A sheepish grin wiped away the hardness from his face. "Sorry about that. I guess my temper still gets hold of me."

"That was great, Dad," Darcy said, grinning.

"Great? Just wait until you hear the lecture you get from me, young lady." He took a breath, his gaze flickering to land on her bloody sleeve. "Jav—Vincent, can you get her home? I'll make sure the ladies get home safely."

"Dad—"

"Sure, Josh." Vincent reached for Darcy's uninjured arm. He grinned at the way her mouth flattened and her eyes took on the same stubborn fire he had seen in Josh's eyes too many times. Some things passed from father to daughter despite the lack of a blood tie, he supposed.

"No arguments." Josh shook a finger in her face. "Just what did you think you were doing?"

"What you always told me to do," Darcy grumbled.

The Plinkney sisters just stood there, dainty mouths hanging open, eyes flicking back and forth between father and daughter like spectators at a tennis match.

"I never told you to take on three gang toughs with knives, with nothing but your bare hands!"

"I found a weapon. Besides, you always say it's up to us, and nothing is worth living for unless you're willing to die for it."

"Darcy—"

"If I don't defend people, who will?"

"You could have gotten killed, baby. Did you think about that?" Josh's voice and face crumpled.

"No," she whispered. Some of the high color from the battle fled her face. "I just reacted."

"Yeah, well..."

"Josh, walk the ladies home. I'll make sure Darcy gets that cut cleaned up." Vincent took a firmer grip on her arm and gave her a tug toward the Center. Darcy resisted for a moment, then let him lead her away. A fine trembling moved through her body.

"How'd I do, teacher?" she half-whispered. She glanced sideways at him, and her mouth trembled a little, too.

"A few points off for style..." He winked, earning a lopsided grin from her. Vincent glanced over his shoulder to see Josh leading the Plinkney sisters around the corner, one lady on each arm, nodding attentively to their chatter. "Extra points for ingenuity, though."

His thoughts flashed through the handful of trained dogs at Quarry Hall, waiting to be assigned as bodyguard and assistant and confidant. There was no rule that the dogs could only go to residents of Quarry Hall. The sooner Darcy had a big dog walking at her side, if she held onto this need to be a hero, the better he would feel.

"Thanks." She stumbled on a cracked piece of sidewalk. Vincent tightened his grip.

They found Geneva in the kitchen. Vincent gave a hurried explanation of what happened as she led them down a section of completed hallway to the single room that functioned as the clinic for now.

"Darcy wanted to be Lancelot when she was a little girl," Geneva muttered as she flipped on the light in the little room. "You—there," she said, pointing her daughter to a cot. Darcy rolled her eyes, flashed a sheepish grin at Vincent, and sat. "That's a result of seeing her father being reduced to defensive measures too many times. Since Josh was her favorite uncle, even. David was just as bad as her, always fascinated with Bruce Lee movies, looking totally harmless one moment and then disarming ten enemies in two seconds."

"Guess it's in my genes," Darcy said, eyes wide and tone just sugary enough to hear her mock innocence. She stuck her tongue out at Vincent behind her mother's back.

Darcy was going to be all right. As for himself, he had a few doubts. At Quarry Hall, he had some control, some authority to keep his girls off the road, off active duty for the foundation, until they outgrew their adventure-loving, reckless immaturity. He had no authority over Darcy, except whatever she granted him through their growing friendship.

Geneva decreed the sweatshirt a loss, then took her scissors and cut the sleeve off. When Darcy protested, she promised her daughter she would cut the other sleeve off so she could keep wearing it.

"No stitches, Mom?" Darcy pleaded, after her mother had cleaned the wound so they could get a good look at the extent of it.

The knife had entered deep near her shoulder and sliced down toward her elbow, a good five inches long, growing shallower as it traveled. Most of the bleeding had stopped, except at the entry point.

"Oh, and how do you think you'll do your kitchen work and help your father if we settle for a few butterfly strips to hold it together? Do you want to be limited to tutoring math and reading classes and helping change diapers in the daycare?" Over Darcy's head, Geneva winked at Vincent.

"Oh, gag," Darcy muttered. "Didn't think it was that bad."

"Better safe than sorry." She stepped over to the supply drawers and picked up several pre-threaded needles, then a bottle of topical anesthetic.

While they waited for the anesthetic to work, Darcy filled them in on what the Plinkney sisters told her, gossip about the neighborhood, who was causing trouble and how many more women had decided to trust the Spike Center with their children while they were at work. Geneva seemed pleased with the information, though she did roll her eyes a few times at the verbatim phrasing of the two elderly sisters.

"I don't know what you were thinking," she muttered, as she took her neat stitches at the deepest end of the cut. "Rushing in like that."

"I wasn't thinking," Darcy admitted. "Those creeps just got me so mad." She shrugged, wincing when the movement affected her wound, and earned herself a gentle slap on the hand from her mother.

"You see what a handful she is?"

"I think you're doing a good job," Vincent said with a grin. Darcy stuck her tongue out at him again. "In fact—"

"Geneva?" a deep, British-accented voice called. "Is Darcy all right?" Hard-soled shoes tapped on the tiles of the hallway. "I stopped in the kitchen to look for you and the ladies told me what happened."

A tall, wide-shouldered, silver-haired man stepped through the door. His chiseled features paled when he saw Geneva tying off another suture, then pause to swab more blood away. He turned sharply on one heel, staring at Vincent, who leaned against the wall to stay out of the way.

Midas.

Vincent flashed back to Josh's words about "four," when he had said "three down and two to go." And yet, he found it hard to believe that

Midas, of all the members of their former team, would be here, and displaying so much concern for Josh's family that he would look physically ill at the sight of Darcy's injury. Of all of them, Midas had the most reason to want Josh killed in as slow and torturous a fashion as possible, and to destroy everything precious to him before killing him.

The years had been good to Midas. He had aged in an elegant, sophisticated manner. Vincent would have known him just by the expensive tailoring of his charcoal suit and the lump of amethyst decorating the handle of his ebony cane. He was a square-cut man, wide-shouldered, with pale blue eyes. Whenever they weren't on assignment, he was always in evening dress, indulging in every cultural event and venue offered by the cities where the team went. Even before he was badly injured, giving him a permanent limp, he walked with a heavy ebony cane that hid his sword. Then again, Midas loved blades of all kinds. Daedalus had learned his love of swordplay from Midas.

Midas stared at Vincent, who stared back. The clearest thought for two long seconds was to wonder why Darcy hadn't mentioned him. After all, she had the photo of their team, with which she had identified Vincent.

His muscles tensed, preparing to dodge the moment Midas made a move to release the cane hiding his sword and come after him.

Why hadn't Midas killed Josh before now?

"Geneva, what has been going on around here? All those women in the kitchen can tell me is that Darcy stumbled in here, leaving a trail of blood." Midas turned his gaze from Vincent, but it was a given all his attention remained focused on him.

"Hardly a trail of blood," Geneva said, somewhat distracted as she tied off the last suture.

"A bunch of Coals came after me and the Plinkneys," Darcy said. "Boy, if I had my sword—"

"You did not attack those gang bangers." Midas closed his eyes. He actually looked sick.

"Vincent and Dad were there before anything happened." She grimaced and nodded at her arm as her mother spread antiseptic cream on the stitched wound. "Well, anything worse."

"Vincent, is it?"

Chapter Eleven

"Oh, I'm sorry," Geneva said. "Vincent, this is — well, you knew him by another name. Before. Karl Van Mournen, now. He's stepped up and is trying to help us with funding, now that we've… well, the missions group funding the Center is having some trouble."

"I'm still rather good with money," Van Mournan said, nodding slowly to Vincent. "I'm always amazed at how good it feels to apply my skills to a worthy cause." A tiny, familiar gesture of his hand, palm out, signaled for peace between them. Vincent nodded agreement.

"Good to hear that," Vincent said. "I'm on assignment with an evangelical, philanthropic organization myself."

"Ah, of course. That's how you've come back into Joshua's life." He nodded again, his shoulders visibly relaxing, and he stepped back against the doorframe, resting both hands on his cane.

"Is everything okay now?" Darcy said, bending her head to look around her mother as Geneva wrapped a thick bandage around her arm. "You're not going to fight?"

"We are different men from who we were very, very long ago, darling," Van Mournen said. "When we did things unfit for ladies' ears. Let's leave it at that, shall we?" He quickly raised a hand to silence Darcy, who opened her mouth to ask the questions bright in her eyes.

Vincent choked, muffling a chuckle. From where he stood, he could see Darcy wrinkle up her nose and stick out the tip of her tongue at Van Mournen, but Geneva blocked her from the man's sight.

"Vincent." Van Mournen nodded to him, a regal gesture that had always irritated the other four members of their former team. "I cannot tell you how grateful I am you were here to protect our Darcy."

Our Darcy? Memories of irritation turned to a chill and a prickle of warning. Vincent hid the sensation behind a smile that grew a little harder to maintain, and shook Van Mournen's hand when he held it out to him.

"She really didn't need much help," he said. "Give her a length of pipe and she's a one-woman army."

"There were three of them, Uncle Karl," Darcy said. "Dad took one, Vincent got the other, and I got the one who did this to me." She gestured at her bandaged arm.

"Three of them? What have I told you about risking yourself?" Van Mournen shook his head. "If you could stay around for a while and teach some caution to this girl of ours, I'd appreciate it, Vincent. It seems that all the ugly experience her father and I share isn't enough to impress her. Someone new might do a better job."

"I'll try." Vincent glanced at Darcy. She rolled her eyes in disgust, mixed with embarrassment. He grinned at her.

"While you're here, do let me show you around. I'm rather proud of what we've accomplished so far."

"We? Oh, that's right, you're helping with funding." He remembered now comments Darcy had made about her "Uncle Karl" and how he enjoyed being their problem solver.

"Karl has been our troubleshooter and fundraiser for years," Geneva said. She nodded toward the door, pausing in throwing the scraps of bandage and dirty gauze into the wastebasket. "All the years we've been in ministry, all the different projects we've gotten involved with. He finds suppliers and saves us money every time we turn around. We wouldn't have half the successes we've known, without him."

"I do what I can, my dear. You and Josh are the true servants and an inspiration." Van Mournen gestured out into the hall with his cane. "Would you care for a grand tour?"

"Why not?" Vincent eyed the cane, wondering how far away in the gutted building they would be before Van Mournen dropped his charming persona and the cane sheathing his sword.

Yet Darcy called him "Uncle," and was comfortable enough with him to sass back at his concern. Vincent knew he had to give Van Mournen the benefit of the doubt, that he had truly changed and reformed, just like he was doing for Josh. That meant discounting his gut instincts and memories every time they shouted for him to remain on the defensive. That meant second-guessing himself every time common sense and experience said to consider every word that came from Van Mournen's mouth a disguised threat and a lie.

"You do have my deepest gratitude, you know," the other man said as they started down the hallway. "Josh's family has become my own. Darcy is a daughter to me."

Van Mournen led him up a flight of stairs. He pointed out the freight elevator at the far end of the hall and all the spots where partitions would be erected to set up the clinic. Vincent listened, waiting for one note of insincerity, of mockery, as Van Mournen proudly detailed all the work that would be done for the good of the community. He detected none, though the tour lasted nearly an hour, going through all four floors of the former factory/warehouse. When all the renovations had been made and funding secured for staff and equipment, there would be classrooms for adults to get their GEDs, woodworking shops and other vo-ed classes, to teach the youth trades to better their lives. A shelter for battered women, runaways and homeless families. An expanded daycare center so single parents could go to work or school and better their lives. Josh's family lived in a hastily assembled suite on the top floor, but when there was enough money, the top floor would be full of apartments for the staff who lived on-site and kept the Center open 24/7.

"All the best, of course," Van Mournen said. "And a fully equipped gymnasium, so Darcy can work out to her heart's content and hone her skills. She will never have to depend on anyone to defend her."

"I'm sure Josh would prefer that she never has to worry about that."

"That is my sincerest desire, believe me." Van Mournen gestured toward the stairs leading down. "However, considering the neighborhoods her parents insist on working in—well, you saw what happened today." He sighed, and didn't continue speaking until they had passed the second-floor landing. "I had my reservations when Roger, one of the board members, started giving her self-defense lessons. I sincerely regretted letting my own skills rust, as it were. There was a day when I could stand with the greatest swordmasters of the world, and I must admit that it pleased and amused me to watch Darcy's fascination with swashbuckler movies grow. She does love knights in shining armor and masked vigilantes fighting for justice. I would have loved to have become her tutor, but... well, we're all much older now, aren't we?" He sighed. "It saddened me greatly when Roger just... up and vanished. I know her regular lessons with him were bright spots in Darcy's day."

"I know. That's how we met up."

"Excuse me?" Van Mournen paused, his head tilting back a moment as if he had been struck. "I assumed you came looking for Josh."

"A friend of a friend asked me to fill in at Roger Lancaster's dojo until he returns. Darcy has been my student for a week now."

"Really. What a... fascinating coincidence. Let's see..." He paused as they reached the first floor again. "To the right. You'll be staying for lunch, won't you?" He smiled when Vincent nodded. "I do hope Roger is all right, wherever he had to go. A terrible thing, these accusations against all the members of the board. It's a tribute to their dedication and faith that Josh and Geneva are continuing with renovating this place, in the face of the scandal that just seems to get worse every day. I do hope the accusations against Roger, in particular, prove to be nothing but someone out to destroy the Center." He shook his head. "For Darcy's sake. I think she has a little bit of a crush on him. He couldn't see it, though. Treated her like a daughter. Which was all to the best, of course, since her parents would not permit a relationship to go any further than friendship."

"Oh, really?" Vincent thought back to Joan's teasing remark about Darcy having a crush on him.

"They're very protective of her feelings. They don't want her becoming too attached to anyone. I think it's partly because they have to move so often in their line of work. Every two or three years, another mission to establish. I admire them, even though I don't quite share all of Josh's spiritual beliefs."

"It sounds like you're very involved in their work."

"I help whenever I see a worthy cause. You see, Josh isn't the only one who has repented of his past."

The rest of the building still waited to have walls ripped out and new walls, circuitry, plumbing, and flooring installed. Van Mournen proudly pointed out the places where the different portions of the mission would someday function. Vincent was impressed, despite needing to reserve judgment until he had spent more time here and completed his assessment. He intended to get Joan to come get involved with the Spike Center immediately, so she could balance his perspective. Vincent hoped his first impressions proved to be truth, because he wanted the Spike Center to not only survive, but thrive. The Center would be a good thing for the neighborhood. Everything that helped the people and gave them their dignity back was welcome.

With the tour over, Van Mournen guided Vincent back downstairs to the livable portion of the building. Geneva asked him if he was staying for lunch, as if it were his regular habit. He excused himself, saying he had business to attend to. He shook his finger at Darcy as he left, earning chuckles from her and Josh.

Darcy was exempted from her regular duties of bussing tables because of her arm. She sat at the table with her parents and Vincent and listened while the two men talked about the different organizations and missions they had been involved with through the years, comparing stories, and even finding a few people they both knew. In some ways, Christian charitable circles were small, and sadly, it was rare when different organizations worked together in total harmony, with no power plays or splinters over ridiculous, extreme interpretations of theology.

"I could tell you a thousand war stories," Vincent admitted.

"But you can't, because they're classified?" Josh grinned. "Never thought you'd go back to working for government-types. Not after the way we were sucked down into a world that justified the means so often, we lost sight of the ends."

"Not the government." He shrugged, glancing at Darcy, who seemed to be holding her breath, listening as intently as if they were talking life-and-death adventures. "The Kingdom."

"I kind of gathered that."

"Covert ops-style work. Dangerous, sometimes. And I can't tell you who I work for... because they sent me here to check you out."

"Not another one of those self-appointed accountability groups?"

Geneva said, disappointment thick in her voice.

Vincent gave an exaggerated shudder and held up his index fingers, crossing them. That earned a chuckle from Darcy and her parents visibly relaxed.

"I've run into that type too often. We're regularly harassed by several of those groups, where I work. No, the foundation I work for is privately funded, as in a private fortune, earned through less-than-ethical methods, now dedicated to the Savior's service. In fact, the future head of the foundation, Joan, is here with me. You have been nominated to receive funds from us — and I'm breaking procedure to tell you this much." He leaned forward, resting on his elbows on the table. The three leaned a little closer. "The thing is, we've learned to trust the Spirit, trust what our guts tell us. Despite what I know about your past as Daedelus... my gut says you're for real. We're on the same side."

"Joan is the future head of the foundation," Darcy murmured. "You guys pretend to be who you aren't to get inside information."

"Inside, yes, and also avoid situations where the people who want our help clean up things, sweep trouble under the rug, put on a false face, just long enough to get funds. We investigate hard and deep and ruthlessly. I'm head of security, and I train my girls to fight hard and dirty and dig until they find the truth."

"How'd you get Saundra to bring you into the dojo?" Josh asked after several moments of silence, just looking at each other across the table.

"Her idea. We're investigating all the members of the board who are facing accusations, digging into their pasts, as well as the pasts, the reputations, of the people making the accusations."

"You're the mysterious friend she won't talk about, except to say that you're making headway on finding the source of the rumors," Geneva said. "Just how powerful is this foundation?"

"If I tell you, I'll have to kill you," Vincent said with a perfectly straight face. To his relief, they laughed, no hesitation.

"Tracking down our enemies is the hard part," Darcy said when the laughter faded. "Everything is rumor, so nobody knows who they originally heard it from."

"You've tried to track them down?" Vincent nodded, pleased. He had already decided Darcy wasn't the type to sit back and merely rely on prayer or complain when her friends were suffering. "We have some pretty sneaky people working for us, and they're tracking down suspicious payments that have been made to some of the people who have publicly claimed to be victims. As for the others who have only been named in rumors, who haven't confirmed, or who you haven't been able to find yet... well, our very sneaky people are very good at finding inconsistencies, digging out and separating the exaggerations from the outright lies. Funny thing, some of these people don't seem to exist."

"How soon can Roger and the others come back?" Darcy asked.

"We need to be solid on our facts. It's one thing to have enough pieces to make our researchers sure the accusations are all manufactured. It's another to have solid evidence we can present to the public to salvage those reputations and convince your wimpy supporters to fulfill their pledges."

Darcy snorted, muffling a giggle, and muttered, "wimps."

"Since Midas—Van Mournen knows me, we should probably tell the truth to the rest of your staff, that you and I know each other from a long time ago. But stick with Joan's cover story. She's one of my students, helping at the dojo, and spiritually searching. If she comes over here and spends time helping out, getting to know people, she should be able to stay under the radar, get people to trust her who might not open up to me because of my connection to you."

"Joan and her dog. He is so cool. So big—and smart."

"How do you know that?" Vincent challenged, exchanging grins with Josh.

"I can tell just by looking at him."

"Yeah, well, you're right. Ulysses is one of the most valuable assets at the foundation. I train our dogs to be partners with the girls. Drug dogs, explosives dogs, K-9 dogs. They're smart and loyal. Don't try to feed Ulysses. He won't take food from anybody but Joan—or me."

"To avoid poisoning," Josh murmured, nodding. His eyes took on a hardness that indicated he understood and could guess all the things Vincent hadn't said.

"So how did Joan start working for you? How does anybody get hired? It sounds like a cool place to work—not that I'll be leaving Mom and Dad any time soon," Darcy hurried to add. "You're stuck with me." She grinned. "At least, until I get my college bills paid."

"I'm raising a mercenary," he grumbled, and *ooph*ed louder than necessary when Geneva dug him in the ribs with her elbow.

"If you'd pay attention better," Geneva said, through their laughter, "you'd have heard Vincent say Joan is the future head of the foundation. She doesn't work for Vincent—he works for her."

"I'm training her," Vincent said. "She's the daughter of our founder. He essentially created the foundation to make up for his past life, and to give Joan the tools and resources to do what she's been trying to do all her life, help the little people, make sure the bad guys don't evade justice."

"So what else do you do, besides train dogs and investigate rescue missions in trouble?" Geneva asked. She glanced sideways at Darcy, and Vincent caught her concern.

He launched into a series of stories about mundane assignments, the everyday routines of training for dogs and girls, how some of them hated the self-defense training, the hours spent driving from one location to another on errands that were better handled in person, rather than through the Internet or on the phone, for security purposes. Whatever would give Darcy an honest picture of the hard work and lack of recognition that made up the majority of the lives and routines of the Arc Foundation's workers. None of the danger and life-and-death situations they sometimes faced.

Although, once he thought of it, he wondered if perhaps Darcy needed a few stories to warn her away from longing for a life of adventure. She needed to know that those who took point in the battle of good and evil lived with targets painted on their foreheads, and the enemy used more than bullets and knives to attack them.

"That was a totally stupid criminal," Josh said, coming back to the table at the far end of the kitchen, in a nook where the people in the main dining hall couldn't see them. He referred to the last story Vincent had told, about a problem three Quarry Hall girls had helped resolve.

The kitchen workers bustled about, refilling the serving trays from huge pots sitting across two burners each on the six-burner stove. A six-spigot dispenser for coffee and tea sat to one side of the doorway out of the kitchen, and Josh had brought back tea for the four of them.

"Most criminals are," Vincent agreed. "Mostly because people think that stealing and intimidating is an easier living than honest work. Crime always seems to take twice as much work, because you have to either keep a façade going, or keep people intimidated or whatever."

"I don't really understand," Darcy said, sitting back and glancing between her father and Vincent.

"What? The stupidity that comes from laziness and greed?" Josh said.

"How could he convince all those people that he was a... well, the equivalent of a prophet, I guess. He couldn't even quote the Bible properly. How could anyone believe him?"

"Lots of people nowadays claim to be Christians, but never look inside a Bible," Vincent said. "That's why what you're doing is important. Bring people in by meeting their physical needs, then they'll sit long enough you can make them aware of their spiritual needs and start teaching them. The basic man on the street wouldn't know if Zacchaeus was a book of the Bible or a variant of leprosy or an ancient city in Mesopotamia. When people don't know what they believe or why, they're easy to fool."

"Sorry. I should know that, already." She grimaced. "Guess that was kind of a stupid question, huh?"

"If you weren't curious, you wouldn't be my girl," Josh murmured. "See what a handful we have with her?" He winked at Vincent.

"You seem to be doing a pretty good job," he responded mildly.

"Most of that is Geneva's work, not mine. I'm a bad influence on this girl," he added with a chuckle.

"Dad—" Darcy groaned.

"No, really. I am so busy trying to make up for all the dirt I pulled, Darcy thinks it's normal to live your whole life looking after everyone else."

"It *should* be normal," she grumbled. "Jesus did it."

"Jesus is God—we're not. What happened today with the Coals is a good example of what a dangerous example I am for my girl. I'm proud of her, though. It just about killed me every time I had to paddle her behind when she was a brat."

"I'm still a brat." She scowled at him, but her eyes sparkled. She hid her twitching lips by taking a big gulp from her mug of tea.

"I have to be the tough one," Geneva said with a chuckle. "At least, when Darcy was a little girl. She needed to be paddled or stood in the corner quite a bit. Neither David nor Josh had the heart to do it." She reached over and rested a hand on her husband's hand. "Thank God we all lived through those years."

"By the grace of God, we'll live through twenty more. If Darcy cooperates," Josh added.

"Vincent, you have to help me. They're picking on me something awful!" Darcy wailed.

"You probably deserve it," Vincent responded, managing to keep a straight face.

She huffed and scowled at all three of them for five seconds, then abruptly stood and started scooping their dishes onto the tray Josh had brought the tea on. Her eyes sparkled, though.

"Hey, don't run away when the fight's getting interesting," Josh said.

"I still have to do dishes." Darcy made a point of keeping most of the weight on her good arm and carried the tray over to the huge stainless steel dishwashing machine, with its long, wall-hugging chute and slots for soap and six-foot-high stack of plastic trays to hold the dishes. Two basins of dirty dishes waited to be washed.

"She's a good kid, despite the heart attacks she gives us." Josh sighed. His humor faded from his eyes fast enough for Vincent to see it.

Chapter Twelve

"What's worrying you, brother?" Vincent murmured.

"Seeing you, remembering the life I used to live..." He sighed and glanced at Geneva.

"When Karl came into our lives," she said, "Josh had nightmares, afraid he would attack us to get revenge. Even when Karl wanted to let bygones be bygones and insisted he had reformed and admired what we were doing."

"Not everybody who comes around here is going to be a Christian, and even Christians aren't always forgiving, willing to let things stay in the past," Josh said. "I've made a lot of enemies in my time. It won't matter to them that I've reformed. Someday, someone *will* go after Geneva and Darcy because they're my family."

"That's why you let Lancaster give her self-defense training. Makes sense." Vincent shrugged. "Didn't you hear any of the stories I told you about my girls, the dogs I train, all the federal connections we have?"

"Yeah, I did. I got hit on the head often enough in the past, my brains should have been permanently scrambled, but I tell you, *Javelin*—" Josh leaned forward, his voice and gaze gaining intensity to the point they could cut the air. "I'm not so trusting, so willing to wimp out and say since everything is in God's hands, I don't have to lift a finger in my defense anymore. Teaching Darcy to stand on her own is just the first step. Common sense. I'm taking your showing up here as an answer to prayer. Will you take care of Geneva and Darcy for me, if anything happens to me?" Josh held out his hand, and he waited.

Vincent stared into his eyes. Peripherally, he felt Geneva waiting, her face paler than it had been just a few moments ago. This concern of Josh's wasn't a surprise to her, and Vincent guessed they had spent many private moments talking about this, praying together, weighing the risks. He admired Josh for being strong enough to admit his fears to his wife, and admired Geneva for staying with him, and not gathering up her daughter and running to safer ground. He sat still, sending up a silent, wordless request for guidance. That sense of right, of balance and harmony, stayed solid and strong inside him.

"You got it," he said, and clasped Josh's hand.

~~~~~

An hour later, as Vincent stepped out the door to walk across the
~~~~~

street to where he parked his car, he saw a brown sedan pull up to the opening of the alley leading to the loading dock. He had to walk past the alley entrance. The driver of the car watched him. Vincent considered either ignoring the watcher or pushing his luck and confronting the man. From what he had observed and the research Sophie had sent him, the presence of the Spike Center and the troubles its leadership faced served to polarize the surrounding neighborhood. People could be defensive, apprehensive about newcomers, and this man could be watching him and trying to decide if he was a friend of the Center or another foe.

Then Vincent got a little closer and saw the man's red, short-cropped curls, his linebacker shoulders, and the hand on the steering wheel that missed the tip of its index finger. He recognized him from the dojo. The man had been there every single day since he had taken over running Roger Lancaster's business, and just two days ago one of his students had filled Vincent in on the man's identity—but not yet his mission or his loyalty in the conflict.

"Detective McGee," Vincent said, putting on a false smile guaranteed to let the recipient know he wasn't happy to see him. He didn't feel like laughing when the detective flinched at this sign he had been outed. "How nice to see you down here. Working on cleaning up the Zone today?"

"What are you doing here, mister defense instructor?" The detective opened the door and climbed out. When he unfolded, he was nearly as tall as Vincent, but he slouched and his hunched shoulders made it look like he tried to be smaller than he was. "Don't you have battered women to teach how to shoot their boyfriends?"

"I don't use guns." Vincent shrugged. "Just having lunch with some old friends."

"Who would they happen to be?" He glanced at the building, his doubt visible in his gaze.

Vincent hesitated, torn between telling McGee it wasn't any of his business, giving him a smart remark about befriending derelicts and homeless families, or telling him the truth.

"Why are you here?" he finally decided to ask.

"Not that it's any of your business..." The detective made a show of adjusting his belt, pushing back his sport jacket to reveal his shoulder holster. "We got an anonymous call that three gang members tried to beat up the Rev's daughter."

"The Coals," Vincent said, nodding. "They actually tried to mug the two little old ladies Darcy was escorting."

"Clay and his family are your old friends?" McGee let out a groan when Vincent nodded. "Should have figured that, with you taking over Lancaster's place."

"Do you want me to come back in while you talk with Darcy?" he offered with his most innocent expression.

"No." The detective headed for the door Vincent had just exited. "If I need to ask you any questions, I know where to find you."

"You certainly do," Vincent said under his breath, and continued toward his car.

Who, he wondered, had called the police? Josh hadn't made any move to get the police involved. Maybe one of the kitchen workers. They had certainly showed enough distress over Darcy's wound.

Vincent suspected something more was going on than the scandal that had driven the members of the board to step back.

Joan was thoughtful when he related what he had learned and discussed at the Spike Center. They met for dinner in the office/safe house on the opposite side of the city. Joan had handled several beginner classes at the dojo while Vincent was at the Center, then she walked around the neighborhood, pretending to look for a second job while talking to more people, asking questions. She then came here to get the latest report from Sophie and bounce ideas around with the research team, while waiting for Vincent to join her.

"My general feeling is that most people like what's happening here. They like the Clays, and they're furious over what's happening to the other leaders." Joan handed over a carton of kung pao chicken.

"Furious enough to get in the way of people who are looking for answers?" He nodded, liking how that fit into the puzzle.

"What's funny is that it seems the Clays earned acceptance by the neighborhood faster than the other leaders." She scooped lo mein noodles onto her paper plate, then picked up two with thumb and index finger to toss to Ulysses.

Vincent groaned as the big dog leaped up from a full reclining position and caught the noodles neatly, snapping them up and swallowing them with minimal mess or noise. "I don't want to know how you taught him that."

"More like he taught me. Are you sure you don't have some kind of mind control gizmo implanted in our mutts, giving them hypnotic control over us? I thought Su-Ma was crazy, the way she babies her BooBoo. The only dog I know that cries if he doesn't get chocolate ice cream at least once a week."

Ulysses let out a whine that sounded clearly nauseous.

"Yes, I know you're too smart to want that nasty stuff," Joan said. "BooBoo is definitely a mutant, if chocolate doesn't poison him like a normal dog." Ulysses let out a snort and she laughed.

"Back to subject?" Vincent said. "Are you saying the original leaders of the Center weren't... what? Welcome? Wanted?"

"They've been in this general area for years, working their way up from a storefront soup kitchen, moving into better quarters as they gained funding, expanded their services to the community. Could be someone caused trouble, got nasty, created some bad history at some point." She popped the top of the can of green tea and paused, lips pursed. "They got labeled as a bunch of loud-mouth, arrogant hypocrites. Even if it was just one of them who stepped over the line, all of them got smeared. But Darcy and her folks arrive and all they do from the get-go is give and love and accept people. First impressions are the strongest." She picked up the can to pour into her paper cup and paused again.

"What?" Vincent prodded. He smiled and slouched a little in his chair, enjoying the almost visible connection of ideas sparking in her eyes. Joan did with instinct and intuition what Sophie did with her custom-designed Internet search programs.

"Everybody I've talked to speaks about Darcy first. They really like her. She walks around with her heart out where everybody can see it. It's always 'that Darcy and her folks,' when anybody talks about them. She's got something that makes people trust her."

"She's innocent and good-hearted and smart. Innocent without being stupid or gullible. That's a hard balance."

"Especially with a guy like Daedelus for her stepfather?" she murmured.

"Especially."

~~~~~

Full night had fallen by the time Darcy finished her after-supper duties in the kitchen. She shoved the last plastic tray of dishes out of the steaming mouth of the dishwasher and slid it down the long chute to the end, to finish drying and cool. The voices of the departing clean-up crew echoed from the dining hall. Darcy listened for a few moments, then looked around. She was alone, and those dishes could certainly sit until morning. She scurried around the massive room, almost slipping on a wet patch in the tile, and flipped all the switches to turn off the various pieces of equipment. She checked the walk-in cooler and turned off the light, then headed for the door.

A light was on in the long meeting room destined to become administrative offices. She glanced in the doorway and saw yet another meeting in the long room, three tables set up end-to-end—her parents, Martha Blaine, 'Uncle Bob' Dempsy and a handful of staffers who had come with her parents from the mission in San Antonio. Darcy didn't pause in the doorway long enough to catch anyone's attention.

She went upstairs to the treasure room. It was in a section of the third floor that wouldn't be renovated for years, even under the most optimistic circumstances. No one else called it the treasure room—the official designation was short-term storage for Van Mournen's personal effects.
~~~~~

The man lived on the road and had no permanent address. As a favor to an old friend who devoted much of his influence and knowledge to helping them, her parents always provided a room for storage wherever they were assigned. He had given Darcy the key to this room at the Spike Center as soon as his trunks arrived and asked her to be the secret guard for his belongings. Her father had the other key.

When she was thirteen, Darcy had gone exploring in the basement of the mission building in Chicago that her parents were helping to upgrade and expand. Her schoolmates had been telling tall tales about Al Capone's mysterious treasure vaults, and she had been sure that the clammy, cobwebby passageways under the big old mission building had to be the gangster's vaults. She had borrowed her father's key rings, taking one ring each day, after school while her parents were busy, until she had tried all the keys in all the doors. She was nearing the end when she found the treasure room. Inside were four steamer trunks. She ignored the three without locks and went directly to the one with the padlock. Anything left unlocked and unguarded wasn't worth investigating. Darcy hefted the jangling key ring she had borrowed for the afternoon, and reached for the big, bright lock.

For some reason, it was unlocked. Glancing over her shoulder, thinking she heard something move out in the dark hallway, she tugged on the padlock.

It came off the loop of the trunk and she lifted the clasp. She took a deep breath, glanced over her shoulder — positive she heard something this time — then lifted the lid.

A sigh of delight escaped her. The trunk held swords. Eight in all, each wrapped in cloth with their hilts showing, inside thick, clear plastic sleeves. Darcy reached for the closest, with bits of blue stone embedded in the woven basket-style guard.

This time, she definitely heard something out in the dark hallway.

It was a long way from the storage room door to the stairs. Monsters liked to hide in the dark — though she was certainly too old to believe in monsters. Darcy considered the swords and knew she would disbelieve in monsters a little more strongly with a sword in her hand.

The one with the blue stones was too heavy. She put it back, pouting a little in disappointment, and reached for the rapier next to it. The sword had a simple hilt like a wide cup with a bar across it and a long curve of gleaming steel with lions embossed in it.

"Lovely, isn't it?" a deep, British-accented voice had said.

"Uncle Karl!" Darcy squeaked and dropped the sword. It clattered and clanged against the other hilts, its velvet-wrapped blade making a dull thud.

"I should have known you would find this trunk sooner or later. Your father and I should have either told you about it or buried it." He chuckled. His silver-gray trench coat was spotted with raindrops and his silver hair was slicked to his head. His blue eyes sparkled palely.

"This is Daddy's?" She was so relieved not to be scolded, she didn't wonder what he was doing in the basement, when he was supposed to have left for New York on a fundraising trip that morning.

"Your father's and mine, actually." Van Mournen came into the room and dropped to his knees in front of the chest. "In our former life, when we worked for the government, fighting the forces of evil all over the world, we gathered... mementoes. Trophies, actually. Memories of battles won and lost, innocents rescued, friends lost in the battle of good versus evil. What grand stories these blades could tell, if they could only speak. And other treasures, which have been entrusted to our care to safeguard until we can return them to their rightful owners. Someday, Darcy, all this will be yours to guard."

"Why are they in these dirty old trunks, here in the basement? Shouldn't they be like... in a bank? Or maybe a museum?"

"There are many evil people still roaming freely in this world, dearheart. If they knew your father and I were entrusted with guarding these treasures, the first thing they would do is threaten those who are most precious to us. You or your mother. Secrecy is a far more effective safeguard than any vault or burglar alarm or even heavy locks."

"I shouldn't have found them, huh?" Darcy sighed, knowing she would not be able to just leave the trunks alone from now on. She wanted to see everything in them, to touch them and dream about all the stories they belonged to, and maybe convince her father to tell her those stories.

"Well... let's make a deal. I will let you come down and examine them and I won't tell your father, if you do two things for me." Van Mournen held out his hand. His mouth fell into a serious line, but his eyes sparkled, like they did when he took her out on surprise trips like roller skating or to the bookstore or to the circus.

"Deal." Darcy grasped his dry, long-fingered hand.

"My dear, you really should find out what the conditions are before you make any promises. What if you promise something that you cannot in good conscience deliver? You must perforce break that promise. Never break promises, Darcy. Ever. I couldn't stand it if you lost your purity of heart and soul."

"I'll never break a promise." She crossed her heart with her free hand. "Tell me what I have to do."

"Let's see, where were we?" He frowned and tilted his head to one side and 'hmm'ed a few times, making her giggle. "Ah, yes! We must educate you. To be a proper guardian, you must understand everything there is to know about the treasures that will someday reside in your care.

We will start with this trunk, and when you are an expert, with nothing more to learn, you can move on to another. To begin, you will study swords and how to use them. Go to the library and read everything you can find. Pay careful attention when you go to the movies and see sword fights on television."

"Like Robin Hood?" She had sat perfectly still, entranced during the Errol Flynn movie just the Saturday before.

"Better than Robin Hood. Watch every movie with Tyrone Power and Maureen O'Hara. They were masters with the sword. When you're old enough, I'll find you a teacher, so you can learn to handle all these swords. And my second condition — don't tell your father you know about the trunk. It would break his heart. He so looks forward to surprising you with this treasure someday. Agreed?"

Darcy wasn't sure about keeping the secret from her father, but she agreed. She had already promised, after all.

Now, two missions and six years later, she had graduated from the trunk full of swords to the trunk full of heavily swaddled bits of antique porcelain. When Van Mournen had left, after giving Vincent the tour, he had nodded to her, winked, and crossed his heart — their secret sign that another item had been added to the treasure trove. Darcy had been on pins and needles all day, waiting until she could sneak up to the room, open the trunks, and figure out what had been added.

She unlocked the door of the treasure room and stepped inside, closing the door before she turned on the light. Her heart skipped a few beats. She didn't know which part she enjoyed more — the thrill of a new treasure to research and learn by heart, or the chance that she might get caught. In some ways, she resented the approach of her twentieth birthday, when this would no longer be a delicious secret to be protected with stealth.

The three trunks sat under a folding table set up in the corner of the room. Papers and notebooks, maps and artist renditions of how the renovated building would look someday covered the table. There were reports of all Van Mournen's fundraising efforts and results, and projected needs for the Center for the next twenty years in a pile at the end of the table. Darcy frowned when she glanced over the figures. It looked as if Van Mournen planned to be the sole source of funding for the Spike Center, and that made no sense. As soon as those stupid, hateful rumors were dealt with and the board came back to work, the money would flow in again. Everything wouldn't rest on his fundraising talents and connections anymore. Besides, once Vincent was done with his investigation, there would be even more money from his foundation.

Shaking her head, she pushed aside those thoughts. Everything was going to work out, just like she had been praying ever since the first hint of trouble came to light. She dropped to her knees in front of the center trunk. The newest item was always in the center trunk. Her hands shook as she pulled out the key and inserted it in the lock.

"Oh," she breathed, as she saw the new sword lying on top of the familiar, cherished pile.

The elaborate basket hilt was worn smooth in places. The crystal chips had fallen out of three sockets. Steel showed through where the gilding had worn off completely. Darcy knew she would have to examine it closely for days and check her secret library, but she thought the sword was a genuine Venetian, a schiavona, not just a flattering imitation.

Who had carried it? Where had they obtained the sword, how — by inheritance, theft, purchase — and when and where? How had they been threatened, that they had entrusted their treasure to Van Mournen for safekeeping? Darcy sat back on her heels, closed her eyes and tried to imagine that very different life, and the drastic changes that had necessitated separating owner from treasure.

With a sigh of regret, she put aside her speculations and closed and locked the trunk. She knew better than to linger over her new treasure this first time. If her father caught her, it would ruin the surprise he planned on giving her someday, when she was old enough to help carry the burden of his and Van Mournen's guardianship.

"Someday, Daddy..." Darcy stood, supporting her injured arm as she moved.

Chapter Thirteen

Vincent stopped and glanced toward the single light glowing in the window of the dojo office. A handful of people had keys to get in to work out or hold classes or provide services after regular hours. However, none of them had keys for the office.

"Somebody's there," Joan murmured. "There goes planning the next couple of classes." She took the lead, heading for the back of the building instead of going in through the front door.

He had a rough plan by the time they reached the back door and he unlocked it.

"I'm up the fire escape?" Joan whispered, when he glanced at the skeleton of metal, dark lines in the shadows where the inadequate streetlight barely reached.

"Backup, while I see what our visitor wants." He detached the key for the roof door from his ring and handed it to her.

Ulysses went up on his back legs and scratched several times at the door before settling back on his haunches.

"He wants to be backup," Joan said.

Vincent muffled a smile and snapped out the gestures that instructed the dog to stay and guard the back door. If he were caught sneaking around some place where he didn't belong, he would choose the exit with the least amount of light. Ulysses whined once, as if he disagreed with his orders. Vincent mentally filed away a complaint about Joan's bad influence on the formerly well-trained dog.

He gave Joan a boost, cupping his hands for her to step and reach the ladder up to the fire escape. She moved lightly, with minimum rattling and squeaking of the rusty bars. Vincent waited until she passed the second floor before he unlocked the back door and entered through the storage room of the dojo. All was quiet. He moved through the darkness, guiding himself with fingertips brushing the edges of the metal shelves. At the door of the storage room, he paused, listening. No light spilling under the door. No footsteps out in the main room. He opened the door, lifting up slightly on the doorknob to avoid the creak that appeared halfway through the swing of the door.

Light spilled through the tall, thin windows down the street side of the first floor. While removing most of the walls to make it one vast room was a smart move in creating an exercise area, it worked against him now, giving him few places to stay out of sight while he approached the intruder. However, the light didn't reach further than halfway across the floor, leaving the rest of the long room in shadows. Those shadows felt thick, solid. Vincent stayed in the darkness of the doorway, stretching his senses through the room to the spill of light from the lamp in the corner office. Whoever had been wasn't there now.

A breath of air warned him. He threw himself into a forward roll as a blade slashed through the air at the height of his neck.

Scrambling to his feet, Vincent raced through the stripes of darkness and street light. He snatched at the lowest of the katanas in the display on the wall and turned to face his attacker.

Icy pale eyes burned in a dark ski mask. A wide-shouldered figure dressed in black lunged at Vincent. Moving on the balls of his feet, wearing soft-soled boots, the man was a literal shadow as he attacked. Vincent threw off the effects of the long day, and let his own blade become part of his arm.

The intruder's sword moved quickly, a silver blur in the shadows and the red glare of the emergency exit sign. Vincent could barely see enough to block and feint, let alone discern the style of blade.

Six times their blades met and clashed, throwing sparks through the darkness. The other man leaped at Vincent, turning at the last moment for a blow more appropriate for football. Vincent sidestepped and brought his elbow down into his opponent's shoulder, knocking him off balance.

A banging erupted at the front door. Vincent pushed aside the distraction and spun, bringing his blade up. His opponent turned, distracted by the sound. The blade glanced off the stranger's shoulder, catching on cloth. The iron-salt smell of blood filled the warm air, mixed with old sweat and floor polish.

"Anybody here?" a man called, accompanied by the creak of the front door opening. That door should have been locked.

Vincent somersaulted backward to avoid a slash that would have eviscerated him. He landed and kicked, catching the other man at the knees and throwing him to the floor. The sword went flying. Vincent took a step backward, straining to see through the darkness and light. Was the newcomer enemy, ally, or innocent bystander?

His enemy fled, pausing long enough to snatch up his sword, then bowling over the man who appeared in the doorway. Three steps took him out into the night, vanishing into the darkness between the streetlights.

"You want to tell me what's going on, or do I have to drag you down to the station?" Detective McGee asked, as he struggled to his knees.

"It's simple," Joan said, coming around the last turn in the stairs. "We came back to work on tomorrow's schedule, we interrupted a robbery in progress, and Vincent used the first weapon he had at hand."

"Looks like the other guy was prepared," the detective retorted.

"He probably thought he was being clever, using a weapon that should scare most people and wouldn't make any noise."

"You sound pretty sure of that strategy—like maybe you use it yourself." He smiled as he said it, but Vincent didn't like it any better than if the man had snarled at her.

"I'm learning the weapon myself. It's romantic, it's fulfillment of childhood fantasies. Heck, with all the sword and fantasy movies out there, who wouldn't think of swords and bows and such? Especially with all the tougher laws for just carrying a gun during a crime."

"Uh huh."

"Something I can help you with, Detective?" Vincent said.

"I came to talk with you about those kids who beat up on Darcy."

"Someone beat up on her? From what I've seen, it must have taken a whole gang," Joan said. "That girl knows how to take care of herself."

"Uh huh. Just as long as you don't make any problems for her, I'm satisfied." McGee glanced toward the door. "You certainly are good with that thing."

"Yes. Isn't it lucky?" Vincent stepped up to the rack and put back the katana.

~~~~~

An hour later, McGee finally left, after asking repeated questions about the Coals and anything Vincent or Joan knew about the gangs in the city. He asked four different times for his version of the attack on Darcy and the Plinkney sisters. Vincent didn't know if the man was relieved or worried that the story didn't change. Was he trying to get more to use against the Coals? McGee didn't ask any more questions about the fight he had interrupted, and Vincent knew better than to be relieved. He had other things on his mind, though.

Joan had brought Ulysses inside during the interrogation. Now they went upstairs to lock up and search the apartment, in case the intruder had started there. Vincent made the rounds of the dojo. He checked doors and windows, searching for signs of force or damage. The only anomaly was the open front door. Whoever his surprise visitor was, the man had managed to enter with no damage to the door. None of the windows showed any sign of tampering. Unless his enemy could walk through walls, the only logical explanation was either the intruder was very good at picking locks, or he had a key. Which begged the question why he bothered with a disguise, if he had the right to come inside after hours.

Josh, at one time in his spotted past, had been a locksmith.

Vincent didn't like the uneasy feeling that thought gave him. He wanted to reject the suspicion immediately, but knew better than to let
~~~~~

emotions and the appearance of righteousness overrule common sense.

Then he saw a shadow approaching the front door. A tall, dark, broad-shouldered figure. Vincent glanced over at the sword rack, then upstairs where Joan and Ulysses were hard at work, checking for signs of the intruder. What were the chances the intruder decided to come back, maybe with a gun this time?

"Javelin?" Van Mournen called, stepping into the light over the door. He paused a moment, then rapped on the glass of the front door. "Are you in there?" Another pause, and he stepped over to the other side, to press the button for the buzzer of the apartment.

"Just a minute." Vincent took slow steps toward the door. Just because Van Mournen had been gracious and open that morning didn't mean the man wouldn't come after his head tonight. Just because he hadn't destroyed Josh for his betrayals so many years ago, that didn't mean he wouldn't take brutal justice on Vincent. After all, he stood at the door and called him Javelin, perhaps indicating the past was more alive to him than the present.

"I'm glad you're here. I wasn't sure if you were using Roger's apartment, or you decided to stay somewhere else," Van Mournen said, as he stepped into the dojo, wrapped in a cloud of a spicy, rich aftershave. He glanced around the half-lit room. "I'm glad you're keeping this place going. In some ways, Roger did as much for the neighborhood with what he taught here as the Center does with food and medicine."

He settled down in one of the deep, old-fashioned windowsills with a grunt and grimaced as he rubbed at his leg just above his knee. "Of course, I could be biased. I still have a passion for a beautiful, well-balanced blade. Since my leg betrayed me, well... I mostly stay in shape to look good in the boardroom. Money is often a better weapon than a sword—don't tell our old friends I said that," he added with a wink.

"What can I do for you?"

"Let bygones be bygones, just as Josh and I have?" He planted his ebony cane firmly in front of himself and straightened his shoulders. His tweed jacket shifted in the half-light as he tilted his head back and studied Vincent for several heartbeats. "What was done to us... I'm sure someone, somewhere, will justify the warping of our souls. Looking back... we were forced to hate and mistrust the only people who understood what we endured." Pain clouded his pale blue eyes. "We are, in essence, the only real family each other has."

"The problem is that most murders occur within families."

"Touché. I just wanted to come by, offer you my hand and—" He stopped as the clatter of Ulysses' claws on the stairs grew louder and closer.

Vincent turned partially. Nothing would persuade him just yet to turn his back on Karl Van Mournen. He watched for Ulysses' reaction to the man. Joan appeared a few seconds after the dog came in and sat down midway between Vincent and their visitor. She met Vincent's gaze and briefly shook her head. Nothing upstairs, no signs of searching or damage. If anything had been stolen from Roger's possessions, they would have to wait until the missing man reappeared to be sure.

"Madam, I seem to be intruding." Van Mournen swept her a bow. He glanced at Vincent, and his eyebrow rose high enough to vanish in the thick sweep of silver hair across his forehead. "Please, accept my humble apologies."

"Everything checks out upstairs. No sign of damage from the intruder. Let's hope we caught him before he stole anything," she said.

"Intruder?" Van Mournen asked.

"Karl Van Mournen, my boss, Joan Carter of the Arc Foundation. We specialize in troubleshooting for Christian organizations."

Now it was Joan's turn for a raised eyebrow. What concerned her more? The false name, or identifying the foundation to Van Mournen?

"We're investigating the accusations against the Board of the Spike Center," she said. "I hope you won't blow our cover. We've found that coming in through the back door and acting discretely and under cover ensures honesty, helps us find the truth much faster than simply walking up to the front door and asking them to open all the files to us."

"How well does that approach work, if they hired you to troubleshoot?"

"They didn't." Joan snapped her fingers and twisted her wrist slightly, bringing Ulysses to his feet to stand in front of her, head lowered, gazing up at Van Mournen.

"We've jeopardized our mission enough letting you know what we're doing," Vincent added. "A gesture of good faith."

"Of course. I'm flattered. And pleased." Van Mournen nodded to them both. "Do Joshua and Geneva know…"

"No, since they're among the targets of our investigation," Joan said. "I hope we can rely on you to be discreet?"

"Absolutely. And I do look forward to learning more about your organization." He stood and bowed to her.

"You should be warned," Vincent said. "Nothing is what it appears on the surface."

"Indeed." He glanced back and forth between them, eyes narrowing for a few seconds, then his face lit up in a jovial smile. "Well, this has been a delightful, profitable evening. Can I look forward to meeting you again, perhaps at the Center?"

"Count on it," Joan said.

When Van Mournen left five minutes later, Vincent walked him to the door to lock up. They shook hands. Van Mournen's hand was cold and dry. Vincent didn't wipe his hand on his pants until after his visitor was out the door and walking down the street. He turned off the light in the entryway, but stayed there in the doorway, watching.

Van Mournen climbed into a dark, newer model sedan. From ten yards away and in shadows, Vincent couldn't tell much more than that.

Joan waited in the apartment. She was taking a glass measuring cup of steaming water from the microwave when he had finished locking up, turned off the lights downstairs, and came upstairs.

"He sounds just a little too good to be true," she murmured, and plopped a handful of tea bags into the water.

"Really?"

"Do you believe him?"

"Since I'm not sure what was a lie and what was truth… no."

"Did you notice if he wore so much scent when you ran into him before?"

"No…" Vincent thought for a moment, then shook his head. "He had something—you can't wear a power suit like that, play the part of the man of culture, without cologne, but it wasn't that strong." He leaned back against the counter and crossed his arms. "Why?"

"Ulysses didn't like how he smelled. It was like a wall pushing him away."

"And?"

"If I had broken into a place, it would be smart to come right back, pretend ignorance, and get feedback from the victims while they were still off balance. That would include dousing myself in something smelly."

"Really, Sherlock?" He grinned, catching on to what she was thinking, and pleased.

"The victims of the break-in associate the over-strong smell with me visiting and not with the intruder, even if just subconsciously."

"Considering the short time between the break-in and Midas coming back, the wound to the intruder's shoulder, and the lack of any sign of injury on Midas… he would have had to plan this, be able to treat his wound by himself—"

"What if he has an accomplice, waiting nearby?"

"True. Except Midas hated needing anyone." He shook his head. "It's a good theory, and something totally in line with his way of handling things. But one little problem."

"He walks with a limp and leans on that cane a lot." Joan sighed. "And my main reason for suspecting him is the way Ulysses reacted to the scent. He couldn't tell me if he was here before."

"Midas wouldn't—"

"You should really call him by the name he uses now, or else he won't use the name you want."

"Smart-alec kid," he muttered. Joan smirked. "Right. *Van Mournen* wouldn't have known Ulysses was here and wouldn't know he needed to disguise his scent." He took a step back. "Unless he was close by, saw us bring Ulysses in, and came back specifically to confuse things."

"It makes my head hurt."

"You and me both."

"I mostly meant the scent." Joan swirled the cup of water and went down to one knee to give Ulysses a good, hard rub. "Imagine what it's doing to his nose."

"Yeah. And that sounds like something Mid— Van Mournen would definitely do. But there's still the cane and his bad leg."

Van Mournen would have no problem pretending to have a handicap to lull his enemies into a false sense of superiority, but that meant he had been faking his bad leg for years — or at least long enough that Darcy and Josh and Geneva didn't remark on it now. For what purpose?

~~~~~

The Coals gathered around a fire in a metal barrel on the far north corner of their territory. The night was warm. Some of them didn't even wear shirts. The fire was for looks, for atmosphere. They were the Coals; they played with fire.

A big black Lincoln with rental stickers pulled up to their corner. Their conversation died as everyone watched Tito, *El Presidente*, to see what he would do about this intruder. No one, especially strangers in big, fancy, expensive cars, came into Coals territory after dark.

"I'm looking for the little boys who tried to beat up on a skinny girl and two little old ladies this morning," a deep voice drawled in a Southern accent.

"Yeah? What for?" Bo Berber snapped. He rubbed at his arm without thinking, massaging the bruised, twisted muscles.

"I just want to see who made such a big mess of such an easy job," the stranger continued. He was nothing but a silhouette wearing a wide-brimmed hat, a shadow in the darkness. The car's interior lights were blue-green, turned down to mere glimmers of color.

"Weren't no easy job," Tito said. He strutted up to within three feet of the car, bending to look inside the driver's side. "The girl, she some kung-fu expert. And she had two big guys come jump us when we ain't looking."

"Poor, abused children," the stranger said, laughter in his voice.

"Watch who you calling children, you—"

"How'd you like a chance to even the score?" The voice turned icy.

Ten long seconds of silence while Tito considered the dark interior of the car. His followers watched him. He glanced at them, noting their eager faces.
~~~~~

"Okay. What we gotta do?"

The door to the back seat clicked and swung open, revealing a lush, cream-colored interior that begged to be spoiled by their greasy, food-stained clothes.

"Step into my office, gentlemen. Ah, just one moment," the man said, as half the gang jumped forward to pile into the car. "Just the three."

A few gang members grumbled and whined, but Tito silenced them with a glare. He tugged his threadbare army surplus jacket straight and climbed into the back seat. Bo and his cousin Jumper followed him. The driver's window closed with a soft hum of electronics.

"So, what's the deal?" Tito demanded, as the car headed down the street.

"All in good time," the driver said softly. He reached over and tapped the controls for the sound system. "Relax and enjoy the ride." Vivaldi spilled from the speakers. The Coals sneered at each other, until Tito caught a glimpse of icy, pale eyes glaring at him in the rearview mirror.

Twenty minutes later, the three Coals climbed out of the car in the crumbling parking lot of the Allied Glass Works. Following the driver's instructions, they went inside and headed for the back of the vast open space of the ground floor. The driver pulled his Lincoln around the side of the building, parking it in darkness.

"Hey, what's that over there?" Jumper said, noticing a shape lying at the edge of the moonlight coming through the broken skylight.

"Whatever it is, it be smelling rotten," Tito replied. He snorted and gestured at the shape. "See what it is, Bo."

Dutifully, Bo stepped through the shaft of moonlight and crouched down by the shape. He made a gagging noise, then abruptly jumped to his feet.

"Tito — man, this dude ain't got no head!"

"What a coincidence," the stranger drawled from the doorway. His voice dropped its accent and twisted into a nasty mimicry of their speech. "You dudes ain't got no brains!"

Gunshots drowned out the cries of the three. They fell, joining the rotting corpse of Roger Lancaster on the shattered floor.

Just before dawn, before the predators and prey retired to their tenements and holes in the ground for the day's sleep, a black Lincoln stopped on McCreedy Street and dumped three bloody corpses in front of the alley where Darcy Clay had defended the Plinkney sisters.

Chapter Fourteen

"Joe," Vincent said, so early on Sunday morning it nearly counted as Saturday night, "thanks for helping us."

"Glad to. Even all the way over here in England, we're hearing rumblings of the problems Josh and Geneva are dealing with." Joe Sullivan's face looked slightly green on the screen of the computer as he nodded somberly to Vincent.

Sophie had tracked him down, along with nearly twenty other friends of the Arc Foundation who had encountered both Joshua Clay and Karl Van Mournen in the last fifteen years. Despite the hour, Vincent needed to talk to as many people as possible, get their assessments of his former teammates in their new lives, before he encountered them at the worship service that coming morning.

"Tell me, how is all this affecting little Darcy?" Joe continued.

"I've been working with her about a week. She's a good kid. Of course, what worries her parents worries her." Vincent shrugged. "Other than that... well, she's a natural athlete."

"She was crazy for Robin Hood and King Arthur when she was over here. Has she toned down her mania for swords?"

"Not much." He glanced at Joan, who was busy on her own computer, checking out more data Sophie had sent her. She met his gaze and rolled her eyes for a moment. "In fact, I'm teaching her. She wants to learn moves for all types of swords."

"Is she good?"

"Very good. How about Josh Clay and Karl Van Mournen?"

"What about them, exactly?"

"Are they 'good'? In a former life they were mercenaries. Have they reformed, or is it all just a trick?" Vincent fought to keep his voice casual, soft. He didn't want to be wrong *not* to doubt Josh and Van Mournen's reformations.

Silence, so complete Vincent could hear the traffic on the street outside Joe's flat. The other man rested his elbows on the table in front of his computer and gave a short, sharp nod.

"Josh Clay's been clean and straight more than twenty years. He lives what he preaches. Karl Van Mournen's been his supporter maybe fifteen years, clearing away legal obstacles and finding money for new projects when other mission groups can't keep their doors open."

"So they're for real?" Vincent knew better than to relax totally.

"You want to know what kind of man Josh Clay is—look at the daughter he raised. He could lie to you, but he can't lie to her."

"Never thought of that," he mused. "Thanks, Joe."

~~~~~

"Hey, Mom," Darcy murmured, settling down on the perimeter of the Sunday afternoon mother-and-child get-together, "I know what I want for my birthday."

"Oh, really? You've changed your mind? Again?" Geneva didn't raise her gaze from the cross stitch project spilling out of her lap.

"Mom—"

"I understand dogs like Ulysses are incredibly expensive. They require intensive training to do all the work they do."

"We could use a whole troop of them. Think how great it would be, security and big furry nursemaids for the kids." Darcy gestured at the gaggle of toddlers rolling around and climbing on Ulysses. The big Akita stoically endured the abusive loving.

It had only taken a few hours of seeing Ulysses in action to fall in love. He had sat quietly at Joan's feet during the worship service and didn't have to be told to stay out of the kitchen when she pitched in to help serve dinner. What really amazed Darcy was seeing how he responded to hand signals, going out into the hallway or fetching Joan's backpack from another room, and just a few moments ago, going after a toddler who decided to slip away from the play group.

After lunch, Vincent and Josh and several men headed over to the room currently being renovated, to get more work done, while Joan joined Geneva and Darcy with the mothers group.

Mothers sat in a large circle around the edges of a dozen exercise mats covering the floor of the small gym of the Spike Center. They talked and worked on stitching or other crafts, studied, read, and two different Bible studies took place in opposite corners of the group. In the center of the circle, the children played. Joan was leading a group of older children, between seven and ten years old, in a series of exercises that reminded Darcy of a merger of Tai Chi and yoga.

At first, some of the mothers weren't too sure they wanted such a big, fierce-looking dog-bear in close quarters with their children. A few mothers belonged to exercise groups at the dojo and had already encountered Joan and Ulysses. More important, their children had played with the dog and had fallen in love with him. They ran to him with squeals of glee. Darcy found it interesting that those children were vigilant in keeping the other children from "being mean" to the big dog.

"They're standard equipment for the foundation," Geneva said, still not looking up.
~~~~~

"Maybe they have some extra—"

"Your father already asked Vincent."

"He did?" Darcy got up on her knees, ready to hug her mother.

"Vincent said you would have to work for his organization to justify giving you one of those dogs." Geneva looked up now, all teasing gone. "It takes a lot of training, and a lot of boring work. It isn't all fun, investigative work, traveling around, like Joan and Vincent are doing."

"It's a lot of the dirty grunt work like we've been doing my whole life," she filled in, guessing where her mother's warnings were heading. "Would it be so bad, working for them? I think it would be so cool. Doing everything we're already doing, but without having to worry about funding. I'd be glad to work for them, if I could work with a dog like Ulysses."

"We haven't told you everything about the foundation," Joan said, coming from behind them.

Obviously, the exercise group had dispersed. Darcy's face warmed. She hoped she hadn't been so loud that everyone could hear her gushing about Ulysses.

"A lot of our recruits come to us after a crisis. Kathryn, my cousin, says we're the walking wounded. God sends us out to tell other people how to find the healing and peace that we have. Just a warning, but wanting to work for us is like praying for patience."

"If you ask God for patience," Geneva said, nodding, her smile turning rueful, "that generally means you're going to go through rough circumstances to teach you that patience. Never fun."

"So if I want to be good enough to be a recruit, I have to go through a war." Darcy shrugged. "Daddy says we're in a war of good against evil."

"It's the difference between a fire and a firefly," Joan said. She settled down on the mat facing Darcy. "I have to admit, though, you would be a good recruit. You can already stand up to Vincent beating up on you. That's half the battle."

Darcy laughed, despite the slight dropping sensation deep inside. Maybe she was just being childish, but she really wanted a dog like Ulysses. After all, it wasn't like she was going to get a kiss and her first real boyfriend by her twentieth birthday. Even if they had made up, Doug hadn't made any moves toward getting closer after that stupid fight they had about Roger.

~~~~~

Mid-afternoon, Detective McGee showed up without warning and interrupted Vincent and Josh in a discussion over whether to put a half-wall in the front room of the clinic, or a service window in a full wall. Neither one knew the man was there until he asked them where he could find Darcy.
~~~~~

"Hello, Jack," Josh said. "Darcy? I think she's in the gym. What's up?"

In answer, McGee dug in his pocket and brought out a clear plastic bag. Inside was a silver, heart-shaped locket. Engraved on it were the words: "Darcy, Sweet Sixteen."

"Where did you find this?" Vincent asked, when Josh paled, and his fist clenched around the bag.

"On the body of one of those street punks who beat up on her yesterday," the detective answered. "At least, that's the theory."

Vincent went with Josh and Geneva, accompanying Darcy downtown to identify her assailants in the morgue. Because it was Darcy's locket, McGee needed her testimony, not just Josh and Vincent's. Their word was needed too, since they had fought with the gang members.

The morgue attendant only tugged down the sheets far enough to show the faces of the three dead youths. Shock was still visible. They looked very young in death, under the grime and smears of blood.

They all look young, no matter how old they actually are, Vincent thought. *No one is ever old enough to die.* He shook his head and followed the others out of the morgue.

McGee led them up to an interrogation room and asked them all to sit down.

"I'm breaking the rules a little, letting all of you be in here at one time, but what the heck." The detective shrugged. "Basically, I need to know where the three of you were last night when those upstanding members of the community were murdered."

"How did they die?" Geneva asked quietly.

"Preliminary exam says they were shot, then stabbed multiple times." He looked around at all of them, his gaze resting the longest on Vincent. "I can guess what you were doing last night, but let's hear it."

Vincent left out Van Mournen's visit, merely saying he and Joan had been together all evening, dividing up the different classes at the dojo. They had stayed up until nearly three in the morning, talking with people in other countries, making phone calls and talking over the Internet with people such as Joe Sullivan. There was no benefit in letting the Clays know they were the subjects of that research. He suggested McGee come back to the Center to meet Joan and get her part of the story and verify his whereabouts.

Darcy fidgeted and fumbled through her testimony, but she stated she had worked in the kitchen, then went up to her room and worked on her Sunday school lessons, then read until she went to bed.

Josh had stayed up until two, painting. He had been alone. Geneva had gone to bed at eleven, after their weekly staff meeting and preparing for the service and Sunday school lesson.

"I believe you folks, and nobody is going to cry over those three down in the morgue, but procedures had to be followed." McGee shrugged again and pushed himself to his feet. "Thanks for coming down. We probably won't call you again on this."

"Jack?" Darcy's voice threatened to crack. She didn't look at anyone as she continued. "I wasn't wearing that locket yesterday. So how did they get it?"

The temperature in the room dropped ten degrees, at least. Someone wanted them to know why those three boys had been killed.

McGee visibly came to the same conclusion, and he wasn't happy about it.

~~~~~

"How about another lesson?" Vincent suggested, when they had returned to the Center.

The ride back from the police station had been too quiet. Detective McGee's car was sitting by the loading dock, so he assumed Joan was talking to him, answering questions about last night. It might be good to arrange for some private time for Darcy and Joan to talk. Maybe she knew more than she realized about who might be her champion. Even without the locket dropped with the bodies, Vincent doubted it was a coincidence that those three particular Coals died.

"My arm," Darcy began half-heartedly. Her face had lit up at his words, though.

"It'll be good for you, hon," Josh said. He nodded to Vincent, gratitude in his eyes. "If you're as good as Vincent says you are, you don't need two arms to handle your sword. You have to learn how to defend yourself while you're wounded."

"Yeah, how many muggers can there be out there?" she muttered. Darcy winced. "Sure, Vincent. That'd be great."

They made arrangements for Josh to come pick her up in an hour. Darcy jumped into Vincent's car ten minutes later, after changing into sweatpants and a loose t-shirt. She laughed as they drove down the street with the windows open, the wind blowing her loose hair into her face. She struggled to braid it and tucked it into the neck of her shirt as they drove. Vincent turned on the radio. Neither of them spoke, but he could tell from the tension lines leaving her body, Darcy felt better already.

"Ready?" he asked, when they reached the dojo. He unlocked the door, grateful that Roger never scheduled classes on Sundays, which in turn gave him some free time.

"I guess. How you expect me to be any good with my arm like this, I don't know." Darcy rubbed at the edge of the bandage poking out from under her sleeve and followed him inside.

"You're good, Darcy. Just listen to your body, your instincts, and you'll do fine."
~~~~~

"Then why give me lessons?"

"You have to learn to listen." Vincent gestured at the katanas hanging on the wall. "Do some warm-ups while I get changed, all right?"

She nodded, her face lighting up as she reached for her usual sword. As he climbed the stairs, Vincent considered giving her the sword to take home for practice. He had checked, and very few people took lessons on swordcraft from Roger, so no one would feel shorted if Darcy took it out of the dojo for any length of time.

She had found the radio by the time he came back down. She did slow leaps and deep bends and twists, moving in time with an old Stephen Curtis Chapman song about the Lord of the Dance. It certainly seemed appropriate for the moment. Vincent wondered what sort of station played any songs more than three or four years old.

Darcy was beautiful, framed in the light coming through the windows, stretching for the ceiling, taking a few leaps in imitation of ballet. Vincent stayed where he was, just watching. He fought down a temptation to pick her up and carry her off to Quarry Hall where she would be safe, hidden from the ugliness that seemed to be gathering around the Spike Center.

Then Darcy turned and saw him and her steps faltered. She blushed and gave him a grin that had probably been the same when she was a gawky adolescent. If she ever was a gawky adolescent.

"All warmed up." Darcy hurried over and flipped off the radio. Her smile went crooked, half eagerness and half wariness. "Are you sure this is a good idea?"

"What's the use of learning how to fight if you stop as soon as you're wounded? You have to learn to fight through the pain and compensate for the wound." He raised his katana. "Might as well take advantage of the situation. It's important to learn to keep your balance no matter what's under your feet or the condition of your body."

"You're not going to make me practice blindfolded, like in *Star Wars*, are you?" Darcy took up her starting position, feet spread for balance on the mat.

"It's a matter of becoming one with the blade and knowing your entire body. You're the one who has to do the fighting, Darcy. Not the Force." Vincent raised his sword and stepped up onto the mat. He saluted her. "Ready?"

"Ready or not, here we come," she murmured.

She learned quickly to balance on one leg while parrying his slashes and lunges, so she constantly turned her injured arm away from him. Darcy learned after a few false starts to use her good arm for the strength of the blow, and her injured arm to merely guide the sword's path.

Her eyes sparkled and her breath came in shallow, rapid bursts. Even when she grunted from a slap to her arm or leg or backside with the flat of his blade, she grinned. Vincent had a sinking sensation in his gut as he realized something he had never noticed before. Darcy considered this all a game, an exercise, something fun and exciting. He had seen this before. And he had no way of predicting how she would react when the day came that the battle turned serious. Would she freeze, would she crack, or would she rise to the occasion and lose her innocent joy in her skill?

She put everything she had into the exercise. She listened and tried to apply everything he told her. She was a good student, yet she lacked that fine edge of seriousness that his girls at Quarry Hall brought to their lessons. They knew what Vincent taught them could save their lives. Darcy grinned through the sweat streaking her face, making her shirt cling to her lean frame, and sometimes laughed when one of her defensive attempts worked especially well. That bothered him.

Vincent feinted forward, forcing her to turn in the wrong direction, putting her injured arm between them. He brought his elbow up and thrust down, aiming for the white streak of her bandage.

Darcy let out a shriek that was part anger, even when he pulled the blow short and didn't even graze the cloth. She twisted sideways, but instead of falling backward as he expected, she dropped her sword and threw herself on him. Vincent flung his sword out of the way as they went down.

"Good move," he gasped, with her elbow in his gut.

"Good move?" For two seconds Darcy stared, her mouth hanging open, sprawled across his chest. "You rat!" Fists clenched, she pounded at him, laughing.

Vincent took three blows to his chest and shoulders before he could sit up and interpose his arms between them. Laughing too, he grappled at Darcy, pinning her arms at her sides. He struggled up onto his knees. She twisted and wriggled and managed to get an elbow into unprotected spots with distressing accuracy.

"Give up?" he asked between chuckles.

"Uh uh." Darcy tried to throw herself forward against the bond of his arms. He grunted and twisted sideways to counter her weight. "I'll call my daddy!"

"Won't do you —" He gasped as she got an elbow into his gut again. "Any good," he finished, and got to his feet. He shook her, swinging her legs from side to side until she turned red from giggles. Then he let her slide to the mats. "Okay, you pass."

"I don't think that was a legitimate test," she said, still somewhat breathless.

"What use is a test that makes it easy for you?"

"True." She sobered a little too quickly for him.

"What's wrong, little girl?"

"Oh, not you, too!"

"What?"

"I'm not a little girl."

"Hmm, no. You're smart, you're strong, you're a hard worker, and you think fast."

"How come people don't take me seriously, then? Do you think I'd make a good worker for the Arc Foundation? I was talking with Joan, and she was telling me that they get recruited. The walking wounded—"

"She's right. You have to be tough, you have to know what it's like to hurt and be scared, so you have the right spirit. In a lot of ways, you're an ideal member of the Arc Foundation, but you're not tested." He shrugged. "And you have another handicap."

"Like what?"

"Well... you're pretty." He chuckled when she glared at him. "The kind of work you would do, working for us, you don't want to be noticed and for people to remember you."

"Am I really pretty?" she whispered. "Thanks." A blush spread across her face.

"What? Nobody tells you you're pretty?" Vincent settled down on the mat. He had the feeling this was going to be a long discussion.

"Mom and Dad and some of our friends, but they're biased, you know?" She sat back and crossed her legs. "I'm in an awkward situation. We move so often, and I'm so busy helping Mom and Dad. I have to be careful about boy-girl things. I realized a long time ago that being a PK kind of makes me a target for the slimes. You know?"

"I think so." He felt a flicker of pity for her. Maybe her impulsive manners were a self-defense mechanism, to break down the walls other people erected around her.

Chapter Fifteen

"Some guys see me as a challenge. It's a game to try to lay the preacher's daughter. Other guys stay away because of the stereotype of PKs always being troublemakers. Then there are the guys who would like to date me, and maybe I'd like to date them, but I never get a chance to find out because Dad scares them off. If Dad doesn't, Uncle Karl does." A shaky laugh escaped her.

"Is there anybody you want to date? Anybody brave enough, that your dad wouldn't try to scare away?"

"Well…"

"Ah hah. Confess."

"I should be talking to someone else about this. Another girl. Do you think Joan—"

"She's not involved with anybody." He thought of Joan's slowly mending friendship with Matt Cameron. If there was anyone who had a claim on her heart, he suspected it was her inventor friend. Vincent feared Joan still had too many secrets and hidden pain to resolve before she ventured beyond friendship. "Who's the lucky guy?" he pressed.

She shrugged. "Doug."

"Doug?"

"Martha's grandson—Martha helps us set up all the missions. He joined up when we moved here. Dad even likes him."

"You like him, huh?" Vincent grinned.

"Maybe it's better if we go slow?"

"If it's real, it's worth waiting for."

"How come I can't talk to my mom or dad about stuff like this?"

"One of the mysteries of the universe."

~~~~~

Ulysses waited outside the loading dock entrance when Vincent arrived at the Center on Monday morning, meaning Joan was already there and busy with whatever Geneva found for her to do. He hoped she found time to talk with Darcy throughout the day, earn the girl's confidence. Maybe talking with Darcy about her boy problems, as petty and innocent as they were, would help Joan in turn. From what he had seen of Matt Cameron, the man would be good for Joan if she would just give him a chance.

Vincent stopped in the kitchen for a cup of coffee before heading over
~~~~~

to the renovation work area, and was pleased when several of the crew, hard at work cleaning up from breakfast and preparing for lunch, welcomed him with smiles and nods. The sharp-eyed little woman with her silver hair cut in a modern, youthfully short style, asked him to take a carafe of coffee and some cups with him, because Josh and his assistants had been hard at work since six and were due for a break. Vincent was fairly sure this was Martha, grandmother to Darcy's Doug. He decided it would be smart to get on her good side from the start. He bowed to her, earning a chuckle from the old woman, and he made a note to himself to get to know her a little better.

Josh was crossing the hall from the supply area to the room he was working in, a hammer in one hand, a box of nails in the other, his carpenter's apron bulging with supplies, when Vincent reached the work area. He grinned as Vincent waved and continued his leisurely stroll down the hall.

"Thanks for coming. We could really use six hands for this job today. My other helpers couldn't come—most of them only show up when they aren't scheduled to work. I thought it'd just be Doug and me and maybe Skinner later on today."

Doug. The name caught Vincent's interest. There couldn't be two Dougs working on renovating the factory building, could there? Vincent could almost hear Joan teasing him about nominating himself a second father, to check out Darcy's love interest. Some of his amusement vanished as he thought about Josh's request that he look after Geneva and Darcy if his past came back to punish him.

"Hey, Doug?" Josh called, as Vincent stepped through the doorway into the half-walled room. "This is Vincent. An old friend. He's going to be helping us for a while."

"Hi." Doug was the redhead who had been working with Josh when Vincent first came in last week. He wore faded jeans and his blue flannel shirt hung open, revealing decent abs—he didn't get that condition from just carpentry work, Vincent decided.

"Nice to meet you," Vincent said, shaking the young man's hand. It was an effort not to keep watching Doug as he got back to work with just a nod and smile. He envied him, having such a clean conscience. On second thought, being so innocent and trusting in an area like the Zone didn't show much intelligence. Maybe he should have a talk with Doug later—or maybe Martha? Shaking his head, Vincent turned to Josh and held out his sweatshirt-clad arms. "What do you want me to do?"

As he and Josh and Doug finished assembling a long section of wall studs and hoisted it into place, then fastened it down and got to work on the drywall, Josh did most of the talking. Vincent envied him as his former teammate brought him up to date on all the things he had done, the missions and outreach centers he had helped renovate through the years. He decided he also envied the freedom Josh had to talk about the past twenty years. Some of the things he had done for the Arc Foundation had to be kept quiet—not because he had done anything unethical, but to protect others. People he had helped go into hiding and change their identities. Or protect the reputations of Christian leaders who had faced threats that had come straight from the pit of Hell.

But there's such a thing as discretion, Vincent decided, as he stepped back to pick up another sheet of drywall to hand to Josh and Doug, who were anchoring the sheets into place. Josh made a few too many veiled references to their shared past. Eventually, someone would put the pieces together and realize what kind of a man Joshua Clay had been before he turned his life over to Christ and dedicated his talents to building instead of destroying. What would an unethical person do with that knowledge? How far would they follow those foolishly scattered clues to dig up Josh's past and perhaps use it against him, just like the current enemies of the Spike Center used falsified accusations against the board?

At lunchtime, Vincent sat at a corner of the table in the kitchen and watched Doug and Darcy interact. They were still at that first blush stage of the romance, he decided.

Darcy had serving duty, filling basins of soup from the huge new electric cauldron, taking them over to the counter and filling bowls for the lunch crowd. Doug stepped over to help her a few times. They stole glances, each time looking away with a grin, eyes glowing, never saying anything. They could have carried on a conversation in a normal tone of voice and nobody would have heard them through the noise of the kitchen and dining hall. Vincent smiled a little sadly, realizing that the two simply couldn't talk with so many other people in the room.

"Dad?" Darcy came over to the table with Doug in tow.

"Yeah, hon?" Josh looked up from a diagram of the next clinic room to work on. He and Geneva had been examining it while they ate.

"We have enough people for dinner duty. Is it okay if I skip out after cleanup and prep, and hit a movie with Doug?"

"I suppose." Josh leaned back to look around her at Doug. He winked, and the young man looked away, grinning crookedly. "I assume you're caught up on your homework." He waited until she nodded. "Let me guess—*The Lord of the Rings* again?"

"It's a marathon of all three movies. And what's wrong with it, anyway?" Darcy whined, bouncing a little on her toes. She grinned.

"Who said there was anything wrong? Did that word even pass my lips?" He pressed a hand flat against his chest and widened his eyes in feigned innocence. Beside him, Geneva just rested her head in her hands and laughed silently, her shoulders shaking. "Sure. Go on. See if I care."

"Thanks, Dad." Darcy brushed a kiss across his ear and headed back to the serving counter.

"But there are other things to do on a date besides sit in a dark room and watch a movie — correction, three movies — that you've seen at least a dozen times each," he called over his shoulder. "This is an official date, isn't it?" He grinned and turned back to face the others at the table. "Doug looks like he wants to fall through the floor. I guess it's official."

"If it's any comfort," Martha offered, looking up from the tablet where she played Joan in chess — and was beating her — "I'll whup my grandson's behind if he tries anything improper."

"I'm not worried about Doug," Geneva said, lowering her voice. She and Martha exchanged grins. "Darcy knows how to take care of herself." She sat up and widened her eyes dramatically. "Maybe we should be worried about Doug." That sent both women into a fit of giggles, which they muffled behind their hands.

An hour later, Vincent headed down to the loading dock for another armful of two-by-fours and met up with Doug there, stooped over a pallet of boxes, searching through different sizes of boxes of nails. The young man jerked, startled when Vincent stepped up next to him.

"Don't scare me like that," Doug said, forcing a grin.

"Sorry. Didn't mean to." Vincent silently groaned, when he realized his worries about Josh's loose lips had come true. Doug had already decided he was a dangerous person to be around. How soon would that translate into a strained relationship with Darcy, maybe even destroying their romance before it got past the puppy love stage?

What should he say? Should he say anything?

"You do know what Romans says, about being a new man in Christ?" He lifted a few four-bys off the smaller stack of two-bys where they had partially fallen on top of them.

"Uh, yeah?" Doug paused but didn't look up at him.

"I can see you picked up on what Josh was saying. The things we did a long time ago."

No response except a hunching of the young man's shoulders.

"It's over. No need to think or even talk about it. Darcy doesn't — "

Doug stood and turned so quickly he nearly lost his balance. "I'm Darcy's friend."

"Good. Don't let what you heard — "

"I'd never hurt her." He jammed his hands into his pockets and took two steps toward Vincent.

He had guts. His reaction showed that he really did care about Darcy, no matter what he might think of her father and his friends and his past.

"That's all I care about." Vincent hoisted four boards to his shoulder. He glanced over at Doug and knew he had just made things worse.

Helping the lovelorn definitely wasn't one of his talents.

Doug stood stiff and still, staring at him. Even taking the harsh light from the bare bulb into account, the young man looked pale. But something in the tightness of his mouth, the way he narrowed his eyes, told Vincent he wasn't completely frightened away.

"Look, I'm making a mess of things, and if I scared you, I'm sorry. Darcy means a lot to me. If you care about her, you won't let anything come between you. Okay?" He wanted to offer his hand to the young man, try to repair the damage he had already caused, but the boards wanted to slide free. "Okay?"

Doug nodded, a short, sharp movement, and stayed there with boxes of nails in both hands. He didn't return to the partially renovated office for another twenty minutes. Vincent called himself a few names for coward as he debated how to tell Josh he had messed things up for Darcy. First, he had to figure out how to tell his former teammate that he had turned into a blabbermouth and was handing out weapons for the enemy to use against him someday. Diplomacy didn't seem to be among his gifts anymore.

~~~~~

"Vincent, can we... ah, talk?" Van Mournen stepped into the room just a short time later.

"Sure." Vincent looked around. Josh had gone to rinse out the paint brushes. Doug had vanished with the empty buckets. The air was thick with fresh paint and he rolled up the dropcloths that protected the smooth cement floor. "Tile's next. What do you think?" He felt justifiably proud as he gestured around the completed room.

"Lovely work. We're further ahead of schedule—and further ahead of budget. That's my domain, of course." Van Mournen nodded out through the door.

His dark blue suit was free of paint or dust or sweat, in contrast to Vincent's now-grubby, spattered sweatshirt and jeans. His cane lightly tapped on the cement floor as they started down the hall and he seemed to put more weight on his bad leg than the day before.

"I truly appreciate the helping hand you're giving here. Especially considering the painful past the three of us share."

"Painful past?" Vincent smiled. Somehow, he couldn't picture Josh using that particular word.

"Yes, the arguments, the threats to each other's lives. I'm somewhat surprised you keep coming back. It's one thing to make peace. It's another—well, even for the sake of this undercover investigation of yours, don't you think you're going a little too far, handing out free labor? Someone is bound to be suspicious," he added, softening his voice and glancing around as if he thought anyone could overhear them.
~~~~~

"It wasn't until a few years ago that Josh stopped rehashing his anger toward you. It's taken a long time for his anger, his sense of betrayal to settle. I don't exactly share all his beliefs, but it makes one reconsider them to see how he's put aside the past. Don't you agree?"

"Absolutely." Vincent kept his expression pleasant. He hadn't been completely convinced of Josh's changed attitude and his claim that he wasn't going to kill him on orders when they had met in Afghanistan so long ago. The last few days were better, more convincing evidence of that change. Strangely, Van Mournen's words now did surprise him. He honestly thought he and Josh had at least started mending their relationship back then. Was it possible Josh had been hiding his resentment for the sake of survival?

Vincent looked at Van Mournen, his expression so open and honest, concerned, and remembered how this man had worn a dozen different masks in a day as he gathered up intel and funds for their missions. He much preferred to think the man once known as Midas was lying.

The question that leaped into his mind, however, was *why*—what would it profit him now to tell lies, try to drive a wedge into their growing friendship and respect and cooperation?

"I truly don't want anything damaging your renewed friendship, so please, consider this word of warning." Van Mournen licked his lips, visibly distressed over what he was about to say.

Here it comes, Vincent thought.

"Josh thinks rather highly of young Douglas Blaine."

Vincent blinked, wondering where that topic had come from.

"We all do. We were rather pleased to see the attraction spring up between him and Darcy, when he first joined his grandmother and started working with us."

"And?" Vincent asked, when the other man hesitated.

"Darcy is rather... upset with you, for frightening away her beau."

"I frightened him away?"

"I overheard him telling her not ten minutes ago that you had threatened him and ordered him to leave her alone. The dear child has somewhat of a temper. You're not in very good odor right now, I'm afraid." Nothing but regret showed in Van Mournen's pale blue eyes.

"Thanks for the warning," he said slowly.

"I'm only concerned for the peace and friendship of everyone concerned," the other man said, nodding. "If you'll excuse me?" They reached an intersecting hall at that moment. He turned to the right, and Vincent continued going straight.

He paused when he reached the kitchen doorway. Darcy was nowhere to be seen. Geneva saw him and waved before picking up a stack of bowls to put on the serving counter. She didn't look upset with him.

Then again, maybe she hadn't heard yet.

Vincent heard running footsteps on the cement. Darcy careened around the corner, face flushed, eyes glistening but no tears on her cheeks. She skidded to a stop when she saw him.

"I know Daddy asked you to look out for me and Mom, but you had no right—" Her voice broke. The look she cast him could have flayed him. "After I told you about Doug and me and..." Darcy shuddered as she pushed past him and continued down the hall.

"Wrong move," Vincent whispered. For a moment, he considered following her. How was he going to fix this? A snort of laughter escaped him when he thought about going to Joan. True, it was human nature to be able to see the solutions to others' problems more clearly than the same problems in one's personal life. On the other hand, if he wanted the friendship between Darcy and Joan to keep growing stronger, it was probably wise not to involve her in the solution at all.

Josh was nowhere to be found. Vincent thought about Van Mournen's words, how Josh had still been angry with him until a few years ago. Anyone could see Josh doted over Darcy. How would he react to Vincent's interference in her fledgling love life?

~~~~~

Doug dropped the dust pan when he emptied it into the dumpster sitting at the end of the loading dock. Snarling, he kicked at the big kerosene tank, then muffled a curse at the momentary feeling that he had broken all the toes on that foot, despite his heavy work boots. For a few seconds, he stared down into the dumpster and considered just letting the dust pan go. He was already late for meeting Darcy. If they didn't leave soon, they would get caught in traffic and not get to the theater in time for the start of the *Rings* marathon.

"Rough day?" a genteel voice asked, that hint of laughter in it making him spin on his heel, mouth open to snarl.

Doug's mouth stayed open when he saw Van Mournen standing at the loading dock door, smiling at him.

"Ah—hi," he said after a few seconds.

"Could you spare me a moment or two?"

"We're running kind of late and I still—" He gestured, wordless, at the dumpster.

"Yes, of course. I know about your plans for the movie. Darcy is so excited. But it's Darcy who worries me. I know how you care for her, so you can imagine how deeply it cuts me to see her so unhappy. Perhaps if we talk, we can figure some way around this difficulty."

"I don't know..." He wanted to snap at the man, so irritating with his smiles and condescending, I'm-in-a-much-higher-class-than-you attitude, and his way of always knowing what was going on in everyone's life.
~~~~~

Doug knew better than to let his opinion show. His grandmother was thoroughly taken in with Van Mournen's manners. If she found out he was rude to the man, she would be upset, and he didn't want to disappoint her—even over a big, arrogant fake like Van Mournen. Martha was the sweetest, most wonderful grandmother anyone could ever want, but she also believed the verse in the Bible that said it was useful for teaching and for *correction*. She had her own way of laying it on heavy when it came to dealing with her erring grandson, and it had nothing to do with the weight of the Bible.

"Please," Van Mournen said with a smile. "For Darcy's sake."

"Okay. Sure." He shrugged. "But can we talk later? Tomorrow?"

"Wonderful. And no, I have no intention of making you late." He raised his cane, gesturing for Doug to lead the way down the hall. "Would you mind meeting me elsewhere? You could help me with some business while we work on your problem." He handed Doug a card with an address neatly printed on it. "This is a site I'm considering buying, as an investment. Would you help me assess it, while we're talking?"

"Sure. Glad to help." Doug took the card, frowning at the address. It was on the other side of the Zone. "The thing is, the movie marathon is going to go until after eleven."

"That's fine. More than fine, it dovetails perfectly with my needs. Someday, my lad, when you've worked your way up in the world, you'll learn that important business does not hold to banker's hours, and you must be ready to take advantage of every opening, no matter how inconvenient for you."

Chapter Sixteen

"All right, what's really wrong?" Darcy said, when she met up with Doug at the concession stand.

It looked like most of the audience had decided to take a break during the intermission between *Fellowship* and *The Two Towers*, yet of those who hadn't returned to their seats after using the bathroom, the majority stood around the lobby, talking—loudly—about their favorite parts of the movies. She liked being able to see all three movies in a row, just to get a better flow of story and action from one to the other.

"'Wrong?" Doug frowned, but didn't take his gaze off the display of vastly overpriced candy.

Darcy deliberately didn't look. She only let herself indulge in popcorn at the theater because she could get refills if she bought the largest bucket. It ruined her enjoyment of the candy to pay four dollars for something she could get for one dollar at the grocery store.

"Did you enjoy the scene where Tom Bombadil showed up in the first movie?"

"He did?" Doug finally looked at her. "Oh, yeah—"

"No, he didn't. You weren't paying attention. What is wrong with you? You're not letting that argument with Vincent bug you, are you?"

"What do you really know about your dad?"

"Huh?"

Doug caught hold of her arm and led her away from the traffic around the concession stand. He leaned down close, so their noses almost touched and lowered his voice to a furtive stage whisper. Still, it felt to her as if he shouted.

"Are you really sure he changed? That he gave up being the kind of guy who makes Rambo look like my Grandma?"

"Oh for—Doug, how can you work with my dad and think that? He's changed. Completely."

"How can you know? Just listen," he hurried on, when she opened her mouth to argue. "If he lets a guy like this Vincent hang around and talk about the things they used to do, has he really let go of the past, put it behind him? And talk about it and smile and make jokes? Sure, they talk about it all tame and use code words, but anybody with half a brain can guess what they really mean. It sure sounds like they enjoy it. And that Vincent, he's even worse—"

"Vincent has changed. Just like my dad." Darcy clenched her fists to keep from grabbing Doug by his collar and shaking him. She thought of some of those self-defense moves Joan had showed her the day before, and wished she knew how to start the attack without being attacked. It would be highly satisfying to flip him over the concession stand, head-first into the big vat of fresh popcorn.

"Yeah, then what's he doing here? You think it's a coincidence, him showing up right now, when we're having all sorts of problems?"

"No, it's not a coincidence." She went up on her toes and leaned forward, pressing her forehead against his, so they really were nose-to-nose. To her delight, Doug's eyes widened and he backed up, but it wasn't enough to cool the sudden flames of her temper. "It's God, that's what it is. Vincent is here checking us out to see if the people he works for will be able to give us money to help out."

"You really believe that?" He backed up and flung up his hands to block her when she lost her balance and reached to grab hold of him to steady herself. "You really are as naïve and stupid—"

Darcy ducked under his arm, tossing aside her bucket of popcorn with one hand, shoving the other into his gut, right under the joining of his ribs. As Doug staggered backward, his face momentarily white, the breath knocked out of him, she turned and fled down the incline of the theater lobby to the doors out to the street.

She hurried away, as fast as she could move with her legs stiff with fury and trying not to run. The surest way to catch the wrong kind of attention on this side of town was to run. Darcy took great gulping breaths of air and blinked fast, refusing to let that heat and pressure in her eyes turn into tears.

Maybe it was a good thing—maybe it was a God thing—that Doug still hadn't gotten up the guts to kiss her. She had hoped tonight, when he took her home, he might try to kiss her. It would be dark, everybody who mattered would be asleep, and they would both be in a good mood from the movie.

"Jerk." She rubbed at her eyes with one fist. "Major jerk."

Without meaning to, she kept walking, going straight through the intersection where she should have turned left to get back to the Center. Darcy replayed their short, stupid argument, her footsteps keeping time with her aching heartbeats, until she saw the dojo up ahead. The lights were off inside—of course, most of the classes had either been canceled or combined to cut down on Vincent's workload and let him spend time helping at the Center.

Maybe she had wanted to come talk to Vincent, without even realizing it?

No, she decided a moment later, as she spied the lean figure with shoulder-length dark hair and the big, bear-like dog, heading for the front steps of the dojo. Not Vincent, but Joan.

Before she could make up her mind whether to call out to Joan or just keep walking and catch up with her inside the building, Joan looked down at Ulysses, then turned to look down the street right at Darcy. She waved and settled down on the big cement steps. Darcy shivered, then laughed at the notion she had for just a moment, that somehow Ulysses had told her... no, that was ridiculous. Still, she was glad Joan recognized her, even from this far away, and waited for her.

"Okay, what happened?" Joan said, when Darcy got within ten yards of her. "Please, please don't let that be a big fight over Vincent's mistake with Doug. He's chewing himself up inside over messing things up for you as it is."

"Doug is an arrogant, self-righteous, Pharisee jerk." Darcy stomped the last few steps to punctuate her words.

"So it *was* what Vincent said."

"No, it was what Doug thought he heard Dad and Vincent talking about. Can you believe him? He actually thinks that just because Dad and Vincent were talking about the horrid things they used to do before they became Christians, that maybe they still like what they did, they like remembering, and they haven't let go of the past. According to him." She let out a half-growl, half-shriek, and dropped down on the rough steps next to Joan. Ulysses whined and got up from his seat on the step two levels below, and put one of his plate-sized paws on her thigh while looking into her eyes.

"You'd swear he knows what I'm taking about."

"He does," Joan said. "The monster here is a lot smarter than most people I run into."

"Oh, Ulysses... I wish I had someone just like you to snuggle with. And scare away the big, mean jerks." Darcy sighed, ending in a hiccup sound suspiciously like a sob when the big dog leaned in and tucked his head between her arm and her side.

"That means you can snuggle away," Joan said.

Sniffling, fighting tears again, Darcy wrapped her arms around Ulysses and pressed her face into his fur. She wished she could sit there all the rest of the afternoon and evening and just hold Ulysses and feel loved and protected—and not have to go back to the Center or face anybody.

"We really need to get inside," Joan said.

"What, you read minds?" Darcy tried to smile, make her words a joke.

"No, it's just that I'm here to run a few exercise classes. Just a half-hour each. If you want to hole up in the office or the apartment and stay out of sight until you get yourself together, that's fine. We can talk in between classes."

"Really?"

"Absolutely." Joan sighed as she got to her feet and dug in her pocket for the jangling ring of keys. "I learned the hard way, no matter how bad something hurts, no matter how stupid you might feel for your part in the fight, you have to talk to someone about it. The sooner the better. Sometimes it helps to talk to someone who isn't part of the situation at all. Kind of a safety zone or buffer or whatever," she added as she unlocked the big front doors.

Darcy elected to stay in the office, where she could curl up on the rug in front of the ugly old sofa with the broken springs, and pet Ulysses while listening to Joan lead the exercise class. In between the three classes, they drank cold coffee, more cream and flavoring syrup and ice than coffee, and talked. Joan confided in her about her amazing, painful, shadowed background, which made it easier for Darcy to talk about the things Doug had said, the things she knew about her father's past.

"See," Joan began as they stood at the table set up in the office and made the next batch of iced coffees, "I'm your modern American kid. I didn't know who my father was until just a little more than a year ago. Dad was what you would call an information broker. He didn't care who he sold information to—he really cares now, and that's part of why Arc does what it does, to make up for his lack of ethics or morals or a soul, whatever you want to call it. My mother was—and still is—a psychotic terrorist. She only kept me to punish my dad. I got away from her and dedicated my life to doing the exact opposite of what would make her proud. None of it really mattered until I gave up and turned everything over to God. You can't buy your way into Heaven."

"Dad tells me that all the time. He kind of hints around at some of the awful things he used to do and then tells me that he could build a thousand rescue missions, it wouldn't make up for one person he hurt."

"Exactly. But that doesn't mean you don't spend the rest of your Christian life doing exactly that, making up for what you did." She paused and glanced over her shoulder. Several people had just walked into the building for the next exercise class. "The big difference is that you're doing all this to say thank you, instead of wiping the slate clean. Make sense?"

Darcy nodded and settled down with her drink and thought hard while Joan worked her exercise class even harder.

"What if he's right?" she asked, once the class had left. Joan settled down on the couch with her somewhat diluted iced coffee in one hand and blotted her sweaty face with a towel in the other hand.

"Who's right?"

"Oh—yeah—Doug—he called me naïve and stupid and a bunch of other things I didn't bother sticking around to listen to."

"Good for you." Joan took a long, slow drink of the coffee. She tipped her head back when she finished and closed her eyes. "He's wrong, though."

"Yeah?"

"You're innocent, meaning your soul is still clean and bright, untouched by all the pollution, and the disease and filth surrounding you, but that doesn't mean you're ignorant. There's a big difference between innocent and ignorant. You're idealistic, too. Not a bad thing, but it does kind of open you up to getting hurt when people step off the pedestals you put them on, or the pretty gold paint corrodes. Know what I mean?"

"I think so."

"You know too much to be ignorant."

"Knowing *about* things doesn't mean much if I don't apply what I know. Yeah, I know *about* pornography and exploitation and drug trafficking and human trafficking and all the other horrid things Mom and Dad have been fighting against all my life. Maybe that's why I was so mad when Doug said I was innocent. I don't feel innocent!"

"You're not exactly the walking wounded, either."

"Guess that means I can't work for you guys, can I?"

"Depends. But it's good that you were listening yesterday." Joan opened her eyes and raised her head and winked at her. "So what exactly did the big Pharisee jerk say, anyway?"

They continued the conversation in between the other classes. Joan made Darcy laugh by proving, through stories that were almost too ghastly and stupid to be believed, that Doug's attitude was mild compared to some of the "Pharisee jerks" she had been forced to deal with in the year since she joined the Arc Foundation.

When Vincent showed up, they were just locking up the dojo to walk to the nearest market and find something to make for dinner. He seemed to know that Darcy had a fight with Doug, in that same way Joan seemed to know what was going on without being told. Of course, it was a pretty easy conclusion to reach, since she was here when she should still be sitting in the theater, finishing the second movie or starting the third. When he asked if Darcy was all right, and made a move as if he would put an arm around her, something broke inside her. She hugged him and a last few rebel tears came out. Joan explained quickly, with far fewer words than Darcy would have used. To her dismay, Vincent insisted that they needed to tell her parents what had happened.

"Believe me, you do not want secrets at a time like this. If Doug has this attitude about your father and what he says about his past, other people might have it, or develop it. Better face it now, kill it before it turns into something ugly. Your dad needs to know."

"I never thought..." Darcy sighed and wiped at her face with her sweatshirt sleeve again. "Never thought about it like that."

"I've got an idea," Joan said. "Let's go get our groceries like we were planning, but make enough for five of us. When we get back, we'll ask your folks to join us here. It might be easier to talk about it here, and not at the Center where other people could overhear."

Darcy liked that idea much better than facing her parents in the Center's kitchen, where Martha might hear, or Doug might walk in and be mortally embarrassed.

~~~~~

At the exact moment Vincent, Joan and Darcy stood in the grocery produce section and disagreed on what vegetables to put on the kebabs they planned to make for dinner, a dark shadow straightened up from picking the lock on the back door of the dojo. The door opened, and the shadow stepped inside. It glided across the hardwood floor, staying in the shadows as sunset colors turned dull gray, until it reached the display rack of katanas. The figure paused there for many long minutes, studying the rack, before reaching up a gloved hand to lift down the sword at the top of the rack. Moments later, it glided back through the supply room to the back door. Soon the door was closed and locked again, and the shadow vanished into the night.

~~~~~

Full night had fallen in the decaying neighborhood. Doug parked his Jeep in the doorway of the abandoned Allied Glass Works and looked around. The place gave him the creeps.

"Hey, Mister Van Mournen? Are you here?" Doug shivered, hearing nothing but his own voice echoing faintly back from the black cavern of the building.

There was no traffic on the streets leading to the abandoned factory. It was like this whole section of town had been cleared out by an invasion from Mars. Buildings were boarded up, streetlights shattered, street signs twisted out of shape or missing altogether. Why would anyone want to invest in property in this part of town?

He stepped through the doorway, trying to decide how long he would wait before he turned around and left.

A shadow disengaged from the darkness just inside the doorway and snagged Doug's collar. With a simple twist, his attacker flung him, choking, backward against the grimy brick wall. His head connected with a loud smack-thud.

Doug blinked frantically, trying to clear the stars from his eyes. Somehow, he had ended up on his back with someone's very heavy foot crushing his chest. He could hardly breathe.

There was a click, and the sound of wood hitting the dirty floor. A bit of reflected light from outside glimmered dully off a long, shiny blade.

It was a sword. Doug stopped breathing.

"Your pathetic attempt at romance has made you a problem," Van Mournen said in a cool, almost casual tone. He ground his heel into Doug's chest, pressing down on a rib until it snapped. Doug jerked in response. He couldn't seem to get the breath to cry out the pain that cut through him.

"On the other hand," the man continued, "that little tiff with Vincent makes you too valuable a tool to let you just walk away."

Doug barely had time to close his eyes as the sword slashed down into his chest.

Early the next morning, the city sanitation crew found Doug Blaine's body in a dumpster bin, partially wrapped in a tarpaulin. A blood-smeared katana was found jammed into the corner of the same bin.

~~~~~

Darcy hurried through the door of the dojo the next morning, a dozen weak excuses bubbling on her lips for being late. The lights were on, the door was open, but Vincent was nowhere to be seen. After a few seconds of careful listening, she realized she heard voices coming from behind the drawn shades and closed door of the office. She smiled, delighted that Vincent hadn't known she was late, and sat down to peel off her boots and socks. She did a few bends and twists to limber herself up. After all the emotional turmoil of yesterday, and crying more than she had done in years, both with Joan and then later with her parents after they got home, she had slept later than normal. Her head hurt a little. She had devoured most of the bag of Hershey dark kisses Joan had slipped her when she and her parents left the dojo. Staying up late and eating so much sugar was not good for someone who usually got to bed by ten and who rarely indulged in sweets.

Other than her headache, Darcy felt good. Better than she thought she would twelve hours before. She finished warming up and started across the mats to the sword rack. Things were fine between her and Vincent again, Joan promised to spend the entire day with her as a shield and hopefully make Doug feel guilty, and her arm was healing nicely. She couldn't wait to see how well she did today in her lessons.

"My sword's missing!" Her wail cut through the unusual silence of the long room and echoed back to her.

Confusion, anger, and a sense of having been robbed cut through her. Darcy stood still for two seconds, then turned to run to Vincent's office. The door opened before she reached it. Detective McGee stepped out, followed by Vincent. The red-haired detective looked as rumpled and frustrated as always. Vincent smiled tightly at her.

"Your sword, Darcy?" McGee asked in that quiet tone of voice that usually meant deep trouble for someone—usually not her—when her
~~~~~

father used that tone of voice.

"Roger lets me use it for practice. I'm the only one who does. What's going on?"

"That explains the mystery fingerprints."

"What's going on?"

"About what time did you get here yesterday?"

"I don't know. Maybe 5, 5:30."

"Was the sword in its rack when you were here?"

"Yeah." Darcy felt her face heat in a blush. "I checked on it. I mean, it's my sword, y'know?"

"We know," Vincent said, nodding.

"You were with Vincent and Joan until when?" the detective continued.

"About eleven. And my parents were here, too." Darcy glanced back and forth between the two men. "Vincent, what's —"

"Somebody killed Doug last night," Vincent explained. He held out a hand, as if he thought she might lose her balance. "That sword was found by the body."

"He died of multiple stab wounds, and someone called the station this morning and left a nice anonymous tip that Vincent argued with your boyfriend yesterday," McGee broke in.

"Doug wasn't my boyfriend. Not yet," she amended. "You think Vincent killed him, don't you?"

"No witnesses, strong alibi, and no fingerprints. Besides, I don't think Vincent here is stupid enough to leave the murder weapon near the body." McGee looked rather sour. Darcy supposed it had a lot to do with the early hour. "I'm going to have to ask you to come down to the station, Darcy."

"Me?" Her voice squeaked. "What for?"

"To see if the fingerprints match."

"I'll drive you," Vincent said. "Do you want your parents to meet you there?"

"No." Darcy shuddered. "For goodness' sake, Vincent, I'm going to be twenty in a few days. I don't need my daddy to hold my hand all the time." Then she gasped as a new thought occurred to her. "What about Martha? This is going to kill her."

"Who?" McGee asked.

"Doug's grandmother. She works for my dad." Tears touched her eyes. "Vincent?"

"I'll call your mother and warn her," Vincent said, and pulled his cell phone out of his pocket.

Chapter Seventeen

Van Mournen was waiting, pacing across the end of the loading dock, when Darcy drove home nearly two hours later. His pale blue eyes burned and he looked furious enough to strangle someone with his bare hands. She shuddered a little as she recognized that capability in him and wondered that she had never seen it before. Uncle Karl was always the third person she ran to when life was cruel or inexplicable. He had been a rock of security, a ready explanation, a source of comfort and treats and wonderful secrets that made her feel special.

Now, looking at him as she walked her motorcycle up the ramp of the loading dock, Darcy felt afraid of him for the first time in her life.

"My dear!" Van Mournen rested a hand on her shoulder, managing to stay out of her way as she locked up her motorcycle, chaining it to the big water pipe. "What they put you through is simply—"

"Where's Martha?" She nearly smiled at the way he stopped short and blinked, momentarily stunned by her temerity in interrupting him.

"I believe your parents have her in the office. Your concern for her is commendable," he continued, the anger returning hot to his voice.

Darcy left him standing there and set off down the long, half-finished hallways at a slow jog. Van Mournen hurried to keep up. At the back of her mind, she was a little startled at how easily he moved. He had always walked with a pronounced limp and that thick black cane for as long as she could remember.

"You must stay away from Vincent," he said, speaking without huffing as they hurried down the hall.

"What?" Darcy stumbled to a halt for half a second, then got going again. Martha. She needed to comfort Martha, as well as be comforted.

"All this is his fault, you know."

"Vincent was nowhere near Doug when he died."

"What do the police know? It was his sword."

"It was stolen. And technically, it was my sword."

"Yours?" Van Mournen did stop for nearly two seconds. He was pale when he lurched forward and caught up with her. The angry sparks in his eyes grew brighter.

"My fingerprints were the only ones on it."

"Vincent used gloves and planted the sword to frame you."

"Uncle Karl!" Darcy stopped, turning to face him, so the man nearly ran into her. "You really hate him, don't you? Why?"

"I don't hate him. I'm acting to protect you." He drew his dignity around himself like a cloak. "My dear girl, do you have any idea how precious you are to me? I would give my life, sell my soul, to keep you safe from pain and danger. You know that, don't you? Your innocence is the most wonderful treasure in this world."

"Please... right now, Uncle Karl, I can't think straight. Doug is dead and someone tried to frame Vincent and Martha needs me."

"Of course. You're a good girl, Darcy. But when you feel better, we really do need to talk."

"Not about Vincent. He didn't do it."

"My dear, that's the kind of man he is. Some things just do not change, no matter how religious someone becomes. This is exactly what Vincent did best, when we worked together. He saw a problem, he dealt with it, and it didn't come back. The ends justified the means. Vincent likely saw Douglas as a danger and felt justified in getting rid of him. He does it almost without thinking."

Darcy didn't want to believe him. It contradicted all she sensed about Vincent from the moment she met him. And yet, this was her Uncle Karl. She had known him all her life and trusted him completely.

"Martha needs me," she repeated.

"Of course, dear." He patted her shoulder. "I'm so sorry your friend is dead."

She nodded and continued down the hall. Van Mournen didn't follow her this time, which she was heartily grateful for.

As she hurried into her parents' office and put her arms around Martha, who was pale, her face bright with tears, Darcy knew one thing. Whoever hated the Spike Center wasn't content with just spreading nasty rumors and trying to discredit the board. True, there had been thefts of supplies from the beginning, and sometimes petty vandalism, but no one had *died*. Who could hate what they did for the Zone so much that they would kill to stop the Center from being renovated? A chill washed over her as a new thought came on the heels of the previous one — what if the escalation in tactics hadn't started with Doug? What if Roger wasn't just missing, but murdered, and the police simply hadn't found the body yet?

Who could she go to for help? Would Detective McGee believe her?

No. She almost smiled, even as she continued holding Martha's trembling body and wept with her. Darcy knew the timing was perfect. She would talk to Joan and Vincent and explain her theory. For all she knew, they already had the same suspicions. Joan and Vincent had finally revealed the name of their foundation, and told her family many stories over dinner, about what the Arc Foundation had done in the past, the special talents of those who lived at Quarry Hall, and how God had used them to do amazing things. Darcy knew they were just the right ones to get to the bottom of all this trouble and solve it, once and for all.

Hopefully before more lives were lost.

~~~~~

Josh Clay had outlived his usefulness. Van Mournen stood in the treasure room and ran his fingers over the brass bindings of the trunk holding his swords as he contemplated the truthfulness of that realization.

"You'll serve me one last time, my old friend," he whispered. His eyes burned with frustration and remembered betrayals. The most recent of which was Josh's refusal to believe that Vincent was his enemy.

He had dropped casual-seeming hints that Vincent had unseemly interest in Darcy. Why else had he threatened young Douglas Blaine, except to drive him away? Josh had laughed at the idea, saying Vincent was too honorable to try to romance his friend's daughter.

Van Mournen had given up on trying to convince Josh that Vincent had tried to steal Geneva's heart when they first met. He simply could not goad Josh into his old sense of rage. If he could only get Josh angry enough, push him past the point of logical thought as he used to be able to do, he could make Josh fight Vincent. The two had come close to killing each other before, when they were teammates. How could they work together in harmony now?

No matter. That harmony was a façade, just as his years of friendship and support for Josh had been. He had manipulated Josh into thinking everything between them had been forgiven. Why, then, couldn't he convince him Vincent was an enemy, merely biding his time until he struck?

Van Mournen had learned long ago that when the unforeseen occurred and got in the way of his carefully laid plans, the best response was to strike quickly, fiercely, deeply, before the obstruction became entrenched and immovable. The longer he allowed Josh and Vincent to solidify this ridiculous, religion-fueled partnership and understanding, the harder it would be for anyone to believe long-buried animosity had exploded between them. The plan needed to unfold today. Suspicion needed to land squarely and heavily on Vincent, before he was brought to the arena to die with Josh. If the duel-to-the-death had to be staged after the fact, no matter. All he cared about was finally being avenged for the betrayals both men had perpetrated against him when they were a team.

Then, he would use Darcy's fury over her father's death, her anger at Vincent, to finish the delicate work that began in her childhood, fashioning her into his perfect, pure, faithful mate. If only he could make sure that Vincent knew Darcy despised him before he died. That would be just another layer of icing on his cake of vengeance. He knew Vincent was attracted to Darcy, even if the fool didn't do anything about it. Who
~~~~~

wouldn't be attracted to her purity of spirit and heart? Who wouldn't want to claim it as his treasure?

In her grief, Darcy would be easily persuaded that Van Mournen had acted on her behalf, to avenge Vincent's betrayal of her father. Then she would be his. A pure heart, trained to trust him completely, convinced that he alone was wise enough to guide her through life.

Van Mournen nodded in satisfaction. Despite the inconveniences, his plan still functioned smoothly. It was a pity that Geneva would be hurt by all this. She wasn't as completely innocent as Darcy, after all, but she was certainly not the traitorous whore other women had been. She was foolish enough to love a liar and cheat like Josh Clay. That was less a crime than a grievous mistake. But what could be expected? Women were so weak that way, unless they were carefully guided and trained from childhood, their purity shielded.

Van Mournen went over his plan in his head and nodded, sure that it was all coming together perfectly. He lifted the lid of the trunk and slid his hand into a side pocket in the cloth lining. He took out a long dagger, an antique, made in Alexandria. It was a collector's piece, but its history had prompted Van Mournen to buy it, in preparation for this day. The dagger's original owner had used it to kill his brother who had betrayed him, and through the years had been a family treasure, used in defense of the family's honor. Van Mournen had killed the last member of that family to own the dagger. He would have paid for the knife, but the fool refused to sell it to him.

<div style="text-align:center">~~~~~</div>

It was almost ridiculously easy to lure Josh to the loading dock, with no witnesses to see where he went or with whom.

"What's going on, Karl?" Josh asked, looking around the empty, shadowy space. At nearly noon, everyone who wasn't involved in the renovation work was helping in the kitchen. They were so alone, the sense of it echoed off the brick walls.

"Vincent is causing trouble, you know," Van Mournen began.

"Come on, can't you forgive him? This grudge you've been carrying is ridiculous." He grinned and leaned back against the wall, his shoulder pressing into the guide rail for the open overhead door.

"Grudge?" Van Mournen let the ice into his voice. It was welcome, after years of pretending friendship. "Is that what you call it?"

"Karl, if you can forgive me for what I did to you, why can't you forgive Vincent?"

"I don't believe the same things you do, Josh. It's impossible." With his back to his prey, Van Mournen slid a tazer from inside his impeccable pinstripe suit coat.

"That's the problem. Give in and let go, Karl. Accept God's way of doing things and let—"

Josh stopped short, mouth open in soundless shock. He bowed his head, staring at the wires protruding from the center of his chest.

"Karl," he gasped, and slowly slid to his knees, his body shuddering.

"I never forgave you." Van Mournen watched his prey's face go pale, savoring the pain replacing the shock. "You asked my forgiveness, but you never actually heard me say the words, did you?"

A final spasm went through Josh's body and he fell forward. He struck his head against the wall and blood smeared the bricks from the gash that flowed across his temple and into his hairline.

Van Mournen frowned at that little inconvenience. He would have to wipe up that blood to leave no clue for anyone to find.

He hurried down to his car, parked conveniently close to the loading dock ramp, opened the trunk, and brought out the dark blue blanket he had purchased specifically for this purpose. He wasn't going to kill Josh. Not yet. He wanted Josh alive for a while longer to think about the consequences of his crimes. He wanted him to suffer, as Van Mournen had suffered all these years. He needed Josh alive, the blood fresh, when the stage was set and the other actor in their little drama joined them.

He knew just what bait would bring Vincent into the trap.

~~~~~

"Geneva? Excuse me, my dear, but has Josh come back yet?" Van Mournen stayed in the doorway of the kitchen. It was hard, now that the end of the charade neared, not to show the distaste he felt for the bustling, steamy kitchen and the presence of so many pathetic, foolish mortals. His philosophy had always been that those who could not take care of themselves were better off ending their lives, leaving the world's resources for those who could use them properly.

"Josh? Come back?" Geneva wiped a strand of wet hair out of her face and frowned a little. "I didn't know he'd gone anywhere."

"Oh. My." He frowned, putting on the mask of fatherly concern he had worn so convincingly every time he persuaded Josh or Geneva to let Darcy do something the girl desperately wanted. "He said he was going to talk to Vincent about young Douglas's death and the argument they had the other day. That was, oh, more than an hour ago."

"It doesn't take more than ten minutes to get to the dojo. Maybe they decided to get some lunch." She glanced back at the slowing lunchtime rush in the kitchen and smiled. "I don't blame him!"

"Yes, well, ordinarily I wouldn't be worried, but with so many odd things happening lately... and Josh did seem rather angry when he left."

"Angry?" For a moment, Geneva's face froze. He could see the flicker of fear in her eyes. Then it vanished as the woman grinned and shook her head. "Josh might get a little steamed. He might yell. But he never gets that
~~~~~

angry anymore. Vincent is the last person I'd expect to get into a fight with him."

"Did I say fight?" Van Mournen shuddered. "No, my dear. I doubt they would get into a battle. Foolish of me to worry." He nodded to her. "When Josh gets back, tell him I need to speak with him, would you?"

"Sure."

Van Mournen muffled a chuckle as he strode down the hall. Geneva tried to look unconcerned, but he could see that the seed of doubt he had planted had not only taken root, it was sprouting. Now, to nourish that plant until the seeds grew in Darcy's heart as well.

~~~~~

Josh hadn't revived by the time Van Mournen pulled into the dark mouth of the Allied Glass Works building. He dragged his prisoner into the rotting darkness, then bound him with chains around his chest, padlocked to a gas pipe.

For a moment, he was tempted to leave Roger Lancaster's rotting corpse where it was, to add to Josh's torment, a preview of what awaited him. The battle he planned to stage between Josh and Vincent would have to take place here, and Darcy was needed as witness for the plan to work. He didn't want her distressed any more than necessary. Josh had revived and started yanking at his chains when Van Mournen returned from that messy chore.

"What do you want from me, Karl?" Josh asked. His voice didn't hold the fear Van Mournen longed to hear. He sounded almost too calm.

"Vincent won't burst in to rescue you, like he did that time you got into a drunken brawl with that axe-wielding fool in Chicago," Van Mournen said. "No one knows where you are. No one will."

"What do you want?" he repeated. A hint of strain hovered in his voice now. Van Mournen savored it like a fine wine.

Like fine wine, his plan required time to come to full flavor.

"You'll figure it out, sooner or later. You're an intelligent man, Josh. I have faith in you." Smiling, Van Mournen nodded to his prisoner and left the dark, dank room, lit only by a shaft of sunlight coming in through the broken skylight.

"Karl!" Josh's chains rattled for a moment, as if disturbed by the cry. Then, silence.

"You'll lose your poise soon enough," Van Mournen murmured as he walked to his car.

~~~~~

"Vincent, I'm worried about Darcy," Van Mournen said, when Vincent opened the door to answer his knock at eleven that night.

"What about her?" Vincent considered for a moment, then stepped back so he could come in.

"She's taking her father's disappearance rather hard. We've talked to the police, but they won't do anything for an entire day after an adult disappears." Van Mournen shrugged delicately. "Can you help us?"

"I don't know what you think I can do." He fussed with the lock on the door and didn't look directly at Van Mournen as he spoke.

It was hard to keep a straight face. He had just finished talking with Darcy twenty minutes ago, and she had reported Van Mournen kept hinting that he was to blame for her father's disappearance. She had been talking with Vincent in the family's apartment and knew he had been nowhere near the dojo when Josh supposedly came by to speak with him. Like her mother, Darcy didn't believe her father could be angry enough to provoke a fight with Vincent.

The only logical conclusion was that Van Mournen was up to something. Whatever it was, Vincent knew none of them would like the answer.

"Please, Vincent," Van Mournen continued, his voice taking on a rasp of intensity. "Darcy's birthday is only a few days away."

"For Darcy, huh?" He pretended to consider.

"You have connections. Surely you know about places where people could vanish, through no fault of their own."

"I'll see what I can think of," Vincent promised.

Van Mournen's gratitude was just a little too hearty. He had always presented himself as a man of restraint and good manners. His rages were cold, and Vincent knew it took a good deal of pressure to bring him to killing fury.

Vincent mulled that thought over after Van Mournen left. He paused in the middle of the dojo floor and stared at the spot where Darcy had knocked him over and they had tussled. The man he had been twenty, thirty years ago… would have taken advantage of the innocent girl, so full of life and energy.

Van Mournen had poisoned a man who stole a kiss from a woman he wanted. Then when he learned she wasn't the sweet, sheltered, innocent that she pretended to be… she vanished.

"No," Vincent whispered, his mind taking a huge leap forward. Just the other day, Josh had mentioned that Van Mournen spoiled Darcy and considered her the daughter he never had. "Not a daughter."

Van Mournen was attracted to young women who were little more than girls, with an appearance of innocence about them. Purity of mind and heart was more valuable to him than actual virginity.

What if all this revolved around Darcy? What if the entire reason why he hadn't punished Josh was that he was waiting… not just for revenge, but for Darcy to grow up?

Vincent prayed, hard, as he pulled out his cell phone.

An hour later, Sophie had dug up everything having to do with the activities of Karl Van Mournan, code name Midas, and the trail of false identities that stretched between both names. The frustrating part of the long report she forwarded to his computer was that every death of a sweet young woman or an interfering boyfriend was listed as suspicious, nothing more, because there was no proof.

Vincent didn't need proof. The man hadn't changed, other than to learn patience.

~~~~~

"How are you feeling this morning, my dear?" Van Mournen said, sliding into a chair next to Darcy at the breakfast table the next day.

"How am I supposed to feel?" She rubbed at her eyes and stared down into her bowl of rice, milk and honey. The last thing she wanted to do was match wits with Van Mournen. "Mostly I'm tired. I didn't get much sleep."

"That's understandable. But I assure you, whatever has happened, your father is a very capable man. I've known him longer than you've been alive. I've seen him fight off danger that would have overcome four men together."

"That just means that whatever did get him, it's pretty bad."

"Or treacherous." His eyes held nothing but sincere concern when Darcy finally raised her head and looked at him.

"Uncle Karl—"

"You know," he continued with a smile and a little shrug, "you're a grown woman, Darcy. Don't you think you could leave off the 'Uncle' from now on? You make me feel rather ancient." He chuckled.

"I'll try." Silently, she promised herself she would never address him by name again. Calling him 'uncle' somehow put a nice, safe barrier between them. She didn't want to lose that protection.
~~~~~

Chapter Eighteen

"Now, I want you to know that I will always be here to look after you," Van Mournen continued. "I promised your father, when you were just a toddler, playing on the living room floor, that I would watch over your welfare."

"You don't have to."

"But it's my duty. I promised Josh."

"Daddy asked Vincent to look out for Mom and me. I heard him," she couldn't resist saying.

A flicker of anger in Van Mournen's eyes sent a chill through her.

"Be that as it may, my dear, you are, as they say, stuck with me." He chuckled and patted her hand. His felt cold and heavy. "Now, to cheer you up, I have decided to give you one of your birthday presents early. Are you ready?"

"No, please—" She stopped short, knowing herself defeated when Van Mournen set a tiny, brown velvet-covered jewelry box on the table in front of her bowl.

The velvet was worn off at the corners. The trim was gold and it had a tiny, sparkling clasp. Darcy hoped it wasn't a diamond.

At his urging, she picked up the box and opened it. Inside, nestled in white satin slightly yellowed at the edges, was a ring of yellow gold engraved with a leaf pattern. Despite the cold, heavy feeling settling into her stomach, Darcy couldn't repress an indrawn breath. It was beautiful in simplicity. Nothing could negate that.

"I knew you'd like it." Van Mournen chuckled and took hold of her hand to slip the ring onto her finger. "I have been waiting your whole life to give you this ring, my dear. It belonged to someone very precious to me."

Darcy managed to stumble through her thanks. He seemed delighted with her response, and chuckled as he walked away. She waited, in case he stopped somewhere he could watch her. Terror froze her at the thought of his fury if she did what all her instincts screamed to do: take off the ring and throw it far away from her. She forced herself to finish her breakfast. It had no taste.

All her new, niggling doubts about this man who had been a doting uncle to her coalesced into the certainty that he did not think of her as a niece. Maybe he never had. She thought of Doug's last words to her, calling her naïve and stupid. Then she thought of Joan's reassurances that innocence did not mean ignorance.

Definitely, with all the rescue missions, all the rotten neighborhoods her parents had lived and worked in over the years, Darcy knew what was going on. She wasn't as innocent as she had thought she was a few days ago.

What did a man like Van Mournen want from a girl her age when he put a ring on her finger? That wasn't costume jewelry, she was sure. Men who put expensive jewelry on women laid claims on them.

It didn't matter if the girls *accepted* their claims.

The ring seemed to burn her finger. Darcy wanted to take it off, but Van Mournen had taken the box with him. She didn't have pockets in her sweat pants. What could she do with the ring? Besides, what would Van Mournen do if he saw her without the ring on her finger?

That was an antique box, well worn. Who did the ring belong to before her?

Darcy decided she didn't want to know, or even think in that direction, because the next logical question to ask was: Why didn't that girl wear the ring anymore?

Her hands shook faintly as she rinsed out her bowl and cup and hurried out of the kitchen.

Her mother was nowhere to be found. Naturally. Vincent was out looking for Joshua, and Joan had classes.

Martha, however, insisted on coming to work despite Doug's upcoming funeral. She said work comforted her. Darcy needed her guidance just as much as she needed to get her mind off her grandson's murder.

Darcy found Martha in the office, alone for the moment. She gave the ring a blank look when Darcy held her hand practically under her nose. When she heard the story of who gave it to her, the sorrow that softened her features faded to flat-lipped concern. She shook her head and then picked up her glasses from where they hung around her neck on her green beaded chain and peered through them at the ring.

"Although it's lovely, I most certainly do not approve of a man his age giving something this expensive to any girl your age." She shook her head and pursed her lips.

"Thanks, Martha." Darcy hugged the woman. She was glad, and feeling guilty about it, that Martha was here for her. "I just have this feeling that this ring, the timing… it has something to do with Daddy disappearing."

"Really? Why?" Martha pushed her glasses up higher on her nose.

"I think I'm in big trouble." Darcy leaned in closer, after glancing around the office to make sure they really were alone.

"Well, just because I retired from the force twenty years ago doesn't mean I haven't kept my hand in. Sit down and tell me everything you can think of."

"Are you sure?" Her heart gave a little leap, and she felt better than she had since Josh vanished.

~~~~~

After Darcy left the office, Martha bowed her head, half in prayer and half in rapid thought. She shook her head after only a few moments, knowing there was no other answer. Sunday, when Darcy plied Joan with an avalanche of questions about the foundation she worked for, Martha had quietly sat in her corner, kept knitting, and listened. There were far more resources at Joan's disposal than she had revealed, but Martha could guess. She had specialized in reading between the lines when she was on the force.

It was time that she had a long, private talk with this Joan Carter and her too-smart dog. Martha had plenty of experience with K-9s, but Ulysses made the most intelligent K-9 look like an undisciplined puppy.

The first rule in dealing with a possible threat was not to step outside of her usual routines and patterns. Martha had duties that morning, so she waited until lunch was over. Then she went searching for Geneva. Martha found her at the loading dock, signing for another shipment of lumber and other building supplies for the renovation. When Martha announced that she wasn't feeling well and needed to go home, Geneva hugged her and told her to take all the time she needed.

~~~~~

"Hi, Martha."

Joan stepped out of the office, wiping the sweat from her face with a towel she feared she should have tossed in the wash yesterday. Her last exercise group had left five minutes ago, and from the intent light in the elderly woman's eyes, the flat line of her mouth, the timing was a little too perfect. Martha had waited until she was alone. Ulysses let out a whine and scurried across the hardwood floor to the woman's side. That confirmed her sudden suspicions.

"If there was good news about Josh, someone would have called me. What's happened?"

"It's what should have happened a long time ago." For a moment, Martha seemed to sway. "We've been fools. He's been right under our noses the whole time. We even knew he didn't believe what we did, but… well, if Geneva and Joshua trusted him, we thought it was just a matter of time… and Darcy loves him so." A sob escaped her, a broken sound like shattered pottery.

"That fundraising guy — Van Mournen?" Joan hurried to meet her halfway across the floor. Martha gave her such a piteous look, she thought the wiry little woman might faint for a moment. Then she felt the tight muscles still evident under her fuzzy sweater. For all her wrinkles, Martha hadn't gone soft and spongy, and her back and shoulders were still straight.

Joan guided her into the office and settled her on the couch. She put Martha's bag on the floor before stepping over to the tiny refrigerator for a bottle of water. The top sagged open and she caught a glimpse of a camera, notepad, Bible, what looked like needlework, and a compact handgun of some kind. A crooked smile caught her lips, as she remembered Darcy saying Martha had been a police detective. She kept up her certification and even took Darcy to the firing range last year on her birthday.

"What did Van Mournen do?" she asked, once Martha had taken a few good swallows of cold water.

"He gave Darcy a ring. I don't know much about jewelry, but it's gold and I suspect it's old, and valuable. There's only one thing a man like him could want when he gives a ring like that to a girl like Darcy."

"To own her," Joan murmured. "She has to be careful. He's… Vincent told me some of the past he shares with Josh and Van Mournen. That man is — I guess the best word is obsessed. Obsessed with purity. Vincent said he latched onto a couple of girls through the years, and when they didn't live up to his image of them, he killed them. And there was a ring." She thumped her fist on the arm of the sofa. "The symbol of his ownership. No wonder… "

"No wonder what?" Martha's hand was steady as she grasped Joan's wrist and looked into her eyes, demanding honesty.

"Vincent was surprised that Van Mournen was working with Josh. He was never one to let a crime go unpunished. Josh stole one of the girls he wanted, a long time ago. What if the only reason he let Josh live all this time — "

"Is to keep an eye on Darcy, train her." A hiccup-sob escaped her, and then she was all steel and determination again. "And when he claims her, he gets his revenge on Joshua."

"He's got Josh somewhere, if he hasn't killed him already." Joan shuddered, thinking of Vincent's anger and pain when he realized how he had been tricked. "From things Vincent told me, Van Mournen would want Josh to know that Darcy belonged to him, before he killed him."

"I came here hoping all your mysterious connections could give me some answers." Martha nodded for punctuation and closed the cap of the water bottle. "We have the answers, the motivation. Now to take the pawn from our enemy's hands before we make our move. I'll keep an eye on Darcy. Maybe I can convince her and Geneva to leave with me, get them some place safe, until you two find Joshua. Then we'll deal with the Judas in our midst."

She glanced down at Ulysses, who had sat at her feet, gazing up at her the whole time they talked.

"I don't suppose he's part bloodhound?"

"We need to figure out where Josh was last before we can follow his trail. Vincent spent the whole morning searching the Center — Sophie even dug up blueprints of the building, to see if there were any tunnels, any hidden rooms where he could have been trapped." Joan shrugged and offered her hand as Martha struggled up from the couch. "He's out canvassing the area right now, to see if anybody saw anything. Chances are good he's nowhere near the Center."

"Where Van Mournen is… no. He's been hanging around the Center all morning."

"We need to spook him into going to check on Josh. Let me get hold of Vincent," she said, as they reached the door and she opened it for Martha. "We'll do some brainstorming, try to figure out where he would put Josh. Then we'll contact you." She paused in the doorway and made a gesture like sign language to Ulysses.

"The more distance we can put between him and Darcy, the happier I will be." She glanced back, as the dog hurried up the stairs. "Amazing. What did you just tell him to do?"

"Get my purse, so I can lock up." Joan sighed as she helped Martha down the front steps. "I'll have to make a sign and hang it on the door, to cancel classes the rest of the day. Saundra was hoping we could keep this place going, business as usual, until they find Roger."

"I know him well enough, he would tell you to dynamite this place, rather than put it ahead of Josh and Darcy's safety for one second."

Joan walked Martha to the curb where she had parked her bright green Volkswagon and waited until she was sure the woman was steady enough to drive herself back to the Center. She watched until the car turned the corner before reaching into her pocket to pull out her phone to call Vincent. A thud on the front door stopped her and she looked up to see Ulysses on his hind legs, forelegs pressing on the glass of the big double doors. His bark came muffled to her.

"Excuse me," a rasping voice said, coming from around the far side of the building. "Could you help me? I seem to have become lost."

"I'll try." Joan glanced at the hunched figure, leaning partially on his cane and partially against the side of the building. She couldn't make out the man's face, covered as it was by a floppy hat. "I'm not really from around here. Where do you need to go?"

"No, it's where you need to go," the man said, his voice becoming clear and rich, tinged with a British accent. He straightened and brought his cane up in a viciously fast arc that clipped Joan across her left temple, stunning her.

Ulysses went wild with barking and growls and thuds as he lunged at the reinforced glass of the door.

Joan tried to fling herself backward, but Van Mournen grabbed her arm while she was still wobbly and dragged her into the shadow of the building. He flung her face-first against the building. Instinct guided her and she went down, ducking and rolling, evading his hands—but he didn't grab at her. Pinprick stabs in her back alerted her just before lightning seared through all her nerves. She couldn't breathe as her face slammed into the dust and weeds. The burning paralysis of the tazer ceased before she lost consciousness, but Joan couldn't make herself move, couldn't regain her breath. A sharp kick to her ribs sent her into a partial fetal position, but at least it got her lungs working again.

"Oh, don't fight so. I'm not going to kill you," Van Mournen said, coming to rest with one knee on her throbbing ribs. "At least, not yet. You're far too useful as bait. Javelin and Daedelus used to fight over women at the drop of a hat. Let's see if they'll be willing to do it again, shall we?" He rolled her over onto her back and stood up, gazing down at her with the expression of a man dissecting animals, not at all concerned that they were still alive and screaming in pain.

Needles bit at Joan's fingers and toes and joints as Van Mournen hauled her to her feet and half-dragged her to the big, black car in the alley between the dojo and the abandoned building next door. Joan studied the trunk with blurry eyes and guessed it was big enough for two bodies, maybe three. What were the chances Josh was tied up in that trunk and she would join him?

To her disappointment, the trunk was empty, neat and clean. She guessed it was a rental, rather than stolen or Van Mournen's personal possession. Could she get under the carpet and find the jack or other tools for changing the tire, to use as weapons? Her captor shoved her hard into the trunk, so she hit her head when she fell into it. He chuckled once, a cold sound, before more pinpricks stabbed into her back, scorching her nerves. This time she went under completely.

~~~~~

Gasping, grinning in some triumph that she could indeed run without passing out, Martha tumbled back into her Volkswagon. She prayed that when Van Mournen pulled out of the alley, he would turn left and not right and wouldn't see her. Not for the first time, she castigated herself for buying such a bright green car. Just because she didn't think she would ever have to tail suspects once she reached retirement, that was no excuse for not being prepared.

Ulysses' barking continued, and she glanced at the building, saying a silent apology to the big dog. If she had more time—
~~~~~

There. The black Lincoln reached the street. She breathed a silent prayer of thanks as it did indeed turn left instead of right. By old habit, she noted the time on the dashboard clock, as if she would be writing up a report when this was all over.

Nine minutes and thirty-seven seconds since she had sighed and called herself a forgetful old fool and turned around. She needed to get Joan's cell phone number, so they could keep each other updated. Why hadn't she thought of that before she left the dojo? She had heard Ulysses barking before she saw Joan stagger, and the ragged figure that dragged her around the side of the building. Before she knew what she was doing, she had slammed her car into park and leaped out, leaving the door open, the keys in the ignition and the engine running. Her former captain would chew her out, roaring to make her deaf, if he ever knew about that bit of carelessness. Then she ran like she hadn't in years, staying close to the front of the building, hiding in the shadows with her old skill. She did remember to snatch her gun out of her bag, but Martha left the safety on as she peered around the corner and recognized Van Mournen. She winced in sympathy as the man shoved Joan into the trunk and tazered her. Rather than shoot the tires and hope Van Mournen wouldn't kill Joan before escaping, Martha chose to tail him. If God was with them all, Van Mournen would lead her straight to Joshua.

Martha gripped the steering wheel and fixed her eyes on the black Lincoln, always keeping at least two cars between herself and it. She had received commendations when she was on the police force in Chicago for her skill at tailing suspects through the worst kinds of traffic, and she hadn't lost her skill.

When the Lincoln pulled into the crumbling parking lot of the abandoned Allied Glass Works, Martha's eyes narrowed. This place should have been demolished years ago. It was a firetrap and a potential hangout for gangs, and she had just signed one of the petitions asking the city to tear it down. Shaking her head at the mulishness of some politicians, she continued down the street, looking for a place to hide her car and keep watch.

~~~~~

"So, Vincent claims to work for you? How convenient," Van Mournen purred. "How hard to believe. Anybody can see, just watching him, there's a great deal of emotional attachment."

Joan blinked blood out of her eyes and tried to focus on the chiseled face leaning over her. She sat on a pile of rubble, hands cuffed behind herself, wondering what new brutality the man would use next. Her whole body felt bruised by the trip from the car into the black pit of a building. Van Mournen had pushed her along, always out of synch with her steps, constantly threatening her unsteady balance. When Joan didn't
~~~~~

move quickly enough, he clubbed her with a convenient scrap of lumber and kicked her when she fell.

A dozen smart-alec remarks clogged at the back of her throat. She had read too many reports of dangerous encounters either her sisters at Quarry Hall had endured, or the people they had helped to rescue. Nothing would convince her to antagonize this madman. Judging by the things he had muttered since taking her captive, he had a use for her. Only an idiot would push him to change his plans or the timeline. All that mattered was staying alive until rescue came.

Messenger, I don't suppose you're hanging around, waiting to jump in and help? Joan almost smiled, but the hint of movement made her cut and swollen mouth ache. No, the angel that sometimes came to give her cryptic guidance wasn't going to show up, though she couldn't argue with the timing.

Or maybe that was the issue? The timing wasn't right? Something else had to happen before this crisis could be resolved?

Okay, Lord, I'm trusting in You. Move people, move things, shelter us under Your wings. We are Your servants.

How come those prayers were so much easier to pray when she was safe in her room at Quarry Hall, contemplating a tricky problem or someone else facing danger?

The flashlight Van Mournen used to illuminate the corner of the moldering room cast his face into a spectral mask. He flashed the light into Joan's eyes for a moment and let out a disgusted sigh when she just blinked at him.

"Too stupid to be afraid, are you?" Another sigh. "No matter. Javelin seems to find some value in you, and I will use that for my own benefit. Do try to prolong your life as long as possible."

Chapter Nineteen

Van Mournen yanked Joan to her feet, then shoved her backward, so she stumbled over the rubble and slammed her head against the wall, hard enough to make her see stars. He unlocked the handcuffs from her left wrist, yanked up hard on her arms, and relocked them in place, cuffing her to a metal pipe that ran along the wall about five feet up from the floor. There was no way she could reach the phone in her pocket. He hadn't taken it while she was unconscious. Why? Was it part of his plan?

He stepped back and studied her like another man would study a cockroach he had partially squashed, trying to decide whether to let it suffer or put it out of its misery.

"How are you feeling now, Josh?" he called, raising his voice so it echoed off the rusty metal ceiling.

That carelessness over being heard told Joan just how isolated this rotting factory building really was.

From another room came the rattling of chains, but no voice. Van Mournen chuckled.

"Dear Josh has decided not to answer me. He thinks he can play his pathetic religious games and outlast me, make me repent and change my ways, even at this late date. If you Christians weren't so useful, such convenient camouflage... well, I really do think you're going to wipe yourselves out before too much longer. That should be entertaining."

Joan kept quiet, letting her hair hang down in her face, slicked to her skin with sweat and blood. At least now she knew Josh was here. She needed to hang on until Vincent got back to the dojo and found her missing. She wasn't too sure about Ulysses' ability to track the car Van Mournen had put her in, but Vincent would know immediately something was wrong. Just as long as he didn't try calling her while Van Mournen was still around to hear her phone ring and take it from her. If he didn't take it, didn't destroy it, Vincent could track her through the enhanced GPS Sophie had designed a few months ago.

All she had to do was hang on and not irritate the man.

All she had to do was pray until he left, so he wasn't here when Vincent came for her.

Lord, surround us with Your angels. Keep Darcy safe.

~~~~~

Vincent returned to the dojo at sunset, hot and frustrated. He had
~~~~~

spent the morning searching every dark, dirty, hidden corner of the Center, looking for some clue to what had happened to Josh. Then he and Sophie had spent a frustrating couple of hours conferring on the phone and with linked computers, backtracking Van Mournen's and Josh's activities since they had reconnected, trying to find some pattern, some threat, some slip-up that revealed their new identities to old enemies. Joshua's comment just a few days ago came back to Vincent to make him shudder: four of the five members of their team had resurfaced, so what were the odds Shadow had found Josh and Van Mournen, and was taking his revenge? Shadow had broken away from the powers-that-be first, but what if he had been recaptured, retrained, turned into a mindless, loyal weapon whose sole purpose in life was to destroy his former teammates?

Vincent spent an hour at the police station, conferring with McGee, following up on leads. Then he had walked the neighborhoods around the Center, asking questions, trying to find some lead, a fragment of something odd someone had noticed and not realized they noticed.

Nothing.

The loft apartment would be quiet and dark and cool. He looked forward to kicking his shoes off and collapsing on that long, comfortable old couch. Just for ten minutes. Enough time to cool down and be still and turn off his brain, before the hunt moved down another trail, tried something new. He hoped Joan had come up with some ideas while she handled the exercise classes.

A low, mournful keening greeted him as he got out of the car and headed for the front door of the dojo. The door thudded and rattled and he saw Ulysses scrabbling at the glass with his forepaws. If the glass of the dojo, windows and doors, hadn't been reinforced and then the security cage around everything, the big dog would have broken through the glass long ago.

"Please, no, Lord..." He took the steps in one leap and snatched at the doorknob. He turned aside quickly, to keep from being barreled over by Ulysses as the big dog shoved the door open and flew down the steps. Vincent ran, following him around the side of the building.

There, Ulysses ran three circles around a spot in the alley and then sat down, looking up at him with human pleading in his big eyes.

Tire tracks. Scuffle marks in the dirt and gravel. No blood. No bullet casings. No other clues.

"What was she doing outside without you?" he muttered.

No one could have come into the dojo and attacked her with Ulysses around. The dog didn't show any signs of being injured, temporarily restrained to keep him from coming to her rescue. Could someone have been able to threaten her and force her to exit the building and leave Ulysses inside?

"We'll figure it out," he muttered, and turned to go into the building. If he was lucky, Joan had left a note, some kind of clue, an indication of who was threatening her.

Maybe she had walked outside with someone after one of the classes, and got caught outside? No—she wouldn't have gone outside without Ulysses. He wouldn't have let her go outside without him, even if there were no indications of danger. Vincent had trained the dogs too well, and as long as they were in unfamiliar territory, Ulysses didn't let Joan go anywhere alone—unless she gave him orders to the contrary.

Vincent had his answer when he opened the door and found Joan's purse lying on the floor in front of the doormat. He saw the scenario clearly in his mind. Joan walked outside with someone and sent Ulysses to get her purse. That meant she was planning on leaving the dojo. She should have called him to tell him what she was going to do.

Whoever took her got to her before she called him.

If he still had hair, Vincent knew he would be yanking it out in handfuls. He stomped over to the office, hoping Joan had at least made one of the signs to put in the door, to let people know the dojo was closed while she was gone. It would give him an idea of how long ago she had left or when she planned to be back.

The answering machine was flashing, and the counter was lit up with a thirty-seven in lurid red lights. Vincent didn't bother trying to remember how many people were in the exercise classes Joan was supposed to cover for him. He estimated at least two classes worth of people—and most of them probably called to find out why the dojo was locked. Did he dare take the time to listen to all those messages, in case one of them was the kidnapper?

Calls. Messages.

He didn't see Joan's cell phone lying on the floor. She always kept it tucked in her pocket, or in her sock if she went into a tricky situation and didn't want an enemy snatching it too easily. Maybe she couldn't call him, but that didn't mean he couldn't find her.

He headed upstairs, planning his next dozen moves. First, turn on Joan's computer, activate the GPS in her phone, and call Quarry Hall while he was doing that, to get everyone praying. Then he would call the Spike Center to find out if there was any news on Josh.

The answering machine sitting on the little baker's table at the top of the stairs flashed for two messages. He hit the play button and headed for Joan's computer, sitting on the coffee table.

"Vincent?" Darcy sounded out of breath. "You better be downstairs. I'll try there next. *He* beat up on Joan and kidnapped her. They're at some place called Allied Glass Works." She rattled off the address, stumbling over it twice before she got it right. "Martha is waiting for us. I'm going over there right now. Don't worry." Her laugh sounded broken, trying to cover fear. "Martha has a gun and I'm taking one of *his* big, heavy swords. Serves him right if I use it on him. We're not sure it's smart to call the police. At least, not until we get Joan out of there. Please, get there soon?"

Vincent closed his eyes and listened to the machine recite the time the call had come through. More than three hours ago.

How long would Darcy and Martha — why Martha? — wait for him to arrive before they went in after Joan? Why had Van Mournen grabbed Joan?

He almost reached to turn off the machine, but it beeped and Van Mournen's voice oozed out of the little speaker grid.

"Vincent? I've finally found Josh. I don't know what's wrong with him. He doesn't seem to know me. I think he's having a flashback, finally reacting to all that damage he took in Kuwait. He's taken your friend, Joan, captive. He's threatening to kill her unless you show up and face him and pay for your crimes. He was ranting about how you've been trying to kill him all these years, so he's going to kill your friends until you face him." Van Mournen paused, then gave the address — for Allied Glass Works.

Ulysses whined and rose up on his hind legs to put both paws on Vincent's chest.

"It's okay. We'll get her back," he murmured, staring at the answering machine while plans and ideas, strategies and options and painful, bloody memories swirled through his mind.

He was still on the phone, relaying the situation to Elizabeth at Quarry Hall, as he locked the front door of the dojo and hurried to his car. Ulysses raced ahead of him and scrambled through the open side window. Vincent slid into the driver's seat and then went perfectly still, gripping the steering wheel, his head bowed.

"Please, Lord," he whispered. "Keep them safe. Don't make our girls pay for the sins of our pasts."

That was all he could manage to pray. It would have to be enough.

~~~~~

Darcy crept through the darkness, trying not to breathe. Something had died in the building not too long ago and the smell was enough to make her lose her lunch. If she had bothered to eat her lunch.

Her legs hurt from crouching behind an overgrown bush at the far end of the long street for more than three hours, watching the black Lincoln that Martha insisted Van Mournen had driven here, with Joan in the trunk. The back of her neck tingled unpleasantly from too much sun at that sharp angle. The wait had been worthwhile. Ten minutes ago, Van Mournen drove away. Neither she nor Martha could guess why the man had left, but now they could investigate.

The plan was simple: Darcy would go inside, armed with her stolen
~~~~~

sword. Martha would stay outside, in hiding, and watch for the return of the Lincoln. When she saw it, she would fire her gun to warn Darcy. She didn't want to stay outside, but Darcy had made her promise. She had faith in her ability to hold Van Mournen off with a sword. If he had a gun, Martha's sharpshooter skills wouldn't do them much good anyway.

Besides, if Van Mournen caught them, someone needed to get away and pass the word about what had happened.

Darkness all around her. Darcy grimaced as her boot sank into something soft that slid greasily under the sole. She sidestepped and tripped over a pile of bricks—or something that at least sounded like bricks when they fell over.

"Who's there?" Joan called, her voice coming from the darker blot of shadows to her right.

"Darcy." Her voice came out a pitiful whisper. She would have laughed if her throat didn't feel so tight.

"Are you crazy? You're the one in the most danger—get out."

Darcy found a doorway and felt her way across the floor by shuffling her feet. "Keep talking so I can find you."

"You have no idea the trouble you're in. Get out!"

"I called Vincent. He'll be here." She choked on a giggle. "As soon as he gets home and gets the message."

Far away, muffled like pops from an air gun, came two gunshots.

"What was that?" Joan demanded.

"Martha." She paused, straining her eyes to see in the dark blob of shadows filling the room.

"What's she doing here?" From the sound of her voice, Joan was only a few feet away, directly in front of her.

"She came back to the dojo and saw *him* grab you and followed you here. Then she called me. We figured the police probably shouldn't get involved. Although Martha is the police, when you think about it." Darcy kicked something that rattled and sounded like plastic. "What the heck was that?"

"Probably the flashlight. He left it to torture me."

Darcy dropped to her knees, trying to remember the direction of the sound as the plastic tube rolled away.

"At least Martha has a gun," she said with a sigh. "I wish she would have gone back and let Ulysses out, if you guys couldn't find Vincent right away."

"Yeah, but she was only supposed to fire one shot if she saw *him* and then get out of here. What do two shots mean?" Darcy felt plastic brush against her fingertips. She pounced. "Got it!"

The brightness of the beam hurt her eyes, but she grinned and got to her feet and hurried over to Joan. Then she saw the handcuffs.

"He doesn't play fair, does he?" she muttered.

"Get out, Darcy," Joan urged again. "Let Vincent get me out of here."

"No. Martha and I figured that's why he took you. It's a trap. He's getting revenge on Vincent. He—" Her voice cracked and for a moment she couldn't breathe. "He probably already killed Daddy. Joan, he gave me a ring—like—like—" She choked, unable to speak all the horrid speculations that had filled her mind since that morning.

"Like he wants to own you," she whispered.

"Yeah, well, this is twenty-first century United States. Slavery went out a hundred years ago." She squeezed the grip on the sword she had once dreamed of owning and using in adventures of daring-do, thoroughly frustrated and hating the pressure coming at her from all sides. The feel of the metal under her hand gave her an idea. "Pull your arm down as far as you can, okay?"

"What are you—" Joan stopped short when Darcy raised the sword, revealing its heavy, curved blade. "Good idea." She grinned and pulled back as far as she could, to stretch out the short chain of the handcuffs.

It took two blows. She sagged almost to the floor and rubbed at her wrists when she was finally free.

"Where did you get that monster?"

"I took it from the treasure room." Darcy shuddered. "All this time, I thought Daddy knew about it, but I bet—"

"Your dad. Darcy, he's here somewhere. Van Mournen beat up on him pretty bad, but I heard him yelling at him just before he left, so he's got to be alive." She gestured at the stinking blackness around them.

Darcy turned and headed for the door leading out, taking the flashlight with her. Four steps later, she stopped and came back, holding out her hand for Joan. They linked arms and headed deeper into the pitch black of the building together.

Something scrabbled through the darkness far to the right, where Darcy had come from the door, past several tumbledown walls. The sound grew closer, and she heard claws on the cement and dirt and debris.

"Please don't let that be rats," she whispered.

Joan let out a muffled yelp as something big and dark knocked her over. She barely let go of Darcy's arm in time to keep from pulling her down. Muffling a scream, Darcy turned the flashlight on her, just as Joan laughed. She stared, unable to put the pieces together for a few seconds, as Joan got up on her knees, hugging Ulysses and struggling to keep him from licking all over her face.

"How did he find you?"

"One guess. The odds just turned completely in our favor," Joan said. She snapped out some words in a foreign language and Ulysses immediately went still. "He'll find your dad in no time, then we can get out of here."

"I'm here, Karl," Vincent announced, stepping into the frame of the faint light coming through the doorway far behind them.

Darcy's knees sagged from the dizzy relief she felt. Joan flashed the light toward the doorway.

"That's what the two shots meant—someone else coming." She laughed, knew she sounded like a dizzy little girl, and didn't care.

"Josh is in here somewhere," Joan called. "I don't know if he's unconscious or just gagged so he can't make noise." She gestured deeper into the darkness.

Vincent hurried to meet them halfway to the door. He grasped Darcy's shoulder with one hand and shook her. "What do you think you're doing here?"

"I found Joan, didn't I? And now we can get Dad!"

Vincent opened his mouth to retort. She could tell from his face, whatever he would say would boil down to one thing: she had to leave the rest of the rescue to him.

A single gunshot broke the momentary silence.

"He's back," Joan said.

"Joan," Vincent began.

"I know." She took a tighter hold of Darcy's hand. "Get Darcy out of here and don't look back."

"You're learning." Vincent took the flashlight from Darcy and pointed it into the blackness. He rapped out almost the same words Joan had used, and Ulysses leaped away, vanishing into the darkness, on the hunt. Vincent followed.

Darcy twisted free of Joan and raced after him, catching up as he stepped through the next doorway and flashed the beam around the room. Vincent turned to her and opened his mouth—probably to tell her to go back. They both froze as the light caught her father, bleeding and unconscious, supported by the chain that bound him to the pipe. His clothes hung on him in bloody rags. Long bleeding slashes covered his face and arms and chest. Vincent jammed the flashlight in a bend in the pipe overhead, freeing up his hands to fight with the chains.

"Daddy!" Darcy dropped her sword and clamped both hands over her mouth. She didn't know if it was to keep from screaming or keep from throwing up. Her knees did give out this time and she slid to the floor. Then Joan was there, kneeling over her, wrapping arms tight around her.

"Come on. Vincent can take care of him. We need to get out of here and give that slimebag as few targets as possible."

Josh groaned as Vincent tugged on the chains. He blinked against the glare of the light. A slow grin touched his face.

"Always the hero, huh?" He shifted his arms, making the chains clink.

"Get out while you can. Karl has traps within traps. He wants us to fight."

"Why, Dad?" Darcy stepped into the light and tentatively reached out a hand, touching the blood staining his chest.

"Oh, baby," Josh moaned. "Get her out. He's been raving. Karl's insane. He thinks Darcy belongs to him. He's going to get his revenge on us and make it look like you attacked her and I killed you for it."

While Josh talked, Vincent searched the chains and found the lock. He yanked it out, trying to get enough chain free of the tangle. No key was visible.

Darcy held out the sword, wordlessly offering its heavier blade for the job. She stepped back, out of the light and out of his way.

"You two get out of here." He took the sword and gestured toward the doorway. "Karl left a message at the dojo, so he has to be waiting for me to come here."

"We'll go out the back way," Joan assured him. "If there is a back way."

Vincent nodded and raised the sword.

"Sorry," Van Mournen said from the doorway in a pleasant voice. "There is no back way."

Vincent swung down. The link he hit snapped with a shower of sparks. The chains rattled and slid to the ground. Josh slumped to the crumbling floor and Darcy leaped into the light to catch him.

"No!" Van Mournen roared. He took three quick steps into the room, reaching out his free hand for Darcy. "What are you doing here?"

"Rescuing my father and my friend from you." She stood, supporting Josh. "You lied to me. All my life."

"Darcy, be careful," Vincent warned.

"I hate you!" She held up her hand, the ring sparkling in the strong beam of the flashlight.

"Darcy—sweetheart—" Van Mournen licked his lips, visibly unnerved.

"I'm not your sweetheart." She yanked off the ring.

"Don't!" Vincent blurted.

Darcy threw the ring. It hit Van Mournen square in the face and chimed sweetly as it bounced off his nose and tumbled into the darkness at his feet.

Chapter Twenty

Van Mournen howled and reached into the waistband of his pants. He drew out a gun.

His face twisted into an inhuman mask as he fired. Joan threw Darcy to the ground and dove into the rubble of the floor right after her. Vincent leaped to the left. Josh went to the right and rolled.

Van Mournen fired again, the sound of the gunshots raining deafening echoes in the shattered room.

"Karl, don't!" Josh pleaded and scrambled up from his knees. He fell back, curling into a fetal ball as a fourth bullet hit him in the thigh.

A wall seemed to hit Darcy in the side, knocking her off her feet, turning her around before slamming her to the ground. The shriek that escaped her choked off as a wave of fire exploded from her ribs.

Light flashed off a dark form that leaped from darkness through the light and into darkness. Van Mournen shouted in shock, the sound cut off with the heavy thud of bodies hitting the debris-littered floor. Ulysses' low, rumbling growl filled the air, punctuated by the rattle of the dropped gun skittering across the floor.

"Darcy? Baby?" Josh coughed, followed by a dragging sound. "Are you all right?"

She whimpered. It was all she could do to keep from breaking out in sobs as throbbing waves radiated from her side. She couldn't take a breath without feeling like blades shifted inside her chest.

Vincent stepped into the light and pulled the flashlight out of the place where he had jammed it in the pipe. He swept the light around the room, briefly illuminating Josh trying to get to his feet, then Van Mournen sprawled on his chest, Ulysses sitting on his back with his muzzle pressed against the man's neck, then finally landing on Darcy.

"I've got her," Joan said, coming out of the darkness behind her. Dim blue light spilled over her. Darcy whimpered when she turned, unthinking, and the pain rose up in a higher, sharper wave. The light came from her cell phone.

"How is she?" Vincent said.

"Bullet across the ribs. Probably cracked some. Bet it hurts like unholy heck, huh? No, trust me, just relax," Joan murmured when she tried to peel back the torn, blood-soaked flaps of Darcy's ruined shirt.

"Sorry—such a—wimp," Darcy managed to say, her throat trying to close up with sobs. Strangely, once she managed to take a breath, some of the pain receded, just enough to be noticeable.

"Not a wimp at all. Bet this is the first time you've ever been shot. Not that it's any comfort, but it doesn't get any easier."

"You've been shot? How many times?"

"Shot at. Beat up. Left in a sweatbox. Tied up. Left in a warehouse fire to die. Sure you want to join us?"

"How is she?" Vincent asked, as he supported Josh in walking over to join them.

"Don't suppose you have a few yards of bandages in your back pocket?"

"Martha has a big first aid kit in her trunk," Darcy offered. Definitely, it was getting easier to breathe. She blinked tears out of her eyes and looked up at Josh. He stared down at her, his face crumpling in misery. "Are you okay, Dad?"

"Me? This is nothing. But you—" His face hardened into a fury she had never glimpsed before as he turned to look out into the darkness, where Ulysses still growled, and where Van Mournen was still trapped. "Why, Karl?"

"Forget about him," Vincent said. "We need to get the two of you to a doctor."

"Please tell me that's sirens I'm hearing," Joan said, as she helped Darcy to her feet.

Darcy couldn't be sure, with her heart thudding in her ears and her own breathing and whimpers sounding loud enough to deafen. Joan supported her on her uninjured side. It helped to be half-carried out of the old factory, but it was awkward at the same time. Joan had to dig her hand in low on Darcy's hip, below the wound in her ribs, to support her. The bleeding continued, so Joan's hand was slick with it and Darcy felt dizzy and cold by the time they reached the parking lot, where Martha was waiting.

Everything turned into a blur for Darcy. She tried to focus on Josh, but everyone fussed over her, getting in her way, so she was reduced to shouting for him every minute or two, to make sure he was still there. Later, she realized how ridiculous that was, because Josh sat in the front seat of Martha's Volkswagen, and they had made her sit in the back seat.

Then the police arrived and EMTs took over and someone gave her a shot, then another one, and she felt like she floated at least a foot above the seat. The cold went away and she felt fuzzy warm as she slid down a long, dark tunnel.

The sliding sensation stopped when gunshots rang out and men shouted and she heard Joan shout for Ulysses and people were running in every direction. Josh wrapped his arms around her, yanking her back to the present and hot stabs radiated from her side again, as if her wound had to remind her it was there.

"Daddy?"

"I'm here, baby."

"What happened? Is Ulysses —"

"He's fine," Joan said, appearing out of the haziness and squatting down in front of them.

Darcy took a deep breath and found herself sitting on the pavement, leaning against a squad car. She could have sworn she had been sitting in the back of the EMT van just a few seconds ago. Her head felt like it would pop off her neck as she raised it to look around. A sigh escaped her when Ulysses came and sat down next to Joan and rubbed his head against her side.

"What happened?" she said. Funny, but her lips felt kind of numb.

"He got away."

"Joan called off her dog, so the police could take Karl away," Josh said, tightening his arms around Darcy. "In those few seconds, he brought a knife from somewhere and stabbed one of the officers and took a gun from another and… gone."

"He got away," she echoed. Darcy shivered, feeling cold again, in a depth that had nothing to do with blood loss.

~~~~~

Detective McGee wanted to put the Clay family and Martha into protective custody. He deferred to Vincent's suggestion that they camp out in the dojo, which was a much smaller building to secure with fewer entrances to guard. Vincent wondered about the man's sudden willingness to not only trust him, but work with him. When he called down to Quarry Hall to have Kathryn and Su-Ma bring half a dozen of his dogs to patrol the building, he found out the rest of the story. Elizabeth had to pull some strings, use her family name and the name of the Arc Foundation, to get a speedy emergency response at the abandoned factory. McGee and his supervisors now knew about the Arc Foundation and some of its reputation.

The doctors kept Josh and Darcy in the hospital overnight for observation, after stitching and bandaging them, and in Darcy's case replacing the blood she had lost. Geneva and Martha stayed at the dojo that night with Vincent and Joan and the dogs. The next morning, Joan went to the Spike Center with Geneva and Martha to protect them while they carried out their day's usual routine. Volunteers from the neighborhood and a handful of police officers who attended services at the Center set up a patrol, inside and outside the building, to make sure Van Mournen couldn't get back in and exact his revenge by sabotaging the renovations. That huge kerosene tank out on the loading dock kept
~~~~~

returning to Vincent's thoughts. What would it take to set it off and blow up the building? How much of the neighborhood would it destroy as collateral damage?

In mid-afternoon, the doctors released Josh and Darcy. Vincent brought them back to the dojo to wash up and get some sleep. Darcy came into the kitchen after her shower, while Vincent was still on the phone with Sophie, getting an update on the search for Van Mournen's trail. Dressed in a sleeveless gray sweatshirt and green, stretchy lounging slacks, barefoot, her eyes wide with dark smears under them in her pale face, she looked like a drowned kitten. She said nothing as he finished and hung up.

"Hungry?" he asked. Darcy shrugged. He stepped over to the stove and picked up the tea kettle, then went to the sink to refill it. "Tea might help."

She nodded and settled down on a stool at the counter and rested her elbows on the edge. Vincent turned the faucet off.

"I should give you a good dose of moss tea. If you hang around Joan long enough, she'll tell you there's a foul-smelling tea for just about any problem, and if you don't keep up the hand-to-hand skills I teach you, the worst of them all is what you have to drink for punishment."

That earned a hint of a smile from her.

Josh was just climbing out of the shower when McGee called to say he was outside. Vincent wondered why the man didn't ring the doorbell. All the dogs were indoors, two on the first floor, two on the second, and two on the flat roof. He came down the stairs and found the first floor dogs lying down, quiet, at opposite ends of the long room. However, one of the second floor dogs stood on the top of the stairs — outside the front door — calmly watching McGee. The pure black Rottweiler was called Dinger, short for Schroedinger. Vincent suspected he was going to have to give in and change the dog's name to Houdini, reflecting his talent for getting out of locked rooms and collars and over fifteen-foot-tall fences.

"Give me your hand," Vincent said, once he let McGee in. Using hand signals, he brought the two first floor dogs over and went through the routine with them and Dinger, having them sniff the detective while he named him as a friend.

"Good system you've got there," McGee remarked as Vincent led him upstairs.

"I'd rather we didn't need to use it."

"Amen to that." He offered the first real smile when Vincent reacted to that unexpected remark.

Josh and Darcy had settled on the couches, drinking tea, trying to read and not doing a very good job of it. They relaxed visibly when Vincent came in with McGee.

"Have to talk with you." The detective's voice was a strained rasp. "Hate to have to grill you after all you've gone through. Procedure." He hunched his shoulders, jamming his fists into his pockets. The corners were torn from the pressure.

"We got an anonymous call last night," he continued after settling down in a couch facing father and daughter. "Somebody really has it in for you. This guy claimed you cut off Roger Lancaster's head and dumped the body out at the old glass works."

"I'm guessing you found his body, when you were cleaning up afterward," Vincent said.

"Got it in one. Please, if you have any idea what's going on—we're pretty sure the killer and the caller were both this Van Mournen creep. What can you tell us that'll help us nail the lid shut on this?"

"My contacts are still following leads, but after what happened yesterday, it's looking more and more like Van Mournen was behind all the accusations," Vincent said. "He manufactured the scandals. He was out to destroy the Center."

"Why?" the detective exploded.

"It's my fault," Darcy said, leaning into her father's arm around her.

"Why? What could you do—I met the guy. He's as straight-laced as they come. Darcy, I even heard you call him 'Uncle,' a few times. Anybody would think he was as gung-ho as the rest of you."

"That's what makes it so bad," Josh said, his voice cracking. "Honey, you don't have to listen—"

"Yeah, Daddy, I do." Darcy sat up a little straighter and nodded to Vincent to take the lead.

"Karl has had his eye on Darcy since she was a child," Vincent said. "He gave her an expensive antique ring for her birthday. I knew Van Mournen a long time ago, and he gave the same ring to another woman he planned to marry."

"Let me get this straight—a ring? Like an engagement ring?" McGee sputtered. He stared at Darcy, visibly begging her to deny the story.

"More like a sign that he owned me," Darcy said. She kept her eyes on her interlaced fingers as she spoke. "Uncle—he gave it to women he wanted to own, and they always died. Murdered. After he found out they were in love with someone else."

"We're guessing now Van Mournen chose her as his bride when she was a child," Vincent said, "and waited for her to grow up. He pretended to support Josh's work so he could stay close to Darcy and watch over her, influence her, keep her from falling in love with anyone else."

"That's sick." McGee swallowed hard and clenched his fists into his knees. "Darcy, you don't have to talk about it if you don't want to, but did he—when you were a little kid—"

"He didn't molest me," she said, shaking her head, still refusing to meet his eyes.

"He's always been fanatical about purity and an innocent heart," Vincent said. "We think he killed Doug because Darcy was on the verge of a romance with him."

"You're lucky, then." The detective winced. "Sorry. Didn't mean it that way. It's just that most of these guys who go after little girls, they don't wait. So, anyway, what's he after you two for? It sure looked to me like more than just getting you out of the way so he could get at Darcy."

"The three of us were in the military together, years ago," Josh said, his voice quiet. He tightened his arm around Darcy. "Karl was the kind of man who never let any insult or betrayal go unpunished. The things he said when he was torturing me... he chose Darcy partly to punish me. He planned to torture me with the knowledge that Darcy was going to choose him over me, just before he killed me."

"Never, Daddy," Darcy whispered.

~~~~~

Vincent woke at the creak of the floor under a footstep. He rolled over on the pallet of blankets he had spread on the floor under the fire escape window and snatched up the flashlight from under his pillow.

"It's just me," Darcy whispered from the darkness near the stairs. She held still when Vincent turned the flashlight on her. She was barefoot, dressed in the t-shirt and stretch pants she had gone to bed in. "I can't sleep," she continued when Vincent got up and stepped around the sofa where Martha snored softly. "I thought I'd go downstairs and try to... exercise or something. If I can," she added, pressing her hand against her wounded side.

"Good idea." He reached for his shirt and pulled it on over his sweatpants. A glance back showed Joan awake, watching them from her sofa. She nodded to him and gestured with her chin at the bedroom, where Josh and Geneva slept in Roger's bed. Ulysses' tail thumped once, but he didn't move to come downstairs with them.

That reassured him more than the utter silence from the dogs on the floors beneath them that all was well, undisturbed and secure in the dojo.

"You don't have to come with me. I don't think he'd come attack here. Would he?"

Vincent didn't answer right away as they descended the stairs. He had already decided the masked intruder had been Van Mournen, using the keys he had taken from Roger after he killed him, trying to confuse him from the beginning. It had worked, too—attack, then show up a short time later expressing concern, and every time he went about in the daylight, he walked with a pronounced limp and leaned heavily on his cane. Who would suspect he had been the nimble attacker just a short time
~~~~~

before?

He stepped past Darcy at the bottom of the stairs and reached for the first bank of light switches. "I can't sleep either. A good workout will do us both good. You need to keep limber, and I can show you how to exercise around your injury."

"Okay." She followed him across the main floor of the echoing silent dojo. The dogs came over to inspect her, sniffing at her heels for a moment, then headed out into the darkness again. Darcy seemed to take encouragement from that, but it hurt Vincent a little that she didn't try to pet them or make friends. Some childlike quality had been lost in the last two days.

For the first fifteen minutes, she watched him and mirrored his movements as he taught her how to stretch while protecting her injury and not straining her stitches. Then as they moved on to using hand weights, her attention seemed to wander, her gaze growing introspective. When he asked her what she was thinking about, Darcy was silent so long, Vincent thought maybe she hadn't heard him.

"The treasure room." She said it so softly, at first he wasn't sure he heard right. They sat down as Darcy explained about the three trunks and Van Mournen telling her that he was guarding treasures for people who could no longer take care of them. "He told me he and Dad were guarding it together, and someday I would take over their job." She shuddered and wrapped her arms around herself. "I can't believe I fell for that stupid story!"

"How old were you when he told it to you, Darcy?"

"Thirteen."

"You trusted him, right? You wanted to believe him. He probably let you think you were part of a big, wonderful secret." Vincent squeezed her shoulder when she just nodded and gave him a shamed look. "He knew how to play your mind and emotions. You were just a kid. Your parents trusted him, so you did, too. You're not to blame."

They sat in silence. The stillness of the hour seeped through the walls, and the dogs on guard duty snuffled in their sleep.

"I hate him!" she spat. Darcy shuddered and gave him a wide-eyed look, as if stunned at her own vehemence. For a moment, Vincent didn't know who she meant. "*Him.* For all his lies and using me and twisting my life around—for hurting Joan and trying to kill you and for Daddy. But hating is *wrong*. I want to take all his swords and go after him and hack him into a thousand little pieces!"

"You can't let your emotions rule you. They'll blind you and get you killed."

"I know. Dad still lectures me sometimes on the mistakes of his past, and how his anger just got him into trouble. He says hating is wrong.

Forgiving makes you strong and keeps your head clear." Darcy managed a lopsided smile.

"He trained you right."

"Yeah, but trying to live like that made us blind, so *he* could trick us. For years!"

"You're going to have to use his name sooner or later," Vincent said with a grin. It was kind of funny, in a warped way, how Darcy refused to use Van Mournen's name.

"Not if he goes away and stays away and never reminds me that he ever existed." A shuddering sigh escaped her.

"I know it's hard to hear, but you have to live what you believe, never let go of it, even though living that way makes you vulnerable. It's that important."

"I know." She knuckled her eyes before the gleam of moisture turned into tears. "Dad always says, if what you believe isn't worth dying for, why do you believe it?"

Vincent wasn't sure what to say. He refused to use empty words of comfort. Darcy wouldn't hear them, and they weren't what she needed. He put an arm around her and drew her head down on his shoulder. She shivered a little, but she didn't cry. Finally a little of the tension seemed to ease from her shoulders. She took a deep breath, relaxed a little more, then rubbed at her face, wiping away more tears that hadn't fallen.

"This is crazy. I know better. I keep praying and I know what's right. I know what I believe. But there's this big empty space between where I am and where I have to go, and I'm standing on the edge and scared to move. I wish I could just close my eyes and make it all go away! Especially the way I felt when I saw what he did to my dad. When I realized how he had lied to me and manipulated me—he was raising me to be his innocent, brainless bride."

"There's a difference between ignorant and innocent, Darcy. You're too smart to be ignorant. Innocence is... a very good, rare thing."

"*He* used to tell me that innocence was a sharp sword that could hurt you or destroy your enemies."

"He's right."

"Barely. I'm not what he thought I was."

Chapter Twenty-One

"Good. The best way to stay alive is to keep your enemy guessing." Vincent tightened his arm around her, shaking her a little. "You're going to be all right, Darcy. God will use you, make you stronger through this."

"Will He? The way I felt back—" Her lips moved for a few seconds, but no sound escaped.

"Scared?"

"I was too angry to be scared!" Darcy jerked to her feet and stomped away from him. "Vincent, I wanted so much to kill him. All I could think about was how he cut up my dad and left him there. How he had Joan tied up in the dark, with that flashlight just out of reach. How he lied to me and used me to hurt other people—and then gave me a ring that belonged to someone he killed, thinking that would make me love him. I want to kill him and keep killing him and make him pay for all the hurt he put us through."

"That's understandable."

"But it's wrong! That's not what I believe in. Now I really understand why Daddy walked away from all that fighting. The feelings that come over you in a fight are horrible." She wrapped her arms tight around herself. "And addicting," she added in a near-whisper.

"It's not the guns and bombs and blood, Darcy." Vincent stepped up behind her and rested both hands on her shoulders. He winced at the tension running through her, making her whole body stiff again, just when he thought she had recovered.

"It's the hatred, wanting revenge. I can feel it eating me up inside." She turned around to face him. "Vincent, what do I do? I keep praying, and there's this silence." She choked, and the sound turned into a chuckle. "I remember when I was in junior high, and I would ask Dad for answers, and he wouldn't give them to me because he said I already knew them. I just had to find and use them. That's what I feel like God is doing to me right now. He won't answer because I already know the answer."

"Then follow what you believe," Vincent murmured, and wrapped his arms around her.

Darcy rested her head on his shoulder. She sighed, and a little of the tension seeped from her body. "Everything's changed."

"Everything around us does change, Darcy. You have two choices. You either let circumstances change you, or you change them. You can hold onto what you believe in and stay true to what you are inside, or you can let the tides move you wherever they flow."

Silence crept in around them.

"Does it get any easier?" she whispered, when a gust of wind had blown past and rattled the windows, like a friend trying to get their attention.

"The stronger you get, the bigger the target the devil paints on you."

"Grandpa Morris used to tell me that. He used to tell me that you knew you were making God really happy when you made the devil really mad."

"We must be doing something right, then."

~~~~~

"So what do we do?" Geneva asked the next morning, putting down her coffee cup. "Live in hiding?" She looked around the room where the six of them were in various stages of assembling or eating their breakfasts.

Vincent paused to pour himself another cup of coffee. The plan that had been forming in his head since his midnight talk with Darcy was still mostly nebulous. He knew he would need their help and full support and trust. Using them as bait was the part he was trying to avoid.

"We have to bring the fight to our home territory, instead of letting him pull the strings and control the circumstances," he finally said.

"A trap," Joan said, catching on immediately. She glanced at Darcy. The girl caught her look.

"I'm the bait." Darcy almost smiled.

"No — " Geneva began.

"He's right," Josh said. "We lure him in before he goes underground. Then strike, on our home territory. We have to choose the time and place. Otherwise, we'll spend the rest of our lives wondering when he'll come back."

"And he will," Joan said.

"Absolutely," agreed Martha. "Men like that are worse than cockroaches."

"We've been getting more information on his activities, between the unit breaking up and him becoming Karl Van Mournen. He isn't the kind of man to just walk away when he believes he's been wronged."

"*He's* been wronged?" Geneva blurted.

"The world revolves around him. That's the kind of mindset he's always operated under. He wants Darcy, and he wants his justice against Josh, and anyone who denies him what he wants is his enemy. Essentially, denying the laws of nature."

"We need to stop him," Darcy said.

"Why does Darcy have to be the bait?" Geneva pressed.

"Karl used Joan to lay a trap for me," Vincent said, "to set up
~~~~~

groundwork for Josh and me to kill each other. He's used the same tactics before, manipulating people into reacting without thinking and doing his dirty work for him. I think we should return the favor. He won't expect us to use his tactics."

"He thinks we're brainless, weak, goody-goody Christian wimps," Joan offered. That earned a few half-hearted smiles from the others.

Vincent looked around the kitchen. "Martha, you're essential, if he tries to come after Darcy during the day. That tazer of his is new. He's always been a little too eager to use new toys. If he catches her alone, he could stun her and carry her away before any of us know. How good are you with that gun?"

"She held off some gang boys who tried to break in and steal the Christmas collection, down in San Antonio," Darcy said. "She shot a line across the doorstep, right in front of their toes." She traded grins of remembrance with Martha.

"Is that good enough?" Martha asked.

"All I need is for you to slow down Karl if he gets too close to Darcy. The battle is mine. I'll keep him busy until McGee and his men show up and take him down."

"How about if I borrow another sword? That should slow him down, make him think twice," Darcy said.

"That will just make him more cautious," Joan said. "We want him to think you're helpless, so he gets cocky. Over-confidence turns into mistakes."

"We hope," Josh murmured.

~~~~~

Darcy and Geneva were back in the kitchen at the Center that morning, in full view of everyone who cared to walk through. Vincent paired up with Josh, never letting him out of his sight, just like Joan and Martha did with Geneva and Darcy. Ulysses took up sentinel duty in the doorway of the kitchen. Chances were good Van Mournen wouldn't dare act so openly against anyone in the family during the day. There was safety in numbers and lots of witnesses.

The other dogs stayed at the dojo, to make sure Van Mournen didn't sneak in, make a nest, and lie in wait for them to return in the evening. Detective McGee took custody of the three trunks from the treasure room. If Van Mournen somehow got around their precautions and the volunteers who were on the watch for him and actually got into the building, Vincent wanted the disappearance of his treasure trove to throw the man off balance.

~~~~~

Vincent was grateful all this was happening in the summer. The supper hour finished long before dusk. The street people and derelicts and the people who had used up their food stamps before the end of the month came and ate and left while the sun was still above the edge of the rooftops.

On his orders, everyone left the Center while it was still daylight. No one was allowed to stay late. No one argued. Teams of volunteers made rounds of the building, checking the empty, gutted and renovated rooms, ensuring there was no one inside each section as the outer doors and inner fire doors were locked.

By 8:30, there was no one in the building except Vincent, Joan, Martha, and the Clays. Darcy and Martha were left to do the last supper dishes and the huge pots and mixing bowls left from cooking dinner. Darcy had recovered her spirits enough to complain a little, claiming Vincent had purposely sent the kitchen clean-up crew home early just to make her wash dishes. He had laughed at her accusation, tousled her hair, earned a mock offended look, and left the kitchen for one final check of the building.

The only door left open was at the loading dock. The plan demanded they control Van Mournen's movements.

Vincent and Joan took one last tour of the perimeter of the building, checking the locks on the doors and windows from the outside. If Van Mournen was watching, they wanted to impress on him the precautions they were taking. There was nothing like a challenge to make him react in anger and arrogance and strike right away.

Vincent imagined the man was perched somewhere, hidden, using binoculars to keep watch on the building. He had to be somewhere he could watch the doors and count the people going out and coming in. The only weak part of their plan was the long wait until full dark, when Detective McGee and his men would sneak back into the building and be there, waiting, guarding, until Van Mournen struck. When the officers arrived, Joan would sneak out of the building and drive to the dojo to bring the Quarry Hall dogs to add them to the security plan. No one would go back to the dojo or leave the Center until Van Mournen had been caught.

"Please, Lord, let it be soon," Vincent whispered as he, Joan and Ulysses headed back into the Center. They made a point of slamming the loading dock door hard enough that it visibly bounced. If Van Mournen was watching, he would think they were over-confident and careless.

~~~~~

Darcy felt a trickle of warmer air snake through the kitchen and nearly dropped the heavy metal beaters for the mixer as she put them away in the floor-mounted bowl. She froze, trying not to turn to look at the storage room where the air came through. She had noted weeks ago how air moved in the storage room when the door to the loading dock was
~~~~~

opened, creating suction. There were enough gaps in the crumbling drywall of the storage room she could see light in the hallway when the lights were off in the kitchen.

Vincent and Joan had come back inside more than twenty minutes ago, and it wasn't dark enough yet for Detective McGee and the other police officers to come inside.

"Martha." Darcy turned and saw the woman watching her, concern deepening the wrinkles around her eyes and mouth. "He's here." She stood up, her legs a little unsteady, and wrapped her arms around herself. "I need to lead him to Vincent and Dad."

Her stomach twisted at the sudden assurance that Van Mournen would gun down Martha with the ease of another man swatting at a bird that flew across his path.

"You can certainly run faster than me. Take my —"

"No." She stopped Martha as she reached into her apron pocket and the heavy burden that made it sag. Martha had kept her gun there all day. "I don't know how to use it. Besides, if we're lucky, he still wants me. He won't hurt me." *Not too much, anyway. I hope.* "You hide and then call McGee — Call Dad and warn him, first."

Martha tugged the cell phone out of her apron pocket and flipped it open. She tapped one button. "Finally figured out how to use the auto-dial," she said, in response to Darcy's questioning look.

That destroyed the blockage in her throat, and Darcy laughed now. It was a weak sound, short-lived, but she felt suddenly much better. She retrieved the flashlight from the shelf next to the pass-through into the dining room, then turned off the overhead lights.

"Your mom and dad know," Martha reported as she snapped her phone closed. Her face suddenly took on more lines, and a tightness around her usually smiling mouth. "You listen to me, Darcy Grace Clay. You be careful with that madman. You're all I have left to live for in this world, you understand?"

"I promise I'll be careful," Darcy whispered. She hugged the woman, hard and briefly. "Now go hide, will you?" She stepped out the kitchen door that opened directly into the hallway and turned right, heading for the intersection with the hall leading from the loading dock.

~~~~~

Martha dabbed at her eyes as she scurried out of the kitchen. One hand slipped into the other unusually large pocket of her thick, sturdy apron, and caressed the police service revolver hidden there. The dimly lit doorway on the far side of the room seemed a thousand miles away.

"Hello, Martha. Fancy meeting you here." Van Mournen chuckled, appearing out of the dim light of the kitchen behind her.

"Doug," Martha whispered, and snapped her arm up, straight and
~~~~~

steady. She got off two shots before Van Mournen reacted, throwing himself to the floor, underneath a folding table. She ran.

Gunfire exploded through the darkness after her. A bullet careened off the wall, spattering her cheek with fragments of brick and mortar. She swallowed a gasp of pain as one fragment sliced her cheek and kept running.

~~~~~

Vincent hugged the wall as he slid around the corner. He tried to interpret the location of the gunshots by the echoes.

Running footsteps led him to the first stairwell. They were hard-soled shoes. Darcy wore Inca boots, and Martha wore sneakers. Geneva and Josh were safely hidden away, and Darcy was supposed to be heading up to join her parents. Vincent listened to the tapping of feet fading away overhead and smiled into the darkness. His enemy was on the run. He couldn't hear Darcy's light footsteps, so that meant she had lost him already. Now it was up to him, to keep Van Mournen distracted, lose him in the maze of new hallways and darkness, in a building he knew far better than Vincent, until the police showed up. Crouching low to the ground, Vincent started up the stairs.

He paused at the first landing, halfway up to the second floor, and listened. The footsteps had stopped, giving him no clue to locate Van Mournen. Vincent continued up the stairs, out onto the first floor landing. No sound. He crouched low as he stepped out onto the cracked tile of the long hallway. Bits of plastic sheeting glistened in the shadows and half-light. Dust hung thick in the air from walls torn down and ceiling tiles removed. Wires hung down, and pipes bulked at the edge of the darkness. It reminded Vincent of a bombed-out building at the edge of a war zone.

A scraping sound over his head made Vincent turn.

"Mine," Van Mournen growled. Fire flared in the darkness of the stairwell leading up to the third floor.

Vincent staggered at a blow high in his shoulder. As he fell, he felt the fiery bite of the bullet. His arm hung useless.

"Does it burn, Vincent?" Van Mournen purred from the shadows. A single footstep dragged on the steps. "Does it eat into you, like betrayal? Like love sullied and innocence destroyed?"

"I never betrayed you, Karl."

"Liar!"

Another bullet screamed through the darkness. Vincent rolled out of the way and the bullet dug out a shower of drywall over his head.

"You can't have her, Karl. She knows what you are."

There was a fine line between irritating Van Mournen so he lost some of his elegant control, and goading the man into savage fury. The longer Vincent could keep Van Mournen talking, venting his fury, the better the
~~~~~

chance of McGee and his people getting there and capturing the man.

"She will do whatever I say!" Van Mournen roared. He took another step down. Vincent caught a flicker of movement at the top of the landing. "She is mine. She loves me. Me!" Three footsteps echoed through the darkness as he came down the steps.

Vincent braced himself for another bullet, but nothing came. Through the thuds of his heart in his ears, he heard more footsteps.

Were they going away? Back up the stairs? Or had Van Mournen stepped into that inky black blot of shadows at the foot of the stairs? Was he standing there now, watching Vincent struggle to stand up?

"Suffer, Vincent," Van Mournen whispered — definitely on the same floor with him now. "Suffer and run from me. I won't kill you right away. In degrees. Piece by piece."

Vincent held onto the wall and pushed himself to his feet. More bullets were his answer, grazing his thigh, biting into his calf, and shooting up trails of sparks and dust as they scraped the wall beside him.

"Run, Vincent! Run and beg my forgiveness!"

In the sudden silence, Vincent heard the slow clicks of a gun cocking, preparing to fire. He threw himself down the hall, staggering, bending low to make a smaller target.

Behind him, Van Mournen laughed.

The laughter followed him as Vincent crossed to the other side of the building. The footsteps grew closer, louder, as he stumbled down the stairs. The only thought in Vincent's mind was to lead Van Mournen outside, away from Darcy and Martha. Hopefully into the hands and guns of McGee and the local police.

He found the stairs and threw himself down. His feet clattered on the steps. Tiles were loose here, not yet removed for renovation, and slipped under his feet. The blood trickling down his leg made the sole of his boot slippery.

A gunshot tore through the stairwell, echoing crazily. Vincent looked up as he made the final turn. The bullet skimmed past him, so close he felt his skin crisp. He saw Van Mournen's pale face above him, stretched wide in a rictus of triumph. He fell, tumbling down seven steps and banging his head hard against the wall so he saw stars.

"Leave him alone!" Darcy screamed, fury turning the sound to a roar.

She leaped forward to grab Vincent by his arm and drag him out of the stairwell, out of Van Mournen's sight. He tried to stand. The movement twisted him away from Darcy's support and opened up the wound in his shoulder.

"Go!" Vincent went to his knees. He saw the wall looming before him as he fell, but he could only raise one arm to catch himself. He saw more stars and felt his cheekbone crack and skin split as he hit the wall.

"Vincent!" Darcy's voice broke with tears. She grappled at his shoulders and rolled him over. She slid her hands under his armpits and started to drag him.

"Darcy, my love?" Van Mournen's voice was a nearly unrecognizable croon.

"You don't know what love is!" she shrieked.

Footsteps echoed slowly down the stairwell as Van Mournen descended.

"Leave him be, darling. He deserves to suffer for his crimes."

"I'm not your darling!"

As long as they argued, Van Mournen wouldn't shoot. He would be too distracted to notice when reinforcements approached. Vincent played dead, curled up in pain, praying, stretching his senses for the first sign of Joan or McGee, willing Heaven's defenses to gather around Darcy and protect her. If Van Mournen pulled out that tazer, Vincent prepared to leap between them, take the jolt, and give Darcy time to run.

"You can't kill him. I won't let you."

"Don't fight me, Darcy. I don't want to have to punish you."

Vincent opened his eyes. Darcy stood over him, a foot on either side of his knees.

"You're too young to know what you're doing," Van Mournen pleaded. "I love you." He took a step closer.

"You don't know what love is!" Darcy cried, her voice cracking. "Love is patient, love is kind. It does not envy, it does not boast, it is not proud. It is not rude, it is not self-seeking, it is not easily angered, it keeps no record of wrongs." She laughed, the sound spilling over Van Mournen's snort of disgust at her words. "Love does not delight in evil, but rejoices with the truth. It always protects, always trusts, always hopes, always perseveres."

"Who taught you that slop?" he demanded.

"It's not slop—it's the word of God!" She stepped away from Vincent, and he fought the instinctive reaction to grab her arm and push her behind him. He needed her to distract Van Mournen. Just a little longer.

"Religion is for fools who die too easily. They need hope. We are masters of our own fate, Darcy. Your father lied to you, keeping the truth of your destiny from you. I have always been here, preparing you."

"Lying to me!"

"Your father taught you to be weak."

Vincent got up to his knees, moving slowly, hugging the shadows behind Darcy.

Chapter Twenty-Two

"When I am weak, then I am strong," she said, fierce laughter thickening her voice. The sound sent a chill up Vincent's neck. He stood slowly, staying in the shadow she cast in the dim hallway. Ready to leap, whatever it took to protect her.

"What are you talking about?" Van Mournen snarled.

"You know, the Bible says to answer a fool as he deserves. The wisdom of God seems foolish to men." Her calm, pale face contrasted with the red, angry flush that made Van Mournen's face look puffy with indignation. "Sometimes, to take that step of faith, you have to jump out into thin air. I understand, Daddy! Now I really understand!"

Darcy stepped within a yard of Van Mournen before Vincent could snatch at her shirt to stop her and held out her empty hands.

"He who lives by the sword dies by the sword. Or maybe I should say, he who loves the sword dies by it." Darcy planted her feet solidly in the filthy hallway and spread her arms wide. Her smile grew. "Go ahead. Give me your best shot."

Van Mournen stared, his face growing redder. A low growling sound emerged from his tight lips. Vincent thought the man would start foaming at the mouth at any moment. There was something almost comical about the scene.

With a shriek, Van Mournen raised his gun. Vincent braced himself, ready to leap, to push Darcy aside and take the man down. Or if necessary, take the bullet for her.

Through the roaring of his pulse in his ears, he heard the scrabbling of claws on linoleum, coming from the right.

Then, footsteps coming from the hallway to the right.

Van Mournen looked right, then left, horror wiping away the fury.

"Mine!" he shouted and turned to aim the gun to the right.

Ulysses leaped into the red-lit stairwell, his jaws clamping on Van Mournen's wrist. They went down, the man shrieking and swearing and twisting, the dog deathly silent.

Joan threw herself down on Vincent and caught hold of his good shoulder to pull him away. A man in black riot gear skidded to a stop and aimed his rifle at Van Mournen. Joan snapped out her command and Ulysses let go, leaping off of Van Mournen. More men in black pounced on him.

"Get Darcy out of here," Vincent barked, shoving Joan's hands away when she tried to pull open his shirt to examine his wound.

She hesitated a moment, looking into his eyes, then nodded. Vincent leaned against the wall, watching, waiting, fighting the spinning sensation that told him he had lost just a little too much blood, until Darcy vanished from sight. He ignored Van Mournen's shrieks and curses and struggles as he was cuffed and hauled to his feet and dragged away. When Darcy was gone, then he let himself slump. Tears blinded him. He let go, and the throbbing fire stole his breath.

It's over. She's safe. They're all safe.

"Paramedics are on their way," McGee said, dropping to his haunches in front of Vincent. "It's over."

Hearing the other man say the same words he had been thinking, Vincent caught his breath and he knew he was wrong. It wasn't over. None of them would be safe until he found Shadow. Four down — one to go.

~~~~~

Sophie came up to the Spike Center and helped in the investigation of Van Mournen's activities. He had apartments, weapons and treasure caches in five different countries. Vincent was willing to let the government confiscate everything. All he cared about was proving Van Mournen had been behind the scandal that threatened to shut down the Spike Center. How Van Mournen thought he could convince Darcy to turn her back on her parents and everything she had been raised to believe in and walk away with him, no one could imagine.

The return of financial support and supporters would be slow, in comparison to the speed with which they had abandoned ship. The Arc Foundation sent an initial infusion of funds to keep the renovations on schedule. More would come after the inspection was completed and an analysis made of what the Center needed, as well as future outreach opportunities.

"When the board is back full-strength," Joan said, "come down to Quarry Hall, get to know us, take some training."

"Work for you?" Darcy sat up and looked around the living room in their apartment, where her parents, Vincent, Joan, Martha and several members of the board had been discussing the latest results of the investigation.

"Hold on, there," Josh began.

"Just get to know us," Vincent said. "We're going to be busy cleaning up all of this for quite a while. And don't you have a college degree to finish earning?"

"Would I get a dog like Ulysses?" Darcy asked. The last thing she wanted to think about was something as boring as required college
~~~~~

courses.

"It all depends." Joan bent and stroked down Ulysses' back as far as she could reach.

"Depends on what?"

"The dogs choose us, we don't choose them."

"You're smart enough to realize that the girls who are out on the road for Arc..." Vincent looked around the table, meeting her father's gaze and holding it. "Well, if they pair up with a dog, that's a pretty good sign they're going to face situations where they'll need a dog's protection. Think you're ready to face that kind of responsibility?"

Darcy wanted to shout yes, she was ready, but the memories of the last few weeks seemed to slam her with all the force of the bullet that had creased her ribs. This was the kind of danger and injury and pain her father had faced, and she kicked herself every time she remembered how she had thought it was an exciting, desirable kind of life. She wanted to shout that yes, she could handle the danger, but she remembered how she had shuddered and felt sickly and dizzy once she was alone in the hospital room, patched up and washed and safe. The crisis had happened too quickly for her to do anything but react. How could she guarantee she would react the right way and protect others, the way Joan and her father and Vincent had dived in to protect her?

"I guess we'll all have to figure that out, won't we?" she said.

Joan nodded to her with a small, thin smile, and Darcy thought maybe she had passed the first of what would be many tests.

END

About the Author

On the road to publication, Michelle fell into fandom in college and has 40+ stories in various SF and fantasy universes. She has a bunch of useless degrees in theater, English, film/communication, and writing. Even worse, she has over 100 books and novellas with multiple small presses, in science fiction and fantasy, YA, suspense, women's fiction, and sub-genres of romance.

Her official launch into publishing came with winning first place in the Writers of the Future contest in 1990. She was a finalist in the EPIC Awards competition multiple times, winning with *Lorien* in 2006 and *The Meruk Episodes, I-V,* in 2010, and was a finalist in the Realm Awards competition, in conjunction with the Realm Makers convention.

Her training includes the Institute for Children's Literature; proofreading at an advertising agency; and working at a community newspaper. She is a tea snob and freelance edits for a living (MichelleLevigne@gmail.com for info/rates), but only enough to give her time to write. Her newest crime against the literary world is to be co-managing editor at Mt. Zion Ridge Press and launching the publishing co-op, Ye Olde Dragon Books. Be afraid … be very afraid.

And please check out Ye Olde Dragon's Library, the storytelling podcast. Interspersed between the chapters will be interviews with authors of fantastical fiction. Listen to the podcast on your favorite podcast app or listen on the website: www.YeOldeDragonBooks.com, and click on the Ye Olde Dragon's Library link.

www.Mlevigne.com
www.MichelleLevigne.blogspot.com
www.YeOldeDragonBooks.com
www.MtZionRidgePress.com

NEWSLETTER:
Want to learn about upcoming books, book launch parties, inside information, and cover reveals?
Go to Michelle's website or blog to sign up.

Thanks for reading!
If you enjoyed this book, would you help Michelle by posting a review on Goodreads?

Are you a member of Book Bub? If so, please follow Michelle on Book Bub, and you'll get alerts when new books are coming out.

As a way of saying thanks, Michelle invites you to the Goodies page on her website. It will change regularly, offering you a free short story, a sample audiobook chapter, sneak peeks at new cover art, inside information on discounts and new release dates, etc. Please go to: *Mlevigne.com/good-stuff.html*

Also by Michelle L. Levigne

Guardians of the Time Stream: 4-book Steampunk series
The Match Girls: Humorous inspirational romance series starting with **A Match (Not) Made in Heaven**
Sarai's Journey: A 2-book biblical fiction series
Tabor Heights: 18-book inspirational small town romance series.
Quarry Hall: 11-book women's fiction/suspense series
For Sale: Wedding Dress. Never Used: inspirational romance
Crooked Creek: Fun Fables About Critters and Kids: Children's short stories.
Do Yourself a Favor: Tips and Quips on the Writing Life. A book of writing advice.
To Eternity (and beyond): *Writing Spec Fic Good for Your Soul.* A book defending speculative fiction.
Killing His Alter-Ego: contemporary romance/suspense, taking place in fandom.
The Commonwealth Universe: SF series, 25 books and growing
The Hunt: 5-book YA fantasy series
Faxinor: Fantasy series, 4 books and growing
Wildvine: Fantasy series, 14 books when all released
Neighborlee: Humorous fantasy series
Zygradon: 5-book Arthurian fantasy series
AFV Defender: SF adventure series
Young Defenders: Middle Grade SF series, spin-off of *AFV Defender*
Magic to Spare: Fantasy series
Book & Mug Mysteries: cozy mystery series
Quest for the Crescent Moon: fantasy series
Steward's World: fantasy series reboot and expansion
The Enchanted Castle Archives: fantasy series

THANK YOU!

Thank you for reading this book from Mt. Zion Ridge Press.

If you enjoyed the experience, learned something, gained a new perspective, or made new friends through story, could you do us a favor and write a review on Goodreads or wherever you bought the book?

Thanks! We and our authors appreciate it.

We invite you to visit our website, *MtZionRidgePress.com*, and explore other titles in fiction and non-fiction. We always have something coming up that's new and off the beaten path.

And please check out our podcast, **Books on the Ridge,** where we chat with our authors and give them a chance to share what was in their hearts while they wrote their book, as well as fun anecdotes and glimpses into their lives and experiences and the writing process. And we always discuss a very important topic: *Tea!*

You can listen to the podcast on our website or find it at most of the usual places where podcasts are available online. Please subscribe so you don't miss a single episode!

Thanks for reading. We hope you come back soon!